He

Leslie Langtry's books:

"Brilliant! Leslie Langtry has once again penned a 'gotta read every page' drama. I loved it, and the end as brilliant...Agatha Christie would be proud!"
—*Kings River Life Magazine*

"Darkly funny and wildly over the top, this mystery answers the burning question, 'Do assassin skills and Girl Scout merit badges mix…' one truly original and wacky novel!"
—*RT BOOK REVIEWS*

"Those who like dark humor will enjoy a look into the deadliest female assassin and PTA mom's life."
—*Parkersburg News*

"Mixing a deadly sense of humor and plenty of sexy sizzle, Leslie Langtry creates a brilliantly original, laughter-rich mix of contemporary romance and suspense in *'Scuse Me While I Kill This Guy.*"
—*Chicago Tribune*

"The beleaguered soccer mom assassin concept is a winner, and Langtry gets the fun started from page one with a myriad of clever details."
—*Publisher's Weekly*

BOOKS BY LESLIE LANGTRY

Merry Wrath Mysteries:
Merit Badge Murder
Mint Cookie Murder
Scout Camp Murder
(short story in the Killer
Beach Reads collection)
Marshmallow S'More
Murder
Movie Night Murder
Mud Run Murder
Fishing Badge Murder
(short story in the Pushing
Up Daisies collection)
Motto for Murder
Map Skills Murder
Mean Girl Murder
Marriage Vow Murder
Mystery Night Murder
Meerkats and Murder
Make Believe Murder
Maltese Vulture Murder
Musket Ball Murder
Macho Man Murder
Mad Money Murder
Mind-Bending Murder

Greatest Hits Mysteries:
'Scuse Me While I Kill This
Guy
Guns Will Keep Us
Together
Stand By Your Hitman
I Shot You Babe
Paradise By The Rifle
Sights
Snuff the Magic Dragon
My Heroes Have Always
Been Hitmen
Greatest Hits mysteries
Holiday Bundle

Aloha Lagoon Mysteries:
Ukulele Murder
Ukulele Deadly

Other Works:
Sex, Lies, & Family
Vacations

MIND-BENDING MURDER

A Merry Wrath Mystery

USA TODAY BESTSELLING AUTHOR
Leslie Langtry

MIND-BENDING MURDER

CHAPTER ONE

———

Ever have one of those days when you wake up in a windowless room with one door and a dead guy five feet away? No? Maybe it was just me. And it was a first because, even during my career as a spy, that kind of thing never happened.

Oh sure, you'd wake up in strange places sometimes, with four empty bottles of Ouzo and a small monkey going through your purse—or in a convent in Belize, dressed as a drag queen with a bag full of knock-off mini bibles. But this was totally new.

Where was I? The simple room had just one door, a table with a box of Lucky Charms sitting on it, an ordinary folding chair next to it, and a small bookshelf against the opposite wall that had more than a dozen copies of a book titled *Boats of the Midwest*.

I found myself lying on the hard concrete floor when I came to. The dead man lying near me was young, maybe in his midtwenties. He was wearing jeans, tennis shoes, and a tucked in polo shirt. And he wasn't breathing. That probably had something to do with the dark red spot over his heart.

At this point, I checked to see what I was wearing. In my experience, it's always a good idea to do this first since you don't want someone bursting through the door to find you naked—or worse, in a banana costume. That once happened to me after a girls' night out with CIA colleague Hilly in Montenegro.

Oh good. I was wearing jeans too. And…huh? The same blue polo shirt as the dead guy. I plucked at the fabric and realized it wasn't mine. I crawled over to the guy to check his pulse in case I was wrong about the breathing thing. It's always a good idea to check this too since I once knew a guy named

Vinnie the Lung who could hold his breath for ten minutes. He was a lot of fun at parties where there was a pool, fountain, or rain barrel.

Was this guy stabbed to death? By who? Had I witnessed whatever happened? And why was I dressed in a shirt I didn't own?

Looking around, I couldn't find my purse. I checked my back pocket in hopes of finding my cell phone, but it wasn't there. I started toward the door but changed my mind, thinking that I'd better see if this guy had a wallet or phone so that I could call the police.

Touching him directly was out of the question, since technically, if it was foul play, I could be considered a suspect. What could I use? Taking off my shirt wouldn't work since anyone could come in here at any moment, and I'd probably get his DNA on my shirt, which was just as damning. The books on the shelf were hardcovers, which would be nearly impossible to manipulate for searching the body.

I walked to the table and picked up the box of Lucky Charms. Unless it was the weapon used (which is unlikely— although what a way to go!), it would make sense to those who knew me if my fingerprints were on it since I ate them practically every day.

Pulling out the bag, I poured the cereal into the box after stuffing one or two handfuls of the sugary goodness into my mouth. You might think that was a bad idea, but one of the most important rules of spy craft was to eat at every opportunity in case you don't get another chance. Of course, the most important rule was to *avoid people with knives or guns who might want you dead*.

Using the bag as a makeshift mitten, I approached the body.

He looked pretty young, which was sad. Very carefully, I lifted his right hip to look for the bulge (a wallet, of course) that should be there.

It wasn't.

I walked around to the other side and did the same thing. Nope. No wallet.

Since I couldn't be caught tampering with the deceased, I poured the cereal back into the bag and, after a couple more handfuls, stuffed the bag back into the box. Then I started for the door.

It flew open before I even touched the knob.

"Hands in the air!" A police officer in all black tactical gear pointed a pistol at me, and I threw my arms up.

Two more cops raced into the room, both toward the body.

"It's him alright," one of the officers said into his walkie. He turned his attention to me. "And it's her too—just like they said."

Well, that didn't seem good.

CHAPTER TWO

———

"Mrs. Ferguson?" The officer walked over to me.

I nodded. "That's right."

He shared a look with the cop whose gun was still trained on me. Then he walked around behind me and pulled my arms back.

"You have the right to remain silent..." he began.

I didn't say a word because I had no idea what to say. Remaining silent seemed to be my best option. This would work out okay. My husband, Rex, was the detective in Who's There, Iowa. These men didn't look like his guys, but if they were County, it was okay because Sheriff Ed Carnack and I went way back.

Metal pinched my wrists as I felt a rough nudge on my back, forcing me forward. I looked back as I was escorted out, to see the third officer talking into his radio. We walked outside into the darkness. Apparently, I was in some sort of shed behind a strip mall in...where was I?

This wasn't Who's There. I was in a town I didn't recognize. I swallowed hard. Was I even in Iowa?

"Merry." Sheriff Ed Carnack came around the side of the shed, and I let out a breath.

"Oh yay!" The words slipped from my mouth. "Hey, Sheriff!"

He looked at me seriously, then asked the officer to uncuff me. Once released, I rubbed my wrists.

"I knew you'd think this was all just a big misunderstanding," I gushed. "I have no idea what happened! I don't know that guy or this place. And hey, this shirt isn't mine."

The sheriff held up a hand to silence me. "I'm sorry, Merry. I really am."

I blinked in disbelief. "Sorry? What for?"

The big man sighed heavily. "I'm sorry to tell you that you are under arrest for the murder of Tyson Pancratz."

I stared at him as if he'd lost his mind. "Who's Tyson Pancratz?"

"The man you just murdered," the officer who'd taken the cuffs off snapped.

"I don't care for your tone," I said. "I'm innocent until proven guilty, right?"

The officer shook his head and went back inside the shed.

"Where are we?" I asked Ed. "And did you get new deputies, because I've never seen these guys before."

He took off his hat and ran a hand through his hair. "We're in Bladdersly. And those men are part of the Bladdersly Police Department. They aren't mine."

Bladdersly. That stinking, fetid hellhole ten miles away from Who's There. Bladdersly was my town's rival in every way, including the annual football game where the Raging Bladders battled the Whorish (an unfortunate mashup of Who's and Irish) in an attempt at some form of athleticism. People from Who's There didn't like people from Bladdersly, and the feeling was mutual.

The medical examiner's van pulled up, and I felt my prospects brighten. Dr. Soo Jin Body was a good friend and had been a bridesmaid in my wedding. She'd be on my side.

"Hi, Merry!" the gorgeous Korean American called out with a little wave. Dr. Body breezed past me and made her way into the shed.

"I'll bet Soo Jin doesn't think I murdered Tyson Pancratz," I pointed out.

Sheriff Carnack sighed again. "For what it's worth, I don't either. But the facts are pretty compelling. You're going to need an attorney."

"What facts? I never met that guy! I've never been here and don't even know how I got here! And, like I said before, this isn't my shirt!"

My name is Merry Wrath, and I'm a retired CIA agent. Born and raised as Fionnaghuala Merrygold Czrygy, I'd been a spy for eight years before I was "accidentally" outed by the US vice president as a way to get back at my powerful senator father, Mike Czrygy.

To add injury to insult, I discovered the betrayal while in a bar in remote Chechnya. Wolf Blitzer of CNN showed my photo, and I barely escaped alive. After some lukewarm apologies and a whopping settlement, I changed my name to Merry Wrath and moved back to my hometown of Who's There, Iowa. My best friend, Kelly Albers, insisted we start a Girl Scout troop, and I eventually married the town detective, changing my name again to Ferguson.

I have the unfortunate reputation of having people drop dead around me…a *lot*. So it wasn't too weird to find one in my immediate vicinity. But this was different. I always knew where I'd been and what I'd been doing. This time, I didn't.

"I'm not going to use the cuffs on you," Ed said. "But I do need to take you in."

My eyes were on the doorway of the shed. "You said I'm under arrest. Which means you *think* you have solid evidence that I did this."

"Let's discuss it back at HQ. I'll make sure Rex is there."

Then it occurred to me. "Why are *you* here? I mean, I'm not complaining. But those officers aren't your deputies. Where's the local chief of police?"

He shifted his feet. "Bryce is on a fishing trip. I told him I'd keep an eye on things. You're lucky it's me and not him. He doesn't like you."

That seemed like bad news. "While I'm never surprised that someone from this swamp of a town dislikes me," I reasoned, "I don't know the man. How can he hate me if he doesn't know me?"

Ed rubbed his chin. "Forget about that for now. At least you're in my custody. Now, please, get in the car."

I did as he asked and stared out the window at the activity. What exactly happened here? And what did I have to do with any of it? I looked around the parking lot, but my silver minivan wasn't here. Neither was my purse or cell. What was happening?

It was at least an hour before we walked into the sheriff's station in Who's There. Rex ran to meet me and crushed me in his embrace. I relaxed against my husband. He'd sort this all out.

"When I woke up in the middle of the night and found you gone, I just thought you'd gone to see Mr. Fancy Pants," he said, referring to the king vulture at the local zoo. I'd adopted him, but that wasn't the reason for my clandestine, late-night visits to the bird. What can I say? He's a great listener.

I melted. "You believe me, right? I didn't kill Tyson Pancratz, whoever he is."

Rex pulled away and searched my face. "Do you really have to ask?"

"Sorry. Of course you don't think that. Did you say I left in the middle of the night?"

"I was asleep. I assumed you snuck out, but I don't know when."

That was disappointing. "I guess you won't be my alibi then, huh?"

"I can't honestly say when you left," he hedged.

"I know. And I don't want to put you into that position. I was just hoping you knew more, because I don't remember anything."

I turned to the sheriff. "What did that officer mean—'just like they said'?"

Ed Carnack took off his hat and ran a hand through his hair. "The call went to the Bladdersly police station. All I know is that there was a caller who said that you had murdered Pancratz. They didn't give a name, just an address."

"Male or female?" I pressed.

"I haven't heard the recording, so I don't know. They only called me because Bryce Vanderzee is out of town and had told his staff to call me if anything happened. Apparently, he doesn't like them working without supervision."

Great. Idiot cops. "So why am I here instead of in a jail cell there?"

Don't get me wrong. I was extremely happy that I was here.

"I might have insisted." He gave me a wan smile. "And they didn't want to do the paperwork."

That was all it came down to? Paperwork? That's what they were afraid of? I needed to remember that to exploit it later.

"Can Rex post bail?" I asked.

"When it's set, yes. It might be 24 hours or more."

Damn. "I have to spend the night here?"

"Yes. We have to wait and see what the judge says."

"I'm sure it's nothing," Rex said. "An anonymous tip is circumstantial. You can't base an indictment on that."

"Yes," Carnack agreed. "But finding Merry at the crime scene, with the body, isn't. I'm hoping this will clear up soon, but right now, it looks bad."

"I think he was stabbed in the heart. Is that what killed him?" I asked.

The sheriff shook his head. "Now, Merry, you know we can't release that information until Soo Jin is finished with her examination."

I looked at my watch. "When will that be?"

Both men looked at each other.

"Okay." I held up my hands. "I know the deal. I'm a suspect and can't investigate."

Oh, I was soooo investigating once I got out. It certainly wasn't the first time I'd been accused of murder, and it probably wouldn't be the last. Wait…that sounded bad. Let's just stick with the first part.

Ed set his hat on his desk. "You're not *a* suspect. You're *the* suspect."

The room went quiet. We stared at each other but said nothing. It was a classic Chechen Standoff. You probably think I mean Mexican Standoff, but that wouldn't be right because none of the three of us were pointing any weapons at each other.

A Chechen Standoff is when three people are looking at each other but don't know what to say. Yeah, the standards are pretty low there.

"Ed," Rex said, his eyes not leaving mine. "We need to get EMTs in here to examine Merry. She was found unconscious, correct?"

"I called them on the way here. They should be here any moment."

"I'm fine," I said. "I'm just not sure what happened. Was I conked on the head or chloroformed?" My fingers searched my head. "I don't have any pain. And I don't have that chloroform aftertaste. It must've been something else."

"Like what?" Rex wondered.

"I don't know. In the CIA, we had some top secret methods. There's that nerve pinch in the neck…"

Ed seemed surprised. "Like in *Star Trek*?"

I nodded. "Yes. Did you know that one of the writers was ex-CIA? The Vulcan thingy came from real experience."

I had never been able to manage it myself. I was told it took a knack, and I didn't have it. Basically, you pinch the right spot, and it temporarily cuts off blood flow. And if you have someone with weird physiology, it won't work. In fact, it may not work on someone with normal physiology either. You just had to have the knack.

There was a woman at the Agency who could pull it off every time. Her name was Roberta, and she could do it to anyone and do it so quickly that it was her only job. She was a specialist who specialized in knocking folks out by pinching them. And she was a rock star. If you needed her, they would fly her out on a private company jet. She walked up behind whoever, pinched, and by the time they hit the floor, she was gone. Roberta the Reaper, we called her. Except that she didn't actually kill anyone.

Rex looked at my neck. "I don't see any bruising. Or any marks at all. Are you sure you weren't chloroformed?"

"No chance. I'd know." And I should too. I'd been chloroformed a few times since I'd gotten out of the CIA. I chalked it up to being a tad rusty, but the fact was, I'd only been a field agent less than ten years. That's about the point where you become a seasoned professional. I was good but not necessarily perfect.

The door swung open, and two EMTs walked in. Carnack nodded at me, and they went to work shining a light in my eyes, asking me to tell them how many fingers they were holding up…the usual stuff. After two or three minutes, they announced that nothing was wrong with me and left.

"That was quick." Rex watched them go.

"Shouldn't they have done a blood test or something?" I asked.

"I'll call your doctor in the morning," Rex said. "I think we need a second opinion."

"Okay." Carnack moved toward me. "Visiting hours are over. And since it's so late, we can have our interview later."

I shrugged. "I don't have much to say since I remember nothing, except going to bed at home and waking up with a dead guy." Which reminded me… "Honey, can you bring me a shirt from home? This one isn't mine."

Rex frowned. "Whose is it?"

"Not a clue—but it's just like the shirt the dead guy was wearing."

Rex ran home as Carnack processed me and led me to a cell. Twenty minutes later, Rex returned with one of my T-shirts. I changed in the bathroom and handed the sheriff the blue polo. Maybe there were trace elements of something that would exonerate me.

Once I was finally alone, I slumped onto the cot. What a bizarre night. I played through what had happened over and over, from the moment I woke up in the shed until the arrival of the Bladdersly police. None of it made sense.

Who was Tyson Pancratz? And why would I have killed him?

CHAPTER THREE

———

All things considered, the cell wasn't too bad. The bed was pretty comfortable, and I had a window and a sink. I mean, I wouldn't want to be here more than one day or anything, but it was certainly tolerable.

Prison cells are different all over the world. In Japan and Sweden, they have state-of-the-art, sparkling clean facilities that could double as vacation rentals. But in Azerbaijan or Nicaragua…well, let's just say you have to be okay sharing a cell made for one person with five or six others and twice that many cockroaches or rats.

I was staring at the mirror image of the window when a movement caught the corner of my eye. Something fell past my window. It was too small to be a man.

A barred owl hooted. Repeatedly. Maybe it was after a possum or whatever had fallen outside. I sat down on the bed and leaned back against the wall. There was a strange sound on the other side of it.

I sprang to my feet and noticed a flashing light outside the window. There was the sound of breaking glass, and then I spotted a small acetylene torch working at the bars.

"Shhhh!" a voice whispered. "They'll hear you!"

"Who'll hear me?" another voice asked.

"The *Man*!" said the first.

I stepped up to the window and peered out.

"Betty?"

A shadowy head popped up in the window. "No. I'm not Betty, whoever *that* is. Cool name though. I'll bet she's amazing."

"Yes, you are. And unless I miss my guess, Lauren is with you."

A figure stepped up and waved. "It's me, Mrs. Wrath! Inez!"

"No, it's not," Betty growled. "That's not Inez, and I'm not Betty."

"What are you doing here?" I asked, although I had a pretty good idea.

"We're busting you out!" Inez said cheerfully.

"Guys!" I protested. "Go home. It's like four in the morning. I'm innocent. I'll get out. By the way, how did you find out I was here?"

"Betty has a police scanner," Inez said as if I were an idiot.

Of course she does.

The torch flared up again.

"Stop! Unless you want to head to juvie, you need to go home!"

"We can't. We told our parents we were spending the night with you," Inez said. "Of course, we didn't tell them about you murdering that guy and all." She turned on her cell phone light, and I could see them better. Both girls were dressed in camo from head to toe. Huh. I would've guessed ninjas.

"You told them that? Where have you been all night if they thought you were at my house?"

"We don't have to answer that," Betty said. "We have veranda rights or something like that."

"It's Miranda, and you aren't being arrested, so it doesn't apply to you." I like to use any opportunity as a teaching moment. "You guys are out running around town in the middle of the night, and I don't need to know?"

"We were at the…" Inez started.

"Don't rat us out, Mac," Betty interrupted. "We aren't the ones who knocked off some sap. We're not on the hot seat."

"Put the torch away." I didn't ask how she came by it, but it wasn't much of a surprise. My troop was not your normal Girl Scout troop, and that was mainly because of Betty. The ten-year-old was a middle-aged spy trapped in a kid's body. She was destined for black ops, hopefully after at least completing elementary school.

"We can do this!" Betty insisted. "We'll bust you out of the joint and hide you in a safe house."

"If you break me out, it'll make me look even more guilty," I said. "Something I'm trying to avoid."

There was a pause.

"I hadn't thought of that."

"It's okay." Inez smiled. "We can get some patsy to take the fall for you!"

"Patsy?" I asked. "Take the fall? Hey, what's up with all the slang?"

"We've been watching old movies. The kind with gangsters," the girl said.

"What are gams?" Betty asked. "The guy in one movie said the dame had nice gams."

"I think he meant gums," Inez reasoned.

"Why would he care if she had nice gums?"

"She didn't have gingivitis," Inez replied. "My dentist says if you don't floss, you'll probably die from that."

Seemed a bit extreme, but I didn't have time to suggest that Inez needed another dentist. Someone could come in at any moment and find them. "Guys, get home and say I wasn't able to have you overnight." I wasn't worried about the girls coming up with a good story. They'd come up with a better one than I could.

"But we brought all this stuff," Inez complained. She held up a bag and shined a flashlight into it.

There was about five miles of paracord, some duct tape, a ping pong paddle, and a rubber duckie.

"Are those maracas?" I asked.

Betty closed the bag with a snap. "We're not going to tell you what all this stuff was for because you're not letting us ninja rescue you."

So it *was* ninjas. "You aren't dressed like ninjas. You're kind of dressed like the military."

"We are revolutionizing ninjahood." Betty sniffed. "Wearing black doesn't blend in with stuff like camo does."

"Good luck with that," I said.

"Betty's smart," Inez said. "She's training online to be a ninja."

"You can do that?"

"Sure. You just need a credit card, and she has her brother's," Inez said.

At least she wasn't using mine this time. I heard a noise in the hallway. These girls needed to get out of here. "Whatever. Take it all home, please."

"Fine, we'll scram," Betty said. "But we'll bust you out before you sleep with the fishes."

As they skittered away, I had to admit it was nice that they'd thought of me. I did need to figure out where they'd spent most of the evening, but I could deal with that later. There were a few hours left to sleep before people started waking up and interrogating me. I decided to make the most of it.

Breakfast was a frozen sausage and egg sandwich they'd thawed in the break room microwave and a bottle of orange juice. I polished it off quickly and noticed a new toothbrush and travel-sized toothpaste on the tray. I brushed my teeth, splashed water on my face, and ran my hands through my short, unruly curls. Until recently, they'd been green, due to an unfortunate dye job in Behold, Iowa. It took bleaching them and then re-coloring them dark blonde to go back to my original color.

I was just starting to organize my thoughts when the door opened and a deputy entered and unlocked my cell.

"You have visitors," he said glumly. He led me down the hall and opened the door on the left, ushering me inside. Then he left the room.

It was a sort of break room with vending machines. Oh wow! Ding Dongs! And me without any money. Maybe these visitors, whoever they were, would lend me some money. I know I'd just eaten, but I was always hungry.

"Merry!" Randi called out as she walked through the door, followed by her husband, Ivan, her twin evil doppelganger, Ronni, and Ronni's husband, Ron. "You poor, poor thing!"

Randi and Ronni were Rex's older twin sisters. Randi loved me. Ronni thought I was the equivalent of an incontinent skunk with halitosis. Their husbands were former Chechens I'd been embedded with back in my CIA days, and they both loved me. Three out of four wasn't too bad.

"We have something for you!" Randi was holding a box.

The twins took baked goods to the town jail every week, which is how they had met Ivan and Ron. My mouth began watering as I thought of their homemade cookies and brownies.

I took the box and opened it.

"Oh. Thanks," I mumbled as I pulled out a diorama featuring a cockroach with a curly blonde wig, using a nail file to saw her way through the bars of a prison cell.

Did I mention that the women were taxidermists? They specialized in bizarre dioramas. Oh sure, they did the typical deer head on the wall or trophy fish like any other taxidermists. But if you also needed an antebellum ostrich in a pre–Civil War hoop skirt with matching parasol, these women were the professionals for you.

"You're the roach." Ronni scowled. "Get it?"

"Yeah, I get it."

Randi patted my arm. "I'm sorry. We didn't have a lot to work with on such short notice."

"Because Ronni hid all the other animals," Ron piped up.

Ronni didn't refute this. Of course she had engineered it so that I'd be a cockroach. The woman hated me for no reason.

"I wanted to put a real file in there," Ivan said. "But they were afraid you would get caught trying to break out."

"And then they might shoot you," Ron added solemnly.

"*I* wasn't afraid of that!" Ronni shouted.

"Of course this whole thing is a misunderstanding," Randi soothed. "I'm sure you'll be out in no time."

"She killed a guy! And she was wearing someone else's shirt!" Ronni snapped.

"I didn't kill anyone, but I *was* wearing someone else's shirt."

Ron frowned, his tiny brain trying to make sense of this. "Why did you put on another shirt?"

"Because her shirt was too bloody, of course." Ivan shook his head and rolled his eyes. Of course these two former blunt instruments for a Chechen strongman would think that.

Ron scowled. "We do not always have bloody shirt after. Depends on the method."

"I didn't kill Tyson Pancratz," I said through my teeth. "I don't even know who he was."

"I know, dear." Randi smiled as she looked at Ivan. "Oh darn! We left the cookies in the car. Can you go out and get them, honey?"

Ivan smiled at his wife. "Of course, my little mutton chop. I will bring them." And away he went.

That seemed promising. "Thank you for everything. But you might have to take the diorama with you." I squinted at it, noticing a small ninja beetle outside the window with a torch. "They won't let me keep this here. Can you take it to Rex?"

"Of course!" Randi patted my arm. "We just wanted you to see it. Everyone is rallying for you!"

"No, they're not!" Ronni took off her cardigan to reveal a #JusticeForPancratz T-shirt. Beneath it was a picture of me in an electric chair.

"Ronni!" Randi narrowed her eyes. "What did we talk about the other day? Merry is family, and we always support family!"

I noticed that she didn't insist I was innocent.

"Um." I pointed to Ronni. "Where did you get that T-shirt?"

Ronni grumped. "I designed them on Zazzle! I bought two dozen and am mailing them to our local clients."

Of course she had. I needed to tell Jane, my lawyer, about this. If we ever went to trial, I wouldn't get a fair one in this county.

"Rex says he'll have you out of here very soon," Randi assured.

I nodded. "He's posting bail this afternoon."

Ivan burst through the door with a plate brimming with snickerdoodles. Yum! I took them from him and dug in.

"Who," I said between bites, pointing at Ronni's shirt, "is Pancratz? Do you know anything about him?"

"How the hell should I know?" Ronni snapped. "But he's a martyr now!"

"Do you want us to find out?" Ivan asked eagerly as he cracked his knuckles.

The men didn't have jobs because a resume that says you can crack ribs and scare people isn't exactly useful here in Iowa. I knew they were bored.

"Do you have your cell phones?" I brushed crumbs from my mouth.

"No. We had to give them to deputy before we came in." Ron brightened. "But we can ask Libarry!"

"That would take too long." Randi smiled at her brother-in-law. "And I don't know if it's open."

"What do you mean?" Ivan asked a question that I imagined the twins got a lot. "Libarry is a person."

Ron nodded. "Every town has a Libarry."

Randi looked confused. I'd given up being surprised by these two a long time ago.

"Explain, please," I asked through a mouthful of cookies.

"Libarry is the guy back home who knows everything. We just find the Libarry here and ask him." Ivan rolled his eyes.

"His name is Libarry?" Randi asked.

"Is short for Libarryanovich."

"We have to go. Now!" Ronni shouted. "I'm president of the Justice for Pancratz committee, and we are making posters!" And with that, she stormed out the door.

Ron turned to me before following her. "I know you are innocent." Then he followed his wife out.

"If there's anything I can do." Randi gave me a quick hug. "Let me know."

"Me too," Ivan said as he crushed me in his arms.

And then they were gone. I was polishing off the last cookie when the deputy came in to take me away. Only he didn't. He announced that I had visitors…again. And left.

"Wrath." Riley and Kelly came through the door.

Riley—my former CIA handler, one-time boyfriend, current friend, and private investigator—walked over and sat down across from me. Kelly, a former nurse who now worked for him as a researcher, hugged me then went to the vending machine and bought me five packages of Ding Dongs before sitting down.

Best friends are awesome.

"I've decided." Riley winked. "That I'm going to take your case."

I tore open the wrapper on the chocolate-covered goodness. "I didn't hire you."

Kelly pulled a file out of her purse and opened it. "Tyson Pancratz is nobody special. He works at Best Bye. Spelled *b-y-e*—I think they're a knock off of Best Buy. He sells computers there."

Riley frowned, endangering his perfect golden skin. "Hey, she hasn't signed on yet. I don't like to hand out info without a retainer fee."

Kelly continued as if she hadn't heard him. "He's twenty-four, grew up in Bladdersly, didn't go to college, and his parents died in a car accident four years ago."

"Kelly!" Riley protested. He probably thought he had the upper hand. I usually solved his cases for him. Now he had a chance to turn the tables on me.

My best friend glared at him. "What? What's the problem?" When he didn't answer, she continued. "If you think I'm going to let my co-leader rot in jail so that you can lord it over her, you're crazy."

"Thank you," I said through a mouthful of chocolate.

Kelly kept going. "We have a Girl Scout meeting tomorrow, and there's no way I'm running that by myself."

"Um." I bit my lip. "Thank you?"

"No problem." She smiled. "Anyway, there's no reason for you to kill this guy. At all."

"I have no idea who he is," I agreed. "Why would I kill a guy like that? And how did I do it? I still don't know how I allegedly pulled that off."

Kelly looked at me for a moment. "I know about that. Soo Jin filled me in. But I'm not going to tell you."

"Why not?"

"Plausible deniability. The sheriff will interview you now that the medical examiner's report is in, and you can honestly say you have no idea what happened."

She had my back, which was awesome.

"I could tell her," Riley said.

"If you do." Kelly turned her stone-cold gaze on him. "I'll not only quit, I'll start my own competing agency."

"And I'll work for her!" I slammed a chocolate-covered palm on the table.

"Fine," Riley relented. "How can we help?"

"You already are. Keep looking into this. Rex is bailing me out soon. And Betty tried to break me out last night. I need you guys to be my eyes and ears until I can use my own eyes and ears."

That didn't make a ton of sense, but I was practically vibrating with all the sugar flowing through my veins.

The sheriff entered into the room and announced that it was time to take my statement. Kelly gave me a quick hug, and Riley winked at me as they left. Now all I had to do was make a complete and thorough statement for a night I couldn't remember.

No problem, right?

CHAPTER FOUR

———

The interview room looked like basically every interview room on TV. Carnack sat across from me. Behind him was a glass mirror, most likely with someone on the other side. I'd waived my right to an attorney for this interview because I didn't need it. I hadn't killed Pancratz.

"Talk me through last night," Sheriff Ed suggested.

"Okay." I thought about it for a moment. "I remember going to bed with Rex. And then waking up on the floor of that shed in Bladdersly."

"That's all?"

"Yup. That's it. Like I told you before, I honestly don't remember any more than that."

The sheriff rubbed his eyes. "I should let you know that it looks bad, Merry. Very bad. There's a witness who saw you shove Pancratz ahead of you into the shed. He heard screaming and called 911."

"Wait, what? Who was it?" I asked more out of surprise than concern. "I thought you said the caller was anonymous."

"The Bladdersly Police Department withheld some intel from me." The sheriff grimaced. I'm sure it galled him that he had to deal with that when he was taking over the case as a favor. "The witness's name is Buddy Malone."

"Who's Buddy Malone?" Why didn't I know anyone involved? "I don't know anyone by that name. Which means he doesn't know me either."

"Buddy Malone is a security guard for the pawn shop that owns the shed. He has a flawless record—everyone knows and respects him. He gives to charity, is a retired pastor, and has never testified against anyone in all his seventy years in Bladdersly."

"Pastor, elderly, beloved Buddy Malone?" I frowned. "That sounds bad for me."

He nodded. "It really does. Are you sure you can't remember anything else?"

"I wish I could. I swear that I've never heard of Tyson Pancratz before. What would my motive be for something like that?"

"This." Sheriff Ed slid a piece of paper over to me.

It was the transcript of a phone call where I allegedly told someone I was going to kill Tyson Pancratz.

"This isn't proof."

"We have the recording. It sounds a bit like your voice. I'm sorry, Merry, but this isn't looking good."

"It can't be my voice because, before last night, I'd never heard of Tyson Pancratz. Someone is poofing me."

"You mean spoofing."

"No, I mean poofing. It's a CIA word meaning someone makes a case against you out of thin air."

"This is real, Merry." Carnack sighed. "I never do this, but I think you really need a lawyer."

I slumped in my chair. This really was bad. Not only did I not remember killing someone I'd never met in a place I'd never been before, but I also seemed to have made a phone call I didn't remember making.

"Okay. I can call Jane Monaghan," I said, thinking about an excellent lawyer who'd helped me out before. "Any news on how he died?"

Ed sat back in his chair. "You're our main suspect. We don't tell our main suspect how the victim was murdered, in case they trip up and tell us."

"Yeah." I rolled my eyes. "But that's just standard operating procedure. I mean, come on. It's *me*."

There was a moment of silence that I didn't like.

"If it helps, I did talk to Dr. Body this morning, and she told me what happened. But we don't have the murder weapon."

For a moment I wanted to blurt out *Aha! He was stabbed in the heart! I knew it!* But I thought about Kelly and plausible deniability and decided to play it ignorant. "You really aren't going to tell me, are you?"

"I've helped you out enough as it is." He looked at his watch. "But the good news is that Bryce Vanderzee isn't back in town, and the judge has granted your bail. Rex is on his way to pay it. At least you'll get a bit of freedom before I have to turn this over to the Bladdersly PD."

I sighed. Heavily. "Hopefully it's enough time to solve this before things get out of hand."

"I really shouldn't be saying this, but be very careful. And get that lawyer. I mean it."

Rex bailed me out twenty minutes later, and I was home in less than five. After carryout of my favorite burgers from Oleo's, my favorite spot in town, I called Jane Monaghan.

"Merry." The petite blonde's voice was warm. "So good to hear from you again! Hopefully under better circumstances."

"Not really," I sighed. "I need your help, Jane. This time it's for me."

Jane agreed to stop by the next day. She would be in court all afternoon. As I hung up, I leaned back into the couch. Rex wasn't in the room, probably doing the dishes or out with our Scottish deerhound, Leonard. I'd just closed my eyes when the doorbell rang. After calling for Rex a few times, I decided to answer it myself.

It was the druidic Cult of NicoDerm. My cult. Well, I was a member involuntarily on my part. Kinda.

"Guys." I held the door open. "What are you doing here?"

The four teens slouched on my doorstep, clad in long, expensive black robes—a far cry from the old ratty bathrobes they used to wear.

"We went to bail you out," Heather said glumly. "But you weren't there."

The others nodded.

Awww, that was sweet. "You didn't have to do that. But it's very nice of you."

"See?" Mike bent down to nudge the diminutive Stewie in the ribs. "I knew Bird Goddess would like that!"

"Save your money for a comic con," I added. "Or one of those druidy things."

Stewie turned as red as his hair. "We're rich now! We can afford to do stuff."

"Yeah," Kayla said. "We sold the rights to *Beetle Dork*. It's gonna be a movie."

"You're joking." This was not good news. *Beetle Dork* was an outrageously fictitious account of a real-life account about me.

Stewie sniffed. "We own the rights. We can do whatever we want with them."

The last thing I needed was a movie based on the lie that I was a bumbling spy. But for now, I could only handle one crisis at a time.

"So we've got a hearse now and everything." Heather pointed to the street.

A black hearse with *Cult of Nicoderm* painted on the side was parked crookedly by the curb.

"Does that say Stewie is a Stewbutt?" I squinted at the writing on the side.

Stewie turned green. "Heather! You were supposed to take that off!"

"It's only chalk," Mike said as he walked over and used the sleeve of his robe to rub it off.

"We painted the Druidmobile in chalkboard paint," Kayla explained.

"Yeah." Heather cracked her gum. "Some of the other kids have been teasing us. So we let them write whatever they want in chalk."

"It's smart…" Kayla's voice trailed away as we noticed that the letters weren't coming off.

Mike stared at it. "I guess it's not chalk. Might be real paint."

"Again?" Stewie erupted. "I am the dread demigod Odious!" He raised his arms and wiggled his fingers in a way that was supposed to be menacing, but just looked jazzy, then lowered them, deflated. "Guys! We have to make that stop!"

"It's your sister, dude." Heather rolled her eyes. "She's the worst."

"Yeah!" Kayla said.

"Totally mean," Heather added.

I stared at the petite, pudgy redhead. "Your sister painted your car?"

"And she spelled everything correctly. Not bad for a kindergartner," Mike said.

I shook my head to clear it. "It's really nice of you to check up on me. Thanks for stopping by."

"We'll sacrifice a chicken to you tonight," Stewie said.

"Well, not a real chicken," Heather added. "'Cuz that would be totally gross."

Stewie shook with rage. "Stop telling people we don't sacrifice real chickens! It makes us look stupid!"

That's what made them look stupid? "Please don't sacrifice a chicken in my name."

"Oh wow!" Kayla's eyes went wide. "She's totally right! We can't sacrifice a bird to the Bird Goddess."

Heather gasped. "That would be, like, so wrong!"

"How about a water buffalo?" Mike asked thoughtfully.

"Where are we going to get a water buffalo?" Stewie whined. "They're from southeast Asia!"

"I've got a stuffed toy one," Kayla piped up.

I waved my arms in front of me. "No, guys, seriously. Don't even sacrifice a stuffed animal to the Bird Goddess."

"Your wish is our command." Stewie bowed deeply.

There was a loud crack, and the short, heavyset redhead whimpered. "I can't move. I threw out my back again."

Heather perked up. "Let's get him to the church and chant over him!"

That got my attention. "Church?"

"Oh," Kayla said. "We bought a church. It's called The Chapel of Despair!"

Mike nodded. "It used to be Lutheran. They have a huge fridge in the basement."

"We've stocked it with Dr. Pepper," Heather said. "For all of our late-night rituals."

Stewie said from his bent over position, "And it has Wi-Fi! We couldn't get Wi-Fi in the woods."

"Some are saying that we're not really druids since we don't do stuff in the woods anymore," Kayla mused. "It's hindered our membership drive."

I looked at the four teens who'd been in it from the start. It was probably for the best that they didn't have new recruits for the cult.

Stewie held up his index fingers. "They will all be begging to join us when we get Xbox for the church!"

I didn't have time for this. "Good luck with that. Thanks for coming by. Good luck with Stewie's back."

They filed out of the house with the hunched over Stewie, who gave me the thumbs-up from his doubled over position. Rex joined me as they started cramming Stewie into the hearse.

"Is that your group?" he asked.

"My cult. Duh," I corrected before shutting the door.

CHAPTER FIVE

———

Rex got called into work in the afternoon to deal with a problem in the office. Apparently, Officer Kevin Dooley, our version of the village idiot, had brought in a shoplifter who, in the course of being booked, stole three staplers, five ink cartridges, and Dooley's midday snack from the fridge. Kevin was obsessed with food, so it didn't go over well, and now both the officer and the shoplifter were in separate cells.

Without Rex here to keep an eye on me, I had time to think. And I used that thinking time to get into my silver minivan and check something out.

As I drove the ten miles to Bladdersly, I realized I didn't really have a plan. Maybe barging into town looking for answers wasn't the best idea, but it was all I had. Riley and Kelly hadn't answered my calls, and I figured this was the only chance I'd have to check out the scene of the crime before Vanderzee got back into town.

There was a car on my tail—a bright yellow Dodge. We were the only cars on the road, so maybe he wanted to pass. In Iowa, on two-lane highways, people passed you when you went too slow. Of course, this was mostly when stuck behind a lumbering piece of farm equipment or a very old lady in a Cadillac that hadn't left the garage since 1974.

I stuck my arm out the window and waved him around. There was no way I was going to get a speeding ticket, because that would only make things worse. The yellow car dropped back a few feet. Maybe they just hadn't realized they were tailgating me.

I pulled into town and tried to remember where the strip mall was. There were many, many strip malls. Bladdersly had aspired to a place above its station in the 1990s by building a lot of strip malls, hoping that would attract business. Unfortunately, no one told them that they needed renters for those places, so they mostly stayed empty.

Turning off the outlying road onto Main Street, I hoped that bisecting the town would make it easier to find the place where it happened. Most small towns in Iowa had charming little downtown areas. Who's There had a park, a couple restaurants, an ice cream shop, and Randi and Ronni's store, *Ferguson Taxidermy—Where Your Pet Lives On Forever!* It was in the historic Peterson Victorian built by the founding family.

Bladdersly appeared to be the exception to the rule. I passed two dilapidated taverns—The Rabid Squirrel and The Dew Drop Inn. There was a gas station that had been boarded up, a comic book shop, two mom-and-pop restaurants that seemed to require a tetanus shot for admittance, and two tattoo parlors. The only decent building was a large old theater, The Opera House, that had a marquee announcing *The Triumphant Return of Hello Dolly!*

Harold Spellman's name was underneath as director, producer, and star. Ugh. Harold and I had worked disastrously together in Central America for about ten minutes. He went on to become a terrible actor here. Hopefully I wouldn't run into him anytime soon.

Pulling over, I tried to think. And that's when I noticed that I was right in front of Pump & Pawn, which seemed to be a combination gym and pawn shop. It was next to The Opera House, and I could see the shed from last night. I drove into the lot and around back.

In the daylight, the shed looked like nothing. The inside had been decent, but the outside was made up of peeling metal siding that, if the sun hit it in just the right spot, you'd go blind. I was rubbing my eyes when I noticed a flash of yellow in the reflection.

Without turning around, I glanced at a papered-over glass window to see the yellow Dodge again. It was parked a few yards away. An average-looking young man with shaggy brown hair stepped out and sat on the hood. The kid wore an Aloha shirt, khaki slacks, and boat shoes. He couldn't have been older than twenty.

I walked toward him. "Can I help you?"

The kid waved me off. "Nah. I'm good. Thanks though."

I tried hard not to grind my teeth. "I don't really want to help you."

He seemed surprised. "Then why did you ask? It seems kind of rude to ask and not mean it."

I closed my eyes and took a deep breath before asking, "Are you following me?"

He blinked for a second or two before answering. "Kinda?"

"You don't know?"

"Oh, I know," he answered amiably.

"Why are you following me?"

"Oh, right. I'm a bounty hunter." He fished around in a shirt pocket and handed me a card that read:

KURT ALLEN HOBBS JR. III ESQUIRE, BOUNTY HUNTER

No felon too *SCARY*, **no crook too** small.

"Too small? What does that mean?"

"It means that I can chase down everything from a shoplifter at the Dollar Store to a serial killer on the lam."

"That's quite a range."

"Thank you. You'd be surprised how many shoplifters we have at all the Dollar Stores in Bladdersly. I could probably work full time on that alone."

"Not really…" I started to say.

"We have thirteen of those stores, and they average two or three shoplifters a day." He gave me a broad, toothy smile. "So thanks for the compliment!"

"I didn't mean it as a compliment."

That seemed to knock some of the wind out of his sails. "Oh."

I pocketed the card, and he jumped off the car, running toward me, hands out. I ducked out of the way and tripped him. Never run at a spy. Never.

Kurt got up from the ground and dusted himself off.

"Sorry," I lied. "Force of habit. Why did you run at me like that?"

He seemed to think it was a strange question. "I need the card back."

I pulled it out and studied it. "Why?"

Kurt put his hands on his hips. "It's the only one I have. It's actually a prototype."

"A prototype of a business card?" I studied it. It was basically white cardstock.

"Yes, and a very expensive one at that." He stared at the card with a pained expression.

For some reason, I sympathized. I took a photo of the card with my phone and handed it back.

"Are you following me because I posted bail? I'm not skipping town. I'm just checking things out."

"It doesn't hurt to be prepared," he said. "I figured I should follow you, and the minute you skip bail—*Whammo!*" He slammed his left fist into his right hand. "I've got you. Then I'll be able to afford more cards. You skipping bail and me catching you will launch my career."

"I'm not going to skip bail. I'm going to find out who framed me."

He deflated. "You're not?"

"No. Who's There is my home. I have no intention of leaving it."

"What if you just skipped bail a *little* so that I can bring you in? It would be great for my reputation."

"No."

"Please? I'm just getting started. I could use the collar." He held his hands up toward the sky as if proclaiming something. "Genius, manly bounty hunter nabs ex-CIA serial killer! Maybe I can get my own reality show!"

"I'm not a serial killer." But it was tempting to start with Kurt Allen Hobbs Jr. III Esquire.

He smiled. "Yes, but you could be. Just knock off someone else. I won't look. I promise." He crossed his heart.

"Are you nuts?"

"Okay." He rubbed his chin. "How about just *murderer*?"

"I haven't murdered anyone and don't plan to. Nor, like I've said several times already, do I plan to skip bail."

His face fell. "Can I just follow you? I told Kayla I was working a case. She said she'd only go out with me if I had a job. She lives in Who's There like you. It would be a huge deal if I could date a girl from Who's There."

That was unexpected. "Kayla? Druid Kayla who works at the ice cream parlor?"

He brightened. "That's her! Isn't she amazing? Anyway, if I can say I was chasing a dangerous perp all day, maybe she'd go out with me. Please can I follow you around?"

I thought about that. With someone out there willing to frame me, it wouldn't hurt to have a witness seeing that I'm not doing anything wrong. But I'd rather have Rex than this loser. However, Rex was at work, ten miles away. I guess this loser would have to do.

I held up one finger. "Today only. And stay out of my way."

"I promise!" He held up the Boy Scout salute. "I swear on the feather cloak of the Bird Goddess…"

That was all I needed. "Don't do that." I froze. "Wait, did you say feather cloak of the Bird Goddess?"

Kurt said, "Yeah. Kayla talks about this Bird Goddess all the time and how she has this incredible cloak made out of feathers. I'm really hoping to meet her someday!"

I held out my hand. "Nice to meet you. I'm the Bird Goddess."

A look came over him that I'd like to describe as awe. "Seriously? I can't bring you in! Kayla would never speak to me again!"

I withdrew my hand. "That's right. And if you don't get in my way, I can put in a good word for you."

And what's this business about a feather cloak? I didn't have one. Maybe it was a surprise? I liked surprises. I decided to drop it so that Kurt wouldn't remember that he told me that.

Kurt mulled this over before nodding. "It's a deal."

That was all I needed—for word to get out to my troop that I'd let a *Boy Scout* help me. I'd never hear the end of it.

"Do you know Tyson Pancratz?" I studied him. He was the same age and size, with the same hair color of the victim. "You kind of look like him."

The kid shook his head. "No. Who's he?"

My patience was wearing thin. "The guy I allegedly killed."

His jaw dropped open. "I look like the guy you killed?"

"Allegedly," I repeated.

He pulled a notepad and golf pencil from his pocket and started to write. After a second, he squinted at the end of the pencil. "You wouldn't happen to have a pencil sharpener on you, would you?"

I turned away from him to face the shed. "Sorry. I usually do, but today I left it at home."

He failed to notice the sarcasm and appeared next to me, staring at the shed. "Why are you at this place?"

"This," I said, wondering why I was even telling him anything, "is where I allegedly killed Tyson Pancratz."

"You killed Tyson Pancratz in the Magnolia Girl office?"

Seriously? My hands involuntarily clenched into fists. The Magnolia Girls. I'd had a rather unfortunate run-in with them at a Civil War reenactment not too long ago. A group of Southern sympathizers, the Magnolia Girls were prissy and mean. It took everything I had to not allow Betty to beat them up.

"There's no sign that says that." I approached the door.

"Oh. That's 'cuz they moved a month ago."

"So it's the old Magnolia Girls office."

The genius, manly bounty hunter shook his head. "No, they still use it. They just do their stuff in another place. It's owned by Pump & Pawn. The owner lets them use it. I think his daughter was in it or something like that. But she's old...like thirty now."

I turned to him. "How do you know so much about the Magnolia Girls?"

"My cousin was in their group for about a year." He grimaced. "She suddenly started acting like she's all that, prancing around, demanding to be treated like a lady, spouting some old junk about the Civil War. My aunt pulled her out and put her in Girl Scouts."

"Sensible woman," I muttered as I stepped up to the door and reached for the knob.

I froze. I didn't need to add any more fingerprints to this place. I raced to my van, pulled some rubber gloves from the glove box, and returned.

"Why do you have those?" Kurt's eyes grew wide. "You really are a killer! Killers have those!"

"So do police officers, doctors, and nurses, to name a few." I snapped them on.

I grasped the doorknob and turned. It was locked. Crouching down, I studied the lock. It was an old one, and if I had my lock picks, I could open it. But I didn't. And kicking it in wouldn't help my situation either.

Moving to the papered-over windows, I tried the sills. They were locked tight too. Great. I walked around the building, taking everything in. Kurt followed, saying nothing. Maybe he was wary of me now that I had rubber gloves. That didn't seem like a bad thing.

Back at the front door, I folded my arms over my chest. I'd have to come back at night and let myself in. Moving under the cover of darkness has benefits because, hey, it's dark. It's also a risk because lights on inside a building that's been shuttered was a bad idea.

"Why don't you just use the key?" Kurt asked.

This guy was getting on my last nerve. Maybe I wouldn't put in a good word with Kayla after all. Sure, she was kind of an idiot, but I felt protective of my druids.

"How can I do that without a key?" I kept my voice measured to avoid exploding.

Kurt opened the mailbox and pulled out a key that he then fitted into the lock and turned. The door swung open.

Maybe he would be useful after all.

We walked into the building. The air was stuffy and stale. It hadn't been like that when I was inside this room last time. I flicked on a light.

The interior of the room was ringed with crime scene tape. Why was it on the inside and not the outside? The police here had a few screws loose. I walked to the table. No box of Lucky Charms. It had probably been confiscated for evidence.

If this had been in Who's There, police officer Kevin Dooley would've eaten the evidence. Kevin was not the brightest nor the best. A paste-eater back in kindergarten (and possibly still now), he'd been slow-witted all throughout our school years. Now he was on the Who's There police force and a bit of a thorn in my husband's side.

Kurt whistled. "So this is where you killed that guy. Why did you pick such a creepy spot?"

I sighed. "I didn't. I've already told you that I didn't kill anyone. I just sort of woke up here." I pointed to a Merry-shaped spot in the dust on the floor. "And found the deceased there." I walked over to the spot where I'd found the dead guy.

"Yeah, right!" Kurt snorted. "You're ex-CIA. How does someone get the jump on you?"

"I've been out of it for a few years," I grumbled. "And I was only in for a short time. I didn't really get all that polished... Wait! Why am I explaining this to you? I don't owe you an explanation."

"Jeez!" Kurt held out his hands. "Don't freak out. I was just asking."

"Well, don't ask any more stupid questions or else I'll waterboard you." I relaxed. "How did you know I was ex-CIA?"

"Kayla told me." He puffed up.

I guess the druids and half of Who's There knew. It just caught me off guard that this kid from Bladdersly did.

"And," he continued, "Harold told me."

"Harold?" My eyebrows went up. "How do you know Harold?"

"He's my uncle. He told us all about how he saved your life in Belize…"

"That. Did. Not. Happen." At any moment, steam could come out of my ears.

Kurt folded his arms over his chest. "Yes, it did. It's all in *Beetle Dork*."

I closed my eyes and counted to ten. It helped. "Just because something is in a comic book, it doesn't mean it's the truth."

And for the record, *I* saved *Harold*. It wasn't the other way around. He was a terrible agent and lasted all of twenty minutes in the field before he was almost killed. The *Beetle Dork* comic had gotten it wrong. Very wrong. But I didn't have time to explain that.

Instead, I walked around the room. There were some empty, cobwebby boxes and some Magnolia Girls pens that I hadn't noticed the night before, but not much else.

Kurt picked up one of the pens. "Someday…" he dreamed out loud, "I'm going to have business cards *and* pens!"

There was nothing here. No clues. No diary from the killer explaining how he'd done it. Not that I'd expected it, but it would've been nice. After looking around once more, we left the building and locked it up. Kurt was about to drop the key in the mailbox when I offered to do it. As he walked away, I slipped it back into the mailbox. Now that I knew where the key was, I was coming back here without Romeo. But he didn't need to know that.

"Maybe we should interview the neighbors," Kurt suggested. "They might know something. Then you can waterboard them."

"Do you know the neighbors?"

He brightened. "Oh sure. I know everyone here. I used to deliver newspapers to the whole town. I quit last month when Kayla said it was a kid's job. That's when I decided to become a bounty hunter."

He might be of some use to me still. "Okay. Tell me who the neighbors are."

"Well, that's The Opera House, where Uncle Harold lives and works. But you already know that."

The waterboarding idea would be far too tempting to try on Harold.

"And Pump & Pawn." He pointed to the strip mall in front of us. "It's owned by Mordecai Brown. And he has Pastor Malone as his security guard. He's very nice. Always tipped me at Christmas."

My witness. "Tell me about Pastor Malone. Is his vision good—can he see at night? Does he suffer from dementia?" All valid concerns for someone over seventy.

"He's a great guy!" Kurt said. "The best! He started up a foundation that gives to underprivileged children."

"Must be most of the town," I mumbled.

Kurt ignored me. "And he started the town's arts council, created the interfaith council, and volunteered for the local chapter of the Boys & Girls Club."

Great. A pastor and a saint. "But how is his vision? Or his mind? Is he a good witness?"

"Mordecai says he's got the eyesight of an eagle." Kurt launched into another stream of praise. "He saved a puppy from drowning last week. And I've heard he has a photographic memory."

It was like having the Pope or Superman as a witness against me. There'd be no fair trial if it took place here. I just needed to make sure it didn't get that far.

"Okay," I cut him off. "I get it. He's unimpeachable."

Kurt nodded. "Why are you asking about him?"

I sighed. "He's the witness against me."

The kid shook his head. "Man, are you screwed. Are you sure you don't want to go on the run?"

"If I did, you'd never catch me. But no, I'm still not planning to go on the run."

"Are you sure you didn't do it?" Kurt eyed me doubtfully.

"Yes." I ground my teeth. "I didn't do it. I didn't even know Tyson Pancratz. I'd never seen him before until waking up with him dead in the same room."

"It's funny, but I don't remember hearing of him before," Kurt mused. "And I know almost as many people as Pastor Malone."

That was funny. "You've never heard of him? How about Pancratz—do you know *anyone* by that name?"

The kid shook his head. "It's not a name from around here. At least, they never took the paper like everyone else."

I thought about what Kelly had said. "But my sources say he grew up here. Maybe you don't know everyone."

Kurt frowned. "That's possible, I guess. I mean, if Pastor Malone reported you two by name, Tyson must have been from here. But then, you're not from here, and he knows who you are."

I needed to get hold of Riley to see if he'd found out anything else about the deceased. Or the cause of death. Yeah, I know, Carnack was helping me out by not telling me. But I needed to know how I had "killed" him.

"I need to call Riley," I mused out loud.

The kid perked up. "Riley Andrews? The private eye?"

How did Kurt know Riley? "You know him?"

The kid rolled his eyes. "Do I! He's only the best private eye in the state! I'd love to work for him."

I gave the young man an arch look. "Best in the state? Where did you get that?"

"Everyone knows that!" Kurt looked defensive. "He's a huge deal in the biz." He paused and looked at me. "That means business."

"I know what it means. But I don't know what you mean. Riley is not the best. In fact, I probably am. I've solved more cases around here than he has."

"Yeah," he laughed. "Right."

I said nothing as I walked to the van and unlocked it.

"Are you going on the lam now?" Kurt shouted eagerly as he ran to his car.

"No. And stop following me," I barked as I got inside and closed the door.

"But I thought I was helping," he pouted.

"Unless you can get someone to prove Pastor Malone a liar, you're not of much use to me."

I watched him in the rearview mirror as I drove away. He was writing in his notebook.

"Riley," I said as my former handler answered on the first ring. "What do you know?"

"Wrath." He sounded irked. "I'm in the middle of a case right now."

Glancing at the dashboard, I realized it was evening. "What's her name? Of course, it has to be a first date since, when she finds out what a jerk you are, you'll be lucky to get a second."

"I'll ignore that," he said. "You're upset and a major suspect in a murder."

I repeated my question. "What do you know?"

"You mean since this morning?"

"Yes. Since then. I understand you're the best PI in the state. How come you haven't solved this by now?"

"Where did you hear that?" He sounded pleased with himself.

"From a delusional bounty hunter."

"You're on the run? Christ, Merry! You could've given me a little more time to figure this out."

"He's a kid, and he's been following me. I'm not on the run. Enough of this crap. Did you talk to Soo Jin?"

"I did. She says he was stabbed in the heart with a stiletto knife. Hey, don't you have one of those?"

I did have one of those. It was at home in the bathroom cabinet.

"Anything new on Pancratz?" I was almost to Who's There.

"Nothing. It's like this guy didn't exist," Riley answered.

I tapped my fingers on the steering wheel. "That's what Kurt said."

"Who's Kurt?"

"The bounty hunter."

"Okay," he said. "I'll call you tomorrow." In the background I heard a woman giggling.

I hung up, and my cell rang. It was Rex.

"Sorry, babe," my husband said. "I'm stuck at the office until late. There was a brawl at the hospital. It'll take a while to sort things out."

"No problem," I said. "See you later."

I needed to hash things out, and I knew the one person who'd listen.

"Hey, Mr. Fancy Pants!" I said cheerfully to the king vulture. "Mrs. Fancy Pants," I said to the female. "Hilly," I said to the chick.

The vulture and I had been through a lot together. But his missus didn't know me yet, and since they had a chick, I didn't let myself into the enclosure like I normally did.

Mr. Fancy Pants tapped on the glass, then looked at my bag with his googly eyes.

Oh crap. I should've swung by the house first. "Sorry. I didn't bring any cookies."

The raptor was obsessed with Girl Scout cookies, and I always brought him a box of crushed shortbread cookies. I'd let him down.

The bird looked at me with disgust and hopped up onto the large tree log, opening his wings wide to show me who's boss.

"I know," I said.

The female studied me for a moment, then started grooming the chick. She didn't find me a real threat, which was good because I didn't want her to think I was trying to steal her man.

"So how are you guys doing?" I asked. When he didn't answer, I continued. "I was arrested for murder. I didn't do it, but…"

"Murderer!"

I'd been so focused on the little vulture family that I'd forgotten about Dickie, the scarlet macaw who kept Mr. Fancy Pants company. A truly obnoxious bird, he liked repeating the things the sullen teenage boy who cleaned up after him said.

"I am not a murderer," I said quietly.

"Mom! You bought me generic deodorant!" the macaw ranted. "I need Axe body spray! For the laaaaaaadies!"

Ugh. I turned back to the vultures to see Fancy Pants centimeters from the window, staring me down.

If you've never seen a king vulture before, it might come as somewhat of a shock. From South America, the birds' bodies are white with black trim at the wings. Their heads look like they came in a prize pack from a box of sugary cereal, drawn by a toddler who watched too many cartoons and ate too much of said sugary cereal.

The bald heads are black and purple. A bright orange wattle flops over the beak. Blue skin forms their cheeks, and their necks are a riot of orange and red. The raptors also have two googly eyes that seem to rotate in different directions.

"I said I was sorry," I explained as he tapped on the glass once more.

"Mom!" Dickie shrieked. "It's not porn! It's manga!"

It took all I had not to turn to the macaw. I wondered if the kid smuggled Dickie home at night.

"So anyway," I continued. "I didn't kill this guy who grew up in Bladdersly but nobody knows, and now I have a bounty hunter on my tail. Granted, he's not a very good bounty hunter. And it looks like the guy was stabbed with a knife similar to one I have. Although I know that knife is at home in the bathroom."

Why do I have a knife in the bathroom? For security, duh. I also have a gun in the oven and a machete under my bed. You can't be too careful.

Mr. Fancy Pants continued to stare but seemed a little less angry.

"But the weird thing is, I woke up wearing a shirt I didn't even own. That's got to be a clue, right?"

"That's not mine! I don't know how it got there!" Dickie squawked.

"The problem is that everyone seems to think I'm in big trouble, including Rex. He doesn't think I did it, but he's very worried because some pastor says he saw me shove Tyson Pancratz into the building where *I* didn't kill him."

Mr. Fancy Pants blinked.

"I suppose I could find a way to discredit him. I mean, I've done that before."

Back in Colombia when I was undercover with Carlos the Armadillo, I discredited his grandmother after she saw me snooping in his desk. When she ratted me out, I told him she was sampling the cocaine in his absence. When he found a baggie with the product in her nightstand, a hidden stash of every season of *The Kardashians* hidden in her knitting basket (I mean, really, what sane person watches that show?), and security camera footage (cleverly edited) of her talking to a donkey at the same time she had seen me in the den, he sent her to a lovely nursing home in Belize.

I've heard she likes it better there.

"It would be tough though. This guy is like the Mother Teresa of Bladdersly."

Still, if worse came to worst, it was a workable Plan B.

"I read the swimsuit issue for the *articles*!" Dickie screeched.

"Well." I got to my feet. "As usual, this has been totally enlightening. But I'd better get back home. I've got a troop meeting, and I'm seeing my lawyer tomorrow."

Fancy Pants nodded as if he understood and went back to his wife and baby.

"That's not weed! It's oregano!" Dickie squawked as I let myself out.

CHAPTER SIX

———

The girls arrived the next morning at my old house across the street. When I'd met Rex, he was my neighbor. After we got married, I kept my little ranch across the street for scout meetings. And because I just couldn't let it go.

Kelly arrived with the Kaitlyns, and I didn't have a chance to pump her for intel. We sat in the living room in a circle. We were trying something new that Kelly thought would put a positive spin on meetings. Each girl was supposed to talk about something they'd read, seen, or participated in that was cool. And it went pretty well—until we got to Betty.

"This"—Betty pulled one of Ronni's *Justice for Pancratz* T-shirts out of a bag—"is really creative."

"Um…" I started to say.

"I mean," the girl continued. "This is out of the box thinking. The kind of stuff we need to do."

"We are not going to do that," Kelly said.

"It is pretty cool," Lauren agreed with Betty, ignoring Kelly. "But aren't they saying Mrs. Wrath is guilty?"

"Yes," I said.

"No," Betty spoke up. "Not necessarily. I mean, don't we all want justice for the victim?"

The girls cheered. I wasn't sure I liked where this was going. I mean, sure, it wasn't right that he was murdered. But it still implied that I was the killer.

"What if we do something that says *Justice for Pancratz* but also *Justice for Wrath*?" Ava asked.

Hannah shook her head. "That's not right. We should be Team Wrath all the way."

The four Kaitlyns agreed with her.

Betty looked at the shirt. "Well, we could find another sap to sell up the river."

"Sap?" Kelly asked.

"She's been watching noir films," I explained. "It comes and goes."

Betty ignored us both. "Some bum to collar and send to the stir."

I wasn't in the least surprised that the girls didn't need translation.

Betty put her hand on her chest. "I vote for the mayor."

"Why the mayor?" Kelly asked. "He hasn't been in office long enough to do anything to make you mad."

"You don't understand, Mrs. Albers," Betty said. "This is a bum rap. No chiseler's gonna make a monkey out of Mrs. Wrath. We need a sucker. And that dupe is the mayor."

Kelly pressed. "Why?"

"Because he's a copper!" Betty said.

"I don't think the mayor killed Pancratz," Kelly said.

"How do you know?" Betty narrowed her eyes. "Were you there?"

"No…" Kelly started to say. She looked at me, but she was on her own.

Betty slammed her right fist into her left hand. "Then we drop the hammer and send him up the river."

"Guys," Caterina piped up. "I think we should focus more on Mrs. Wrath not doing it, instead of Pancratz being dead and all that."

"How about *Free Wrath*?" one of the Kaitlyns asked.

"She's not wasting away in the stir." Betty pointed at me.

"How about *Don't Put Wrath In Jail*?" another Kaitlyn suggested.

Hannah suggested, "Or *She Didn't Do It!*"

"We don't need any T-shirts," I insisted.

Ava, whose goal was to become CEO of an insurance corporation, said, "Yes, we do. We need to counter their message!"

"Technically, their message doesn't implicate me directly," I reasoned.

Betty turned the T-shirt over. *Merry Wrath Is The Killer!* was written in dripping red letters on the back.

I stood corrected.

"Okay. Then ours should say *Merry Wrath Didn't Kill This Guy.*"

Inez thought about that. "But that implies that she's killed other guys."

"Which she probably has." Lauren nodded.

"I haven't killed anyone…" as a citizen.

"I think *Merry Wrath Has Killed Lots Of People But Not This Guy* is too long for a T-shirt," Ava said.

"It has a nice ring to it," Betty said.

"We are not going to put that on a T-shirt." Kelly held her hands up. "That's not what our meeting is for. So let's move on, please."

"We've got your back, Mrs. Wrath," Hannah said.

"Thanks," I said. "Now, Mrs. Albers is right. We planned this meeting a long time ago to talk about goals for this year."

"Absolutely." Kelly nodded. "The school year is starting. You guys are in fifth grade. It's time to talk about what we'd like to achieve this year."

Betty raised her hand. "I think our goal is for Mrs. Wrath not to kill anyone this year."

My jaw dropped open. "*That's* your goal?"

"Well." The kid thought about it. "She should only kill bad people."

"We agree!" said all four Kaitlyns at once.

No one seemed to notice that Betty had stopped talking in noir. It probably got old after a while.

"That is not one of our goals," Kelly said. "Our goals should be what we want to accomplish as a troop."

"Right!" Caterina said. "Our goal is that we don't help Mrs. Wrath kill anyone nice."

Ava held one finger up. "But if she does, I think we should have a plan to help her."

"And to dispose of the body," Inez agreed. "We've never covered that. So it's new."

"You guys, that is so sweet and thoughtful." I was touched.

"But." Kelly narrowed her eyes on me.

Oh right. "But this isn't about me. This is about your new year in scouting."

"She's right," Hannah agreed. "We are a lot older this year."

"I'm glad you mentioned that." Betty pulled a stack of IDs from her bag. "I made everyone fake IDs so that we can help her investigate in places like the Cornhole."

The Cornhole was a dive bar outside the city limits with a University of Iowa theme. There were fights almost every night, and the crowd was dangerous. It was the closest thing we had to a biker bar.

Kelly confiscated the IDs, and I joined her to study them. They were really good. Professional, even. Each of the girls' faces had been aged up to look like they were 21 or older.

I held Betty's up to her little kid face.

"Yeah, no one is going to fall for this. You're ten, not twenty-one."

Betty snatched it out of the air. "I'm eleven. Which is practically a teenager."

"Where did you have these done?" I asked. Kelly shot me a look, but I ignored it. "Our guy at the CIA couldn't have done much better."

Betty appeared to preen. "My grandpa has contacts. Some Russian guy in Des Moines who used to work for the FSB," she said, referring to what used to be known as the KGB.

"Oh really?" That got my interest piqued. "I wonder if I know him?"

"You can't use fake IDs!" Kelly snapped. "Now, ladies, can we please get to work?"

"Mrs. Albers is right," I said with a smidge of regret.

We divided the girls into two groups of five, with Betty, Lauren, Inez, Ava, and Caterina in one, Hannah and the four Kaitlyns in the other. The two groups would get fifteen minutes to brainstorm ideas, and then we'd come together and see what they came up with.

"Any news?" I asked Kelly after she'd handed out the paper and pencils.

My co-leader and best friend took me off to the side. "Not much yet. Riley's confirming cause of death with Soo Jin. And I have to tell you, I can't find anything else on this kid. It's like he did nothing but eat, sleep, and go to work."

"Give me an address," I said. "I'll go search his place."

Kelly gave me a look usually reserved for when I did something stupid. Which, in all fairness, I did a *lot*.

"Do you really think it's a good idea for you to break into his apartment? Wouldn't that make you look guilty if you were caught?"

Aha! "So! He has an apartment. That's something."

My best friend shook her head. "No. You can't go there. It would only make things worse."

"Of course *I* can go there. I don't want *you* getting busted."

Kelly folded her arms over her chest. "I have no intention of breaking into a dead guy's apartment. You're my best friend. It would look just as bad."

I threw my arms in the air. "Well, I can't have Rex do it. It would ruin his career if he got busted. What about Riley? He's handling this case for me."

"That's a thought," Kelly mused. "But he's got a personal connection to you too."

Argh! "Everyone does. But you're right. I can't ask anyone to do this on my behalf. That's why we're back to me doing it."

"When are we breaking in?" Betty appeared at my elbow. "I have some new tools I want to try out."

"*We* aren't doing anything," I said.

"You can't go alone," Betty scoffed. "What if you get caught? Who's going to signal you to let you know someone's coming? And besides, you can't fit into a duct. I can."

"No," I said.

"Betty!" Lauren yelled, and the girl returned to her group.

"Alright," Kelly said. "You can break into the apartment."

I stared at her. "What changed your mind?"

"I'd rather it was you than Betty. Seriously, Merry. You're a bad influence on the girls."

"I am not," I said weakly. "I'm a model of maturity, remember?"

Her eyes grew round. "Where on earth did you get that idea?"

"You called me that," I pointed out. "Or something like that. Once. It might have been a while ago."

"I most certainly did not," Kelly insisted.

"Guys!" Inez shouted. "Are you done arguing? We've got ideas."

We joined the girls as the Kaitlyns selected Hannah to read their list.

"Okay," the girl said. "Here's what we want to do. 1) Go camping. 2) Pet horses. 3) Visit Mr. Fancy Pants, Mrs. Fancy Pants, and Hilly."

"Those are nice, but we do those things every year," Kelly said gently. "You girls are older now. Isn't there something new and a bit more ambitious you'd like to try?"

Hannah said, "I'm not finished. We also want to cure the common cold, give everyone in the world ice cream, and lastly, make world peace." She sat down, and all five girls eyed us triumphantly.

"That's definitely more ambitious," I said. "You asked. They delivered."

Kelly, for once, was speechless. I took it upon myself to call on Betty's group.

"We kinda went in a different direction," Lauren said as she lifted the sheet to read.

"1) Travel to South America to adopt all the king vultures, 2) Set up an exchange program with girls from Catalonia."

Betty was obsessed with Catalonia and used every opportunity to advocate for them. I often wondered if they were paying her.

"3) Have the Magnolia Girls arrested for crimes against Girl Scouts, 4) Go camping, 5) Pet horses, and 6) Look into this murder and elect Mrs. Wrath for president so that she can't be arrested ever again. Amen."

I looked at Kelly and shrugged. "Makes sense to me."

"Okay." She ignored me. "Well, there are *some* workable ideas in there. I especially like the idea of an exchange program. But maybe with some other country that's closer. Maybe Canada?"

Betty squinted. "Are the Canadians free?"

"I don't think so," Inez said. "The queen of England bosses them around too."

Betty and the other girls whispered for a few seconds. I decided not to correct them because I wanted to see what they came up with.

"We'll do it," Betty announced. "We will free Canada."

"And go camping and pet horses," Hannah said.

All ten girls stared at us so intensely that I was worried I'd catch fire.

"Okay," Kelly said at last.

Canada had no idea what was about to hit them.

CHAPTER SEVEN

———

"Merry! Over here!" Jane waved me over to a quiet table in the corner of Oleo's. She'd already ordered appetizers. She was my favorite lawyer for that reason. Well, and for being good at what she does of course.

"Thanks for ordering!" I said as I sat down and dug into the potato skins—all at once.

"I got you a burger and fries. I remember from last time." My lawyer grinned.

Jane Monaghan was a petite blonde powerhouse who at one time worked on my father's campaign. She had helped me recently, but this would be the first time she actually represented me directly. Considering how clever she was, I figured I was in the clear.

"I got the files from the sheriff's office. I have to be honest. At first glance, it doesn't look good."

Why did people keep saying that? I deflated like a popped balloon, but kept eating because not doing so would be wrong.

"Before we do anything." She pulled a pen and pad folio from her bag. "Why don't you tell me what happened?"

It took all of two minutes to explain. Seriously, there wasn't much more to going to bed at home and waking up in Bladdersly with a body.

Our food arrived, and I began to dig in.

"We can try to discredit the witness," Jane mused. "But we need to know what you really were doing that night."

I toyed with suggesting that the druids would alibi the Bird Goddess but decided against dragging them into this.

"I'll look into a few things," Jane continued. "Don't worry. It looks bad because they found you at the scene of the crime with the body, but everything else is questionable. I'll need to find out how they got that phone call transcription. That part seems dicey."

"Have they found the weapon?" I took a breath from inhaling french fries.

Jane thought about this before answering. "No. They think it was a stiletto knife. And if they find it, it could have your fingerprints on it. If I were framing you, I'd place the knife in your hand."

"Then why wasn't it at the scene?" I asked.

"A valid question. I need to dig around on some statutes. But don't worry. It looks bad on the surface, but there's nothing solid beneath."

While she ate, I told her about my troop and how they wanted to help. Then I went off the rails with some interesting stories about Betty.

"She may need my services by the time she's a teenager," Jane laughed. "Either that or she'll make a crack investigator."

I nodded. "It's kind of a fine line between law and crime with her. But we have a few years yet…I think."

I snatched up the check when it came and paid it. Jane protested, but I told her that since I was giving her such a problematic case, the least I could do was buy her lunch. I left Oleo's and went home feeling better about the whole thing.

I was even cheered by the fact that, as a ten-year-old, Betty already had a lawyer waiting to represent her should she pursue a life of crime.

"In my professional opinion, it looks bad, Merry," Rex said later, back at home. "They've got a ridiculously credible witness who saw you shove Tyson into the building and heard him scream."

"Witnesses can be bribed," I said as I poured a glass of wine.

His right eyebrow went up. "By who? Who bribes a retired pastor into lying to convict someone of murder?"

"It's not that strange. Once, in Estonia, I bribed a Greek Orthodox priest to rat out his bishop. It only cost me a llama and five pigeons." I pointed my glass at him. "And if you think it's hard to find a llama in Estonia…you'd be right."

"Merry." Rex ran his hands through his hair. "This is no joke. You have to take this seriously."

"I'm not joking. Bribing Father Kokkinos was a hard sell! It took me weeks to land that deal!"

Rex sat in a chair. "It doesn't help that Bryce Vanderzee is calling for your head. He really doesn't like you."

"About that." I set down my glass of wine as Philby, my cat who looked like Hitler, entered the room. "Why doesn't he like me? I've never met the man."

His dark eyes studied me. "Your reputation precedes you, I'm afraid. He knows that you've meddled in several cases here and in the county."

"I haven't meddled," I groused. "I've investigated."

"You've meddled, and you know it," my husband insisted.

Philby trotted over to my wineglass. She sat her enormous bulk down and looked from it to me.

"Don't do it," I warned.

Philby cocked her head to one side. She stood up and kicked the glass over with her back leg. Then she sat down and stared at me again.

"She hasn't forgiven you for bringing home the golden poison frog." Rex pointed at the intruder in question. The frog swallowed.

I scooped up my glass that fortunately hadn't broken. "Rufus isn't bothering her in the least. He's in his terrarium."

As I walked to the kitchen, I gave the frog a little nod. He blinked. We had a bond. At least, I think we did. After returning to the kitchen with paper towels and cleaning up the mess, I sat back down sans glass of wine, which made me sad.

"Philby." I stroked her fur. "You are my first pet. How can anyone replace you?"

The feline führer narrowed her eyes.

"You've even helped me solve cases…"

"Meddle in cases," Rex amended.

I ignored him. "You have nothing to worry about. That frog won't replace you."

"She's waiting for you to get another glass of wine," Rex pointed out.

"I'm not wasting another glass. That's the wine from New Zealand by the guy who was in *Jurassic Park*! I will, however, have a glass of the cheap chardonnay."

Rex sighed as he got to his feet. "This conversation is not over. I'm worried about you."

I waved him off. "Riley and Kelly are helping me."

He paused in the doorway. "You hired Riley's firm?"

"No, of course not. He owes me. This one is pro bono."

Rex stretched his six-foot-three frame. "And how much has he done so far?"

"And Sheriff Carnack is on the case." I shook my head. "You worry needlessly. Ed Carnack is always on my side."

"About that…" My husband came over and started to rub my shoulders, which was either a good sign or a bad one.

"What?"

His fingers dug into my shoulders. "Since Bryce Vanderzee is back, Carnack had to hand the case over to him."

I turned to look at him. "He's back?" Then I faced forward and indicated that he should go back to massaging me.

"And he's fast-tracking it. He's been bragging that you're going to be his big catch." Rex let go and went into the kitchen.

"You'd better bring me the whole bottle," I shouted. "Of the good stuff."

I stared at Rufus. He gulped. I totally agreed.

CHAPTER EIGHT

———

Bladdersly is weird at night. Sure, most small towns only have streetlights on after dark, and there's usually no traffic except at a tavern. But Bladdersly was creepy. No streetlights, and I think I spotted a couple of tumbleweeds blowing down Main. The only real action I spotted came from The Dew Drop Inn and The Rabid Squirrel. And they weren't my targets tonight.

I pulled off onto Fillmore Street, double-checking the addresses. The streets of this town appeared to be named after failed presidents, from Hoover and Harding to Buchanan and Nixon. Huh. I guess I'd never noticed that before. Why did they do that? Did they do it to distract from Hoover—Iowa's only president who was considerably loathed? Or was it because they were idiots? My vote was for the latter.

That was one mystery that could wait. I pulled up to a duplex with Tyson's address. I double-checked Kelly's handwriting, which was despicably perfect. Yup. This was the place. A one-story duplex. It shouldn't give me too much trouble.

Lights were on in the attached apartment, but nothing was on in Tyson's. That was good, but I'd still need to be careful not to draw the neighbors' attention by making any noise. I parked around the corner and worked my way to the building from behind.

No one was in the shared backyard. And there were no porch lights. Very carefully, I slid up to the back door and tried it.

Locked.

I started to pull out my lockpicks, but I thought of my visit to the shed. It was worth a shot. Easing my way around to the front, I slipped a gloved hand into the mailbox, and my fingers closed around a key.

What was with this town? Did everyone leave a key in the mailbox? What if people figured that out? Were there a rash of burglaries that the Bladdersly PD could solve if they just remembered that everyone did this? The thought made me smile, but there wasn't time to worry about this town's stupidity. I slid the key into the lock and heard a satisfying snick.

Looking around, I made sure no one had spotted me. I very slowly slipped inside, closing the door behind me. The place smelled like it was brand new. Like it had just been painted and cleaned. Had the real killer come over and taken care of the evidence?

The front door opened directly into the living room. I closed the blinds and curtains. Nice. Double blackout. It was still too risky to turn on the lights, but I had a flashlight and turned it on.

Oh sure, I could've used the one on my cell, but it would drain my battery, and I'd need to call Carnack if the killer helpfully showed up. After I beat him to a pulp that is. Whoever was framing me would be in big trouble when I found them.

The living room consisted of one very generic sofa, a coffee table with a remote on it, and a large screen TV. Well, he did work at Best Bye. I'd probably find all kinds of gadgets, which made me study the walls and ceilings. Maybe Tyson had security cameras.

What was I thinking? This guy left his key in the mailbox. Still, I was very careful, checking for cameras as I went but never finding a single one. It was important to find out if there was something that stood out as the reason why Tyson was murdered.

Things like this were usually blackmail material. Maybe this guy had photos of someone doing something they shouldn't. Or he had proof his employer was embezzling. You never knew what would be important. In Lithuania several years ago, I'd been hunted by a Mossad agent because I'd inadvertently picked up the wrong receipt in a restaurant.

His name was Alexei, and he was pretty nice about things once he found out that, even though I was CIA, I really had thought I'd picked up my receipt for two tuna bagels with chips. Why did he need it so badly that he stalked me for a week? Because that receipt proved that he was cheating on both his wife and the Mossad with a Russian agent, which meant he could end up divorced *and* thrown in prison for treason. He turned out to be a nice guy. Even gave me a few Krav Maga tips.

Another possibility was that maybe someone really hated him. There could be death threat letters lying around. Or he could be involved in the criminal underworld—although that seemed like a bit of a stretch. My point was that you had to look at everything, even if you didn't know what you were looking for. In fact, that was something they'd trained us on: looking for something that you could never imagine would be important.

So I began to make a thorough search. First, I searched the back of the TV, which was mounted on a wall. Then I checked under the coffee table and behind and under the couch and its cushions. Nothing.

In fact, there was nothing personal here. No photos or posters or tchotchkes. But then, he was a young guy, and either he didn't have much, or he just didn't care. The living room opened into a tiny kitchen with a small table and two chairs. I searched them carefully before moving on to the cabinets.

This was where I'd probably run into trouble. Opening cabinets was a dicey move. People (like me) sometimes had crammed so much into them that things loudly shifted or fell out when the door was opened. I'd have to make sure the neighbors didn't hear anything.

In fact, I went over and pressed my ear to the adjoining wall. It sounded like someone was either washing dishes or bathing a sink full of armadillos. You'd be surprised to know how much those things sounded alike. I'd once gone undercover with Armadillo Rescue in Mexico. By the way…never volunteer to bathe a bunch of armadillos. Trust me. They do *not* like it.

I started with the fridge. There was a six-pack of cheap beer and a quart of milk. I guess he didn't eat here much—another single, young guy trait. After examining the contents, I checked the freezer. Two bags of pizza rolls, two frozen pizzas, and a quart of ice cream.

The sink was next. There were no dirty dishes, and there were no recently washed dishes. He might've been a neat freak. Underneath the sink was an empty garbage can with a fresh bag in it. Someone must've been here. There was a bottle of glass cleaner, a bucket, and a couple of rags but not much else.

The cupboards were basically barren. I found a frying pan, two *Star Wars* juice glasses, two dinner plates, and two forks, spoons, and knives. The pantry cupboard held four cans of tomato soup, five boxes of instant macaroni and cheese, a loaf of bread not yet broken into, and a new jar of peanut butter. This guy was really just starting out. It made it easy to search that way, but I still found nothing.

As I walked down the short hallway, I once again noticed the lack of pictures. Not even a poster. You can tell a lot about a person by the art on the walls. I'd known a Finnish counterfeiter who displayed thousands of palm tree fronds on his walls. In Bogota, there was an art forger who collected those weird paintings of little girls with giant eyes. And in Okinawa, a Yakuza boss wallpapered his office in Barney the Dinosaur posters. Now he was an interesting case. Botan did some work on the side as a Barney impersonator for kids' parties—when he wasn't killing off rival gang members. He was very good. Always got high marks on Yelp.

But Tyson Pancratz was a blank. So far I'd found absolutely nothing that could tell me about the kind of guy he was. If he were an ice cream, he'd be vanilla. If he were a paint color, he'd be beige. If he were a dog, he'd be a yellow lab. He'd be adorable, but he'd still be a dull, blank slate.

The end of the hall had two doors—a bathroom on the right and a bedroom on the left.

Just like everything else, both were barely stocked. There was one towel and a fresh bar of soap on the sink. The shower just had a bar of soap too. There wasn't even a *bath mat*. What kind of Neanderthal doesn't have a bath mat? The medicine chest had a bottle of aspirin, a toothbrush, generic toothpaste, a razor, and generic shaving foam.

Tyson Pancratz was a mystery. A boring one, but a mystery nonetheless. I couldn't find a single thing that told me anything about his personality.

I still had one last room to check. Hopefully, the bedroom would solve the mystery. I went straight to the closet and carefully opened the doors. My flashlight revealed five blue polo shirts, like the one I'd worn at the scene of the crime, five pairs of khakis, neatly pressed, and two pair of men's dress-casual brown shoes. There was something odd—all the clothes were hung up. What twenty-something did that?

I closed the door and began searching the bed and single nightstand. I found a box of tissues, a small lamp, and a book that seemed strangely familiar. I held my flashlight up to it. It was *Boats of the Midwest*.

The same book from the crime scene. Maybe I should've grabbed one from the crime scene. I stuffed it into my jacket and searched the bedding. Rex once told me that when they searched houses for contraband of any type, eighty percent of the time, it would be between the mattresses. Isn't that weird? I guess it's like people whose password is *Password*. Go figure.

I was holding out hope that I'd find something there as I ran my hands between the mattress and box spring. But I didn't find anything. Not even a mattress tag.

I was just about to pull out the book to examine when I heard a creak that sounded like it came from the kitchen. Turning off my flashlight, I dropped to the floor behind the bed, looking underneath it while attempting to slow my heartbeat.

It could be that the neighbors had made a very loud sound that simply sounded like a creak once it passed through the wall. But then again, it could be an intruder. In my former business, it was always a safe bet to err on the side of *intruder*.

To be fair, I was "technically" an intruder too. But I had business being here because I was investigating Tyson's murder to get myself off the hook. What was this guy's excuse?

The light switched on in the hallway. What an amateur! You don't turn lights on! Everybody knows that! Yeesh!

Footsteps came down the hall very slowly. Was it someone who'd seen me come in and had decided to investigate? Was it the real killer? Hopefully it wasn't the Bladdersly police. That was all I needed. I slid my hand around behind me to touch the .38 revolver I'd tucked into my waistband. Normally, that would be comforting, but now that I thought about it, bringing a gun may not have been the best idea. If I was arrested, fully armed and sneaking around the victim's apartment, it might look a smidge suspicious.

On the other hand, if this was a bad guy, I didn't want to get into a shoot-out in the middle of the night, in the apartment of the man I'd allegedly killed. Looking at it that way, there wasn't any option that this would end well.

What the hell had I been thinking in coming here? Seriously, my inner spydy sense should have talked me out of this. Had I gone soft over the last few years I'd been out of practice? Was civilian life ruining my killer instincts? Was it all the sugar I was eating? *Nope...don't go there, Wrath!* Sugar was my favorite everything. It must be the gone soft thing.

"Effie!" a man's voice barked, bringing me back to the present. "Effie! Where are you?"

Effie? Who the hell was Effie? It didn't look like anyone else lived here. Hell, it barely looked like Tyson lived here. So who was this guy, and why was he shouting for a woman?

That's when I heard purring as two green eyes peered at me beneath the bed.

While I was flattered that this kitty liked me at first sight, she was also sort of ratting me out. I moved my hand to the cat, gently spun her around on the floor, and shoved her to the other side of the bed just as a man's legs entered the room.

"There you are." Two arms reached down and scooped the cat up. "Let's go."

I didn't let out a breath until I heard him walk down the hall. My heart stopped pounding when I heard him close the front door.

Holy crap! That was close. It's kind of crazy how my mind went straight into danger mode when it was obviously someone who knew that Tyson had a cat and decided it needed rescuing. Gradually, I got to my feet and peered out the window, just in time to see a dark car disappear.

I was almost done and didn't see any need to leave before I was ready. Slowly, hugging the wall, I made my way down the hall, dropping to my stomach as I reached the doorway to the living room.

Peeking around the corner to make sure the guy hadn't just pretended to leave was smart (which was good because I'd really started to worry about the sugar thing). If it wasn't just a cat rescuer and this guy knew I'd been there and was waiting for me, he'd have his eyes trained on the level of an adult's shoulders. It wasn't a huge advantage, but looking at him from the floor would give me a few seconds to play with. You can't get complacent with these things. You had to assume the worst. Maybe the car that drove off belonged to the neighbor.

He wasn't there. I let out a very long, deflating breath and shook it off.

That left the basement. If there was one. Living in the Midwest, everyone had basements. It was rare, but sometimes a developer would chintz out and just build onto a slab. Which was a scenario that usually ended with torches, pitchforks, and a good tar and feathering.

Iowans needed basements. Where else would we put the women and children when tornados blasted through the area? I say women and children because, in this state, they were the only sane people in a twister type situation. The men, and I mean all of them, usually stood on the porch and watched. It took a lot to rattle an Iowan, and tornados were a source of entertainment in a state where we literally watch the corn grow.

If there was a basement, access was most likely through the kitchen. I was right. There was a very nondescript door in the corner opposite the table. I turned the knob and opened it. Stairs descended into a dark void. And it occurred to me that maybe the two duplexes shared a basement.

Hugging the wall, I went down the stairs as quietly as possible. At the bottom, I waited for my eyes to adjust to see that, in fact, I'd been right. On the neighbor's side, there were endless boxes filled with all kinds of junk.

But on Tyson's side, there were maybe a dozen, again generic, boxes stacked neatly against the wall. I was just reaching for the top box when the door on the other side creaked open and a light came on.

"Yeah, I think it's down here," a gruff voice shouted. "Probably next to the chairs you and the kids sit in when we get a tornado."

I eased back up the stairs as the neighbor descended, completely unaware that anyone was down there. Closing the door very softly, I tiptoed across the floor to the back door on the other side of the kitchen. Peeking out, I didn't see anyone. I let myself out and made it back to my car.

As I was driving away, it seemed like something had been off about the place, but I couldn't quite put my finger on it. It wasn't the empty, generic nature of the apartment. It wasn't that his clothes were hung up or, in fact, that everything had been neat and tidy. It was something else in the back of my mind.

It came to me so suddenly that I slammed on the brakes in the middle of Nixon Avenue. How had I missed that? It was so obvious! I really was losing my edge.

The thing that was out of place was something that wasn't there. In my search of the entire duplex, I hadn't seen a single pet dish, litterbox, or any cat food.

So what was Effie doing there?

CHAPTER NINE

———

"Merry?" Rex was waiting in the living room when I walked in carrying a plastic bag.

"Hey, babe!" I said a little too cheerfully as I kissed him. Something was wrong. He held me at arm's length, studying me.

"A call went out on the scanner." His eyes never left mine. He was looking for a lie. "Did you break into Tyson Pancratz's house?"

"What?" I brushed him off. "No! Where would you get an idea like that?"

"You were seen. An anonymous tip came in that a woman matching your description was at the duplex where the deceased lived."

Who the hell had seen me? Had there been a neighbor out walking a dog or someone taking out the trash? I really needed to deal with losing my touch. And no, it wasn't the sugar. It will never, ever be the sugar.

"Well, that's just crazy!" I laughed. "Why would I do that?"

"Where were you, then?" Rex asked simply.

"I stopped by the store," I lied.

My husband's eyes shifted to the bag in my hands. "Can I see that?"

"Of course!" I opened it, pulling out a package of Oreos, a bag of cat food, and three tins of tuna.

You didn't think my gloves, jacket, and gun were in there, did you? I may be losing my touch, but I'm not an idiot.

Rex's eyes came up to mine. "Merry, this is serious. Carnack warned me that Vanderzee is back in town and is probably going to call here any minute to see if you were home."

I hated putting Rex's job on the line and felt a little guilty. "And you don't want to lie about it, right? Just tell him I was at the store."

And I had been too. Last week. I always kept a bag of staples in my car for just such a purpose. And the great thing? We actually were out of cat food!

My handsome husband ran his hands through his short black hair. "This isn't good. You're playing fast and loose with your alibis. It's going to trip you up."

I took out the package of cookies and tore into them. "I don't want to get you in trouble, but I really was at the store…" *Last week.* It's important to be honest, and it counts even if you aren't honest *out loud.*

"They have security cameras with time stamps," Rex said.

I shoved a cookie into my mouth and started to chew. "I know," I said.

And I did. I also knew that if I paid a little trip to the store, I could erase the digital recording of my not being there before anyone was the wiser.

"If they have witnesses who saw you at the victim's house…" he started.

"Why were they anonymous?" I countered. "Doesn't sound like something a credible witness would do."

"You have to stop doing this," Rex said.

"I'm not doing anything," I lied again, although technically, at that moment, I wasn't doing anything. "Besides, don't worry. I used to do stuff like this all the time." And if you follow up the lie with the truth, it cancels the lie out. Maybe the truth too, but I don't like to overthink it.

Rex asked, "Did you know that they are looking for a murder weapon that matches that knife you've been hiding in the bathroom?"

The cookie, en route to my mouth, froze in midair. "How did you know about that?"

Rex evaded the question, which seemed fair since I was evading the truth. "It sounds a lot like that stiletto of yours. Do you still have it?"

"Of course I do!" I marched up to the bathroom with my husband hot on my heels. "It's right here!" I pointed to the back of the toilet where I kept it duct taped.

Rex bent over and inspected the area. "No, it's not."

I stepped up and looked. Sure enough, there were two empty strips of medical-grade tape hanging down from the back.

The knife wasn't there.

"Maybe I misplaced it," I said flippantly, even though I was starting to internally panic on my way back to the living room.

Philby was furiously pawing away at the aquarium in an attempt to attack the golden poison frog. Rufus blinked sarcastically. It was a good thing the enclosure was steadfast and that the frog wasn't poisonous anymore, or I'd be in the market for a new cat. Hey, maybe I can get one that resembles Stalin this time!

"You misplaced a stiletto from its hiding place behind the toilet," he said doubtfully.

I shrugged. "I think I used it to unclog the blender the other day."

Rex stifled a grin. "No, you didn't. Because *I* unclogged the blender."

"Oh right." Had my knife been used to kill Tyson? Whoever was framing me was doing an incredible job. A++ to him. Until I found and destroyed him that is.

Rex sat down on the couch. "If you're not going to clue me in on what's happening, I can't help you."

I plopped down next to him. "I'll be fine. I've always come out of these things on top."

"This time is different," my husband pressed.

I snuggled against him. "I've been accused of murder before."

He put his arm around me and held on to me tightly. "Not with this much evidence against you. You were found with the body. A pastor spotted you and Tyson going into the shed. Your knife may be the murder weapon, and now it's missing. There's a phone call where you threatened the deceased. And now people have seen you breaking into Tyson's apartment. Can't you see how this is adding up?"

I sat up and looked out the window thoughtfully. "I suppose I'm going to have to break into the Bladdersly PD if I want to see what they actually have on me."

Rex sighed. "You do realize that you said that out loud. To me."

"Sorry about that." And I was. It was too bad Rex was a cop, because it would be fun for both of us to investigate all these murders that always seemed to frame me. Oh, I know most normal people wouldn't think of being a suspect in a murder as *fun*...

"Merry." Rex turned toward me. "You know that this has been a problem for some time."

"I know." I pouted. "And I always promise it will never happen again. But what am I supposed to do? The Bladdersly police department hates me. Which means that an entire police force hates me. And since Bladdersly is made up of your garden variety village idiots, there's no way they're going to solve this! I'll go to prison!"

"But..." Rex started.

I cut him off. "And you can't help me. Vanderzee isn't going to listen to you. He isn't going to listen to Carnack, and since he believes he's got everything he needs to convict me, he won't look for the real killer!"

"I know, but..." Rex said.

"And then," I kept rambling, "I'll have a jury from Bladdersly, and considering that they name all their streets after bad presidents, it might as well be a jury of goats."

That caught him off guard. "Goats?"

I nodded. "They actually do that in parts of Moldova and Uzbekistan. And those goats are corrupt as hell."

Rex opened his mouth and then closed it.

"Since I don't want to get you in trouble or run the risk of you losing your job, I have to investigate this myself."

He held up one finger. "Technically, you have Riley and Jane Monaghan."

I rolled my eyes. "Yeah, well, unless killers are a cabal of hot, slutty blondes, I wouldn't put too much weight on Riley. After all, I solve most of his cases." I thought for a moment. "Jane's really good though."

I stretched. "Let's hit the hay. We can talk about this more tomorrow."

Rex got to his feet and offered me his hand. "Good idea, but I'll be working most of the day tomorrow. Someone is stealing those little libraries all over town."

I stood up. "Are you kidding? Who would do that?"

"That's classified, Wrath." Rex took me in his arms.

I kissed him. "I'll bet I can get it out of you."

He kissed me back. "Nope. This is one case you're not involved in." He walked to the stairs and then looked back at me. "But I think I should see what you had in mind."

I joined him, and we went upstairs.

Later that night, while he was sound asleep beside me, I realized what I had to do in order to keep the peace around here.

I had to leave.

CHAPTER TEN

———

"You are calling me?" Kurt asked eagerly.

It was midmorning the next day when I got up. Rex was gone, so I packed a small bag with a few essentials and told him I wouldn't be home because Kelly and I had a sleepover with the troop at her house.

Then I called Kelly and told her we had a sleepover with the troop at her house, except that I wouldn't be there and (if she was lucky) neither would the girls. She took it pretty well and said she'd lie to Rex for me if I kept in touch and texted where I was every few hours.

And then I pulled up a number on my cell and called my bounty hunter. I figured I'd head him off before he got all excited and thought I'd skipped bail. It was a simple courtesy call. Nothing more.

He answered on the first ring, and I started to talk. "Hey, Kurt. I wanted to let you know that…"

"This is my *first* business call!" he shouted. I imagined him pumping his fist in the air.

I congratulated him. "That's great and all, but I just wanted to…"

He cut me off. "Hold on." It was silent for a minute. Then I thought I heard a click. "Okay. I'm back."

Back from what? "You'd better not be recording me," I warned.

"Oh! I'm not! I just wanted to take a selfie of me on my first business call so that I can send it to Kayla. But I couldn't take a picture of me on my phone with my phone, so I had to use my iPad."

"I'm sure Kayla will be impressed," I deadpanned. "Are you done? Can I talk now?"

"Huh? Oh yeah! Sorry about that. I was just excited. What do you want?"

It was just too damn tempting. I couldn't resist. "I'm going on the lam. Leaving town, the state, and the country, and you'll never find me."

There was a moment of tense silence, and then his voice exploded as he began screaming in all caps, "*Are you serious? That is awesome! Yes! Yes! Yes!*" He grew quiet for just a second. "Kayla wouldn't like me bringing in the Bird Goddess, but she would like me making my first collar, because then I'd be successful at this. Aw hell, I'll go for it!"

Well, I couldn't let this go on. "No. Of course I'm not serious. You don't really believe that someone who skips bail is going to give you a heads-up, do you?"

It was a little harsh, but I wasn't in the mood.

Kurt sounded a bit sad. "I guess you're right. I didn't think about that."

Now I felt bad. "Look, I was just giving you a heads-up that I am, in fact, not staying at my house. I'm not on the run or anything, but I'll be staying somewhere else for a little bit."

"Okay," Kurt said. "But I'll have to put a device on your car…or maybe an app on your phone so that I can see where you are every moment of the day and night."

"I'm not under house arrest, Kurt. So, no, you won't be tracking me, thank you very much."

"I think." He sounded dubious. "That I can do that legally."

I shook my head, even though he couldn't see it. "Only if I allow it, probably. But I'm not allowing it."

Kurt sighed. "I'll just tail you 24/7, then. It's just…it's just that when I sit too long in a car, I get a rash on my…"

I cut him off. "Nope. Do not go there. You can't tail me."

"I'll come right over," Kurt agreed. "Where are you so I can do that?"

"Fine." This conversation had been over five minutes ago. Kurt just didn't need to know that. "You know the Cornhole outside of Who's There?"

There was a gasp of hushed reverence. "That place? I've never been there!"

The Cornhole was a dive bar outside of town. It was an Iowa Hawkeye bar supporting the University of Iowa. If you weren't wearing black and gold when you went in, they'd probably beat you up. If you ordered beer that had a brand name, they'd probably beat you up. If you looked at people funny, they'd probably beat you up. In fact, the hospital emergency room was so used to treating fight injuries from the Cornhole, they had a code for it: Code Twit. They wanted to call it Code Dumbass, but the CEO said that wouldn't send the right message to civilians overhearing in the waiting room.

It was one of my favorite places. I had taken my friend Hilly, the assassin (who isn't an assassin), there once or twice.

"Yeah, I'll be staying there." It felt a little mean, considering I was lying to get him off my tail. "But don't go in there. I'll be pitching a tent in the cornfield. Never go in there."

There. See? I gave him good advice. He'd never survive the Cornhole. They'd eat that kid alive.

"Roger! Over and out!" Kurt said cheerfully.

"That's not…" I started, but he'd already hung up.

It was only a few seconds later that I realized my error. Kurt might be my best resource. He knew the town and almost everyone in it. I called him back and asked him to meet me for breakfast at a fast-food place in Who's There.

When he arrived, I had a makeshift map of the downtown area, including the shed where Tyson was murdered and all the businesses around it. It was time to start talking to people in Bladdersly. And it would go much easier if I had the right intel for the job.

After ordering breakfast burritos, we sat down, and Kurt took the map, redrawing the parts I'd missed and filling in the blanks.

"You have the two sides of Main Street," he explained. "On the left is the Pump & Pawn, the shed where you killed Pancratz…"

I ignored it.

"On the other side of that is The Opera House, run by Uncle Harold."

I studied his diagram. It wasn't half bad. "Yeah. Him, I know."

Kurt continued, "And on the other side of that is Elrond's Comics."

As a *Lord of the Rings* fan, I couldn't help but smile. "Elrond's Comics. Huh. That's the most literate thing I've seen in this town."

Kurt seemed surprised. "What do you mean?"

I explained, "Elrond is the elf leader in Rivendale in the *Lord of the Rings* books."

He shook his head. "No. That's the owner's name. Elrond Shire. I don't think it's a literary thing."

"Shire is also from *Lord of the Rings*," I insisted.

"I don't have any idea what you're talking about." Kurt was confused. "Is that a band or something?"

I gave up. "What about the other businesses? They might have seen something. Because, obviously, I didn't unconsciously frog march a dead Tyson into the shed."

Kurt went on. "Then you have the two restaurants, Ela's and Ella's."

I stared as he wrote out the same name, exactly across the street from each other. "They have the same name? Is one like an offshoot of another?" I mean, I'd heard of Starbucks that were on opposite corners from each other. Maybe it was like that?

He snorted. "Of course not! They don't have the same name. They're *spelled* totally different. Besides, they have different menus. Ela's serves burgers and fries. Ella's serves hamburgers and french fries."

Even though I love burgers and fries, I decided I did not want to know the difference.

Kurt explained, "And don't go into one thinking you'll also eat at the other. The rumor is that Ela and Ella hate each other so much that they have been known to poison your food if they see you at the competing restaurant."

My jaw dropped open. "They poison people?" That seemed extreme even for Bladdersly.

He waved it off. "Well, it's not fatal or anything, but you'll *wish* you were dead."

I did not have time to get poisoned, or whatever, by rival diners. "Then the plan is we go in there and ask but don't order anything."

He waved his hands in front of him. "No, I can't go to Ela's. My family are Ella's patrons. If you're one, you never go to the other."

That, I sort of understood. We have two grocery stores in Who's There, and everyone goes to one or the other. No one ever goes to both. Ever.

"Okay," I decided. "We'll split them up. You go to Ella's, and I'll hit the other. Is it the same for two taverns?"

"No." Kurt wrote the names of the bars where they sat, opposite the Pump & Pawn and The Opera House. "There's The Dew Drop Inn, opposite the Pump & Pawn, and The Rabid Squirrel next to it. They're owned by the same couple. They just have different themes. The Rabid Squirrel is classier."

In spite of it being morning, I was thinking I really needed a drink in order to make sense of Main Street in Bladdersly.

"What makes it classier…" I started to ask, but then I decided that I didn't care. Besides, I'd find out soon enough. "Never mind. You left out the two tattoo shops."

Kurt drew one on the other side of Ela's and the other directly opposite on the other side of Ella's.

I squinted to read his handwriting, which was terrible. "And both tattoo shops are named Tattoo Shop?"

His eyes grew wide. "Are we getting tattoos?"

I shook my head. "This is just intel gathering. No tattoos."

Kurt started bouncing in his seat. "Because that would be awesome! You could get one that says something like *Property of Kurt Hobbs, Bounty Hunter*, and I could get one with *I Captured The Bird Goddess Serial Killer*!"

"No."

He looked doubtful. "Are you sure? Because why else would we go into those shops? Both of them are run by bikers. Dangerous bikers."

Now that was interesting. Dangerous bikers sounded murdery. "Like Hell's Angels?"

Kurt Hobbs shuddered. "Worse. Like guys who rode with Lance Armstrong."

My cell rang, taking me away from this idiocy. "Hey, Ivan. What's up?"

"Merry! My favorite sister-in-law!"

"Don't let Ronni hear you say that," I warned. "She'll stuff you and have you holding toilet paper in her bathroom."

He didn't seem the least bit phased. "She has already done that with an emu. You should see it."

"What's up?" I cut him off before he could tell me any more.

"We are bored." Ivan sighed to prove his point. "Ron and I have not found jobs. I wondered if you would like us to hurt someone for you? We will give you a family discount!"

The thought of hiring these two former Chechen goons was tempting, and maybe I could have them threaten Kurt if he even thought of getting such a tattoo. And then I had an idea.

"I could use you to help me get some information."

"Will we get money?" he asked hopefully.

"Give me a day to work out the specifics, but yes. Can you meet me tomorrow at Oleo's for lunch? Bring Ron."

Kurt looked up. "Are you hiring someone to help you? I thought *I* was helping you."

"You are." I tapped the map. "I need a little more information on Bladdersly."

We spent the next two hours there with him telling me all the boring stuff about the town, including zoning laws (that seemed unnecessarily draconian) and tax incentives (there were none). My head was spinning when he left. I grabbed a burger and shake to go and headed over to Riley's office.

"Wrath." Riley ran bronzed fingers through his golden, slightly too long hair. "I can't hire Ivan and Ron to work for me." He leaned closer so that Claire and Kelly wouldn't hear. "I can barely afford the staff I have."

"You can*not* fire Kelly," I declared.

"And I would never do that. She's a really good researcher. And I sure as hell can't fire Claire."

I glanced at the glamorous, super smart redhead at her desk near the door. "What does she do exactly?"

Riley waved his arms around him. "Everything. She keeps this place running. I don't even know how it's organized."

"Tell you what," I said, taking out my checkbook. "I'll cover Ivan's and Ron's salaries. Just don't tell them."

I was running out of time before Vanderzee issued a warrant for my arrest. Paying Riley to hire my brothers-in-law probably sounds idiotic, but I had received a very nice settlement from the US government when I was "accidentally" outed. In addition, I'd recently inherited a relative's (who wasn't a relative) estate. And since I wasn't a big shopper and didn't have any flashy needs, it just sat there in my bank account. I pitched in to household expenses and all that, but Rex and I lived pretty simply.

"I can't do that, Merry," Riley said. "It wouldn't be right." A thought occurred to him, and he brightened. "Unless, of course, you are paying me for this case."

My first reaction was, like back in the county jail, *no*. But I thought about it. I needed help to hit the street, and I had a feeling that since everyone there creepily watched everyone else, it might not make people very forthcoming with the truth if they'd just seen me at their competitor. Besides, my retainer could cover the expenses of Ron and Ivan and would make their employment more like a probationary period.

"Fine. Have Claire send me an estimate." I stuffed the checkbook back into my purse.

"Of course." Riley grinned. "It's a pleasure doing business with you. Now, how are we going to handle this?"

"First, you are going to let me crash in your guest room, and you aren't going to tell Rex that I'm there."

His eyebrows wiggled suggestively. "Go on…"

I held up my hands. "Whoa there, slugger. Don't get any ideas. I just need to distance my husband from my investigation so he won't get in trouble."

"Right." He grinned. "Whatever you say."

"And you're staying at the Radisson."

Riley started typing. "Adding that to your bill…"

"And tomorrow we meet up for lunch at Oleo's with the guys and take it from there." Simple. Easy. I stretched. I hadn't realized how tired I was.

"It's the middle of the afternoon, and you're tired?" Riley asked.

I looked at my cell. "You have one hour to pack whatever you need. It's only for tonight. I'm going to eat, do a little digging on my laptop, and crash."

He got up from his desk. Riley knew how to pick his battles. You might think I was being bossy and unreasonable, but if you'd had to put up with all the crap Riley put me through these last few years, you'd do the same.

I ran to the grocery store and bought way more junk food than I needed. Riley was a health nut. Glucose and flour never graced his kitchen. Maybe I'd leave a little behind in case I had to stay at his house again.

Riley's home was an adorable, fully restored craftsman with gorgeous woodwork, expensive furniture, and Tiffany lamps. It was kind of strange for a bachelor pad, but he had expensive tastes, and it probably scored him points with the ladies, if they were into such things.

After making a platter of Oreos, Ding Dongs, and potato chips, I poured a glass of wine and sat down in his living room with my laptop. For several hours, I looked up everything I could on Bladdersly. I even searched their newspaper's online records, *The Bladdersly Beard*. It's surprisingly one of the more normal small-town papers in the state.

And there she was—Medea Jones, intrepid reporter. That girl with the pink hair used to write for our paper. Then she made me her mission to score a Pulitzer Prize. The obnoxious and angry young woman figured that someone who gets accused of murder so much must have a closet loaded with skeletons.

She was right, but she'd never found that out. Eventually, she fled Who's There and set up her quill in Bladdersly. Medea was probably having a field day with this. My name and face would soon be blasted all over town, which was why we were doing our interviews tomorrow.

I took a break and texted Rex good night. He responded with the same, thinking I was currently wrangling ten little girls at Kelly's house. It sucked that I had to deceive him. But there was no time. I had to move on.

Into the night, I read boring article after boring article online. Bladdersly, for all its morons, was boring. There was no mention of Tyson Pancratz. There were hundreds of articles on how wonderful Pastor Buddy Malone was.

I read those too. Which was a bad idea. The man was an absolute saint. When they told me he was loved by all, they understated it. With a sinking feeling that made me feel worse with every word I read, I realized that this witness truly was unimpeachable. I'd need to come up with a strategy to interview him.

It would be tricky, considering the fact that he'd allegedly seen me kill Tyson. But I'd come up with something. I had no choice.

I fell asleep around three in the morning and woke up at eleven the next day. After racing through Riley's state-of-the-art shower, I changed and raced over to Oleo's to hire two Chechen goons to not rough up the people of Bladdersly.

CHAPTER ELEVEN

———

"You want us to get tattoos?" Ron asked as our burgers arrived.

Oleo's was the best burger joint in Iowa. Thick slabs of well-seasoned meat, with just the right amount of grease, went a long way to steeling my nerves for the rest of the day.

"No, I…" I looked at Riley, who discreetly cleared his throat. "I mean, your new boss, Riley, wants you to carry out a little investigation."

Ivan turned to Ron. "It is a good thing we did not kill him if he is our new boss."

Ron agreed. "We have only killed two bosses before. We did not realize it would end our jobs."

Riley's right eyebrow went up. "It took two times for you to learn that?"

Ivan looked at him curiously. "Of course. I kill one. Ron kill the other."

Any normal person would worry about this. But these guys only ever worked for bad guys, so it wasn't an issue. Well, not for me.

"Obviously." Riley rolled his eyes, and I kicked him hard under the table. Ever the consummate professional, he didn't even wince.

"There are two tattoo parlors in Bladdersly," I said. "You two will take one. You go in, inquiring about tattoos, make small talk…"

Ivan frowned. "What is small talk?"

"I think," Ron replied, "that it means you talk to very small person." He held his hand out at about three feet high for good measure.

"Oh. Got it." Ivan nodded.

"You just chat about the town or something," I explained. "Small talk is meaningless chatter that puts people at ease. Then somewhere during that, you ask about the murder. Were they working that night? Did they see anything?"

"And then we break their legs." Ron nodded as though he knew this was coming all along.

"Um, no. Just questions. That's all," I said.

"Gentlemen," Riley said without the slightest hint of sarcasm. "I'm sure when you worked for Wally," he referred to their latest boss, deceased not by them. "You had to interrogate people. Get information."

Ron smiled. "Yes. We hurt them to get the answers we liked."

Riley corrected, "You mean the answers you needed."

"No, I mean the answers we liked. What good is information if it is not what you want to hear?"

"That's not how it works…" I started to say.

"You aren't going to hurt anyone," Riley said firmly. "Just ask if they saw anything that night. Or if they've heard anything relating to the case."

"Okay." Ron nodded. "And then we get tattoos."

"It really isn't necessary to get tattoos," I insisted. "You just go in there, ask to see some artwork, and tell the guy you need to decide later."

Ivan looked disappointed. "But we want to get tattoos."

I gave in. "Okay, fine. Get tattoos."

"But you said we could not," Ron pointed out. "I am confused."

"Forget I said that. Just go into the shop and tell them you are thinking of a tattoo…"

"Which one are we thinking of?" Ivan asked.

I was getting frustrated. "I don't have a clue. Just come up with something on the fly."

Ron scowled. "I would not get a fly. Flies are weak and can be smashed. I would rather get a goat."

Ivan looked at his friend. "But I want to get a goat."

"You can both get goats," I said. This was quickly getting away from me. "Just make sure you get the information to find out if anyone else saw me at the shed with Tyson Pancratz."

"Justice for Pancratz!" Ron said, tearing open his shirt, buttons flying, to reveal the shirts Ronni was making.

"That is not very loyal to Merry." Ivan shook his head.

"But is loyal to my wife," Ron insisted.

"That might work for us," Riley said, ignoring the fact that my brother-in-law was wearing a shirt that pretty much implicated me in murder. "Your shirt may do all the talking for you."

Ron seemed confused. "How can shirt talk?" He thumped his chest. "*I* talk for me. Only me."

Ivan studied Riley. "You do not seem so smart. Maybe we should not work for you."

"What he means," I interrupted, "is that by wearing that shirt, the tattoo shop guy might start talking to you about the case without you having to bring it up."

"That would be helpful." Ron rubbed his chin. "But I never have had a shirt talk for me before."

"In America," Ivan intoned. "People wear their opinions on their shirts. Not so back in Chechnya. We can talk for ourselves there."

Ron nodded. "Yes. I think we can agree that America, while is a wonderful country, can be very silly."

"Agreed," Ivan said.

This line of thinking wasn't getting us anywhere. Or maybe it was. It was kind of hard to tell. I almost wished Betty were here. She'd probably do a better job with the tattoo guy than these guys. Then again, she'd probably convince the artist she was a thirty-year-old midget who was old enough to get one. I wondered what she'd have done? As my mind went through a dizzying array of ponies, Catalonians, and king vultures, I remembered where I was and what I was doing.

"Who's going to handle the second shop?" I asked Riley.

"We can go together to second shop," Ivan said.

"I can do it," I suggested. "I don't think you guys should be seen leaving one and going into the other. It might look suspicious."

"Maybe I should go," Riley said.

"You?" I looked him up and down. "You look like you're on your way to a country club golf fundraiser." I pointed to his black polo shirt tucked into khaki slacks. "They'll never believe you want a tattoo."

"I could totally get a tattoo," Riley sniffed.

"These guys are bad news according to Kurt. Bikers." I left out the part where their wheels were not the motorized kind.

"Let's go together," Riley said. "We've portrayed a couple before."

"You cheat on my brother-in-law?" Ron had a stormy expression.

"Guys," I said. "It's just for pretend. And that might work. If they recognize me and it's bad, I have backup. If they don't, we might get a little closer to finding out what we need to know."

The backup plan was Betty. Good thing I had her number on speed dial. Of course, I would never let a ten-year-old get a tattoo. That would be very irresponsible, and Kelly would probably kick me out of the troop.

"Okay," Riley said. "It's settled. We drive to Bladdersly and park somewhere off of Main. Ivan and Ron will take the shop on the same side of the street as the shed. Merry and I will take the one across the street."

We took my very nondescript silver minivan and drove the ten miles to Bladdersly. By the open-mouthed, wide-eyed gazing that I saw in the rearview mirror, it quickly became apparent that my brothers-in-law had never been here before.

"This is just like Grozny!" Ivan said in astonishment.

"Reminds me of home!" Ron said, a little misty in the eyes.

I guess it did a bit. Grozny had its charms but mostly rocked a sort of shell-shocked, third world vibe. Just like Bladdersly.

"I changed my mind," Ron said. "I am not getting tattoo of goat. I am getting Chechen flag."

"You could get a goat wearing the Chechen flag," Ivan suggested.

We drove down Main Street to look things over. Sure enough, there were the two tattoo shops, both inexplicably named Tattoo Shop.

"Why do you have two diners with same name?" Ivan asked upon seeing Ela's and Ella's.

"Because they are morons." I turned to look at them in the back seat. "Bladdersly is not a good town—unlike Who's There, which is amazing and would never have two tattoo shops named Tattoo Shop or two diners named after the same woman."

The men nodded as if they realized this.

"We can go get food after tattoos," Ivan mused.

"But which one?" Ron asked. "Ela's or Ella's?"

Riley agreed. "We have to check those places out too. We could have the guys check Ela's after they see the tattooist. We can go to Ella's after visiting our shop."

"Okay. That just leaves the two taverns, Elrond's Comics, and the Pump & Pawn."

Riley's eyebrows went up. "Do you think we should do all of those today?"

"Let's play it by ear." I pointed out a side street, named after Millard Fillmore, with plenty of parking, and Riley pulled over.

"Okay guys, this is it. You'll take the shop across the street and Ela's. When done, text me." I held up my phone.

Ron patted his flat abs. "I want dessert. We should eat first."

"This is a job," I reminded them. "You are working for Riley now. You go to the tattoo place first. Then the diner."

Riley added, "And don't mention Merry at all."

"How are we supposed to do this without mentioning Merry?" Ivan wondered.

I shook my head. "Just don't unless they bring it up. Act like you don't know me." I thought about the bitter rivalry between our town and this one and added, "And don't mention that you live in Who's There."

The men got out of the car first. Riley and I stayed behind to wait until they'd gone into their shop. Otherwise, it would look like Bladdersly was suddenly getting a huge influx of business, and that might seem suspicious.

Ron and Ivan walked across the street. Then they started talking to each other.

"What are they doing?" Riley asked.

The men began to argue. Muscled arms were flailing around, and faces were getting red.

I called Ivan and put him on speaker. "What are you doing?"

"Oh! Hi, Merry!" He waved at the van, forgetting everything we'd said.

"Go in, and stop arguing, please," I said through gritted teeth.

"We are discussing goat tattoos. Not fighting."

I heard Ron's voice, "Ask Merry if she thinks you should get big goat, and I should get goat wearing clothes like stuffed animals that our wives make."

"I don't care," I hissed. "Get whatever you want. Just go in there!"

Ivan shrugged, and the two men entered the shop. Once they were in, we got out and made our way to the shop on this side of the street. Riley put his arm around me as we walked through the door.

The inside was dark and dingy. The walls were covered with artwork I assumed were of tattoos.

"I guess the guys should've come to this one," I whispered while pointing at a whole wall full of goat tattoo art.

"What do you want?" A large, gruff man who resembled a bear walked through a door in the back. He had a long, bushy black beard, a bandana around his head, and a leather jacket that said *I Believe Lance Armstrong*.

"Hello!" Riley said cheerfully. "My wife and I are thinking of getting matching tattoos for our anniversary."

"Oh really?" The bear man sneered. "I suppose you want something cute like hearts."

"No." I pulled away from Riley's embrace. "We were thinking of something edgier." I turned toward my "husband." "Right, honey?"

"Oh, Cuddlepuss!" Riley took my hand and brought it to his lips. "I was thinking you could get *Property of My Hunk of Burning Love*."

Cuddlepuss?

"You're still joking about that?" I laughed and then turned to the tattoo guy. "We were thinking of something interlocked." My eyes went around the room to spot five racing bicycles in the corner. "Like two bike wheels."

"I love that idea!" Riley pulled me into his arms and dipped me, planting his lips on mine. It took all I had not to flip him.

"Bikes, huh?" the guy said. "What could you guys actually know about bikes?"

"Well." I pushed myself free of Riley. "My husband rode in the Tour de France once."

Riley transitioned smoothly as the giant eyed us suspiciously. "Well, now, Sugar Buns, that was a long time ago. And I was just an alternate on the US Team. Thank God nothing happened to Lance Armstrong, or I would've had to step up."

Bear softened slightly. "You knew the Great One?"

Riley waved him off. "Not well. I was nowhere near his league. But he was a very humble and gracious man."

The giant looked him up and down for a moment. "Name's Bear."

"I'm Alan," Riley said. "And this is my wife, Eunice."

Eunice. He knew I didn't like that name. We once had a contact in Belarus named Eunice. She set fire to my shoes. While I was wearing them. Just for fun.

"You want bicycle wheels?" Bear asked.

"That's what we were thinking," I said, looking out the window. We were across the street from Elrond's Comics and The Opera House. "How long have you been in business, Bear?"

"Nine years." He grunted, hefting a huge binder onto the counter. "Why?"

"Just checking to see how long you've been tattooing." Was that a word?

"Twenty as an artist." He flipped the binder open to a page full of bicycle images.

"Do you work mostly at night?" I wondered.

"That's when most people want to get them. I usually get a lot of business from The Dew Drop Inn and Rabid Squirrel. I'm not open every night. There are some zoning regulations."

So he preyed upon drunk people when they're stupid. This guy should've been in the CIA. He looked like he could handle himself.

Bear grunted. "This your first tattoo?"

Riley jumped in. "My first one. But Kitten Thighs here has one already."

I didn't like where this was going.

"It's my name in huge cursive letters on the high, inside part of her thigh."

I could've killed him.

"I think," Riley continued, "that you should get my name around the edge of the two interlocked wheels."

"Not happening." I forced a smile.

"Names are not a good idea." Bear pushed up his sleeve to reveal a list of crossed out names, seven in all—all female.

I flipped through the binder. He really did have a lot of bike stuff. "I like this one." I pointed to a bicycle with tires made of dragon scales.

Riley came over and nodded. "Do you have anything with a lot of cats? I mean a *lot* of cats. Eunice here is a bit of a cat hoarder."

Bear scowled. At least, I think he did. It was hard to tell with that beard. "I specialize in bikes and goats. If you want something else, go across the street."

I saw an opening as I followed his finger pointing to the street. "Hey! You have a nice view! And working late, you probably see all kinds of strange things."

"I see some." Bear turned his attention back to Riley, who appeared to be enthralled by a tattoo of a dragon giving birth (graphically) to a bicycle.

"I really don't know much about Bladdersly at all," I said. "We're from Des Moines and staying with Alan's family out in the country. But I did hear there was a murder somewhere on Main Street recently."

Bear didn't respond. But his eyes were on mine, and it was uncomfortably intense. Like he was trying to see into my skull.

"That's right, my little Pickle Lips," Riley said casually. "Some poor young man. Pancratz or something like that. I heard some woman did it."

I went to put my arm around him but pinched him savagely on the back. "I heard she was framed," I added.

Bear interjected, "I did hear she's some bimbo from Who's There."

Bimbo?

"I heard that too," Riley said. "They said she murdered him in cold blood."

"Some idiot woman. That blowhard Mordecai from the Pump & Pawn said Pastor Malone saw the whole thing." Bear shook his head and flipped ahead in the book. "How about this one?"

He pointed to a drawing of Lance Armstrong's head with two intertwined bike wheels behind his head. "That's original art. I drew that." He looked across the street and scoffed. "That other bastard has no talent. He couldn't do something like this. Hell, he even copied my shop's name."

"Mordecai?" I asked innocently in an attempt to get back to the subject at hand. "That's an unusual name."

Bear nodded. "It is. Weird. Just like that guy."

Not as weird as Bear, obviously.

"What makes him weird?" Riley asked.

"Acts like he's the whole chamber of commerce or something. That man's a gossip. Thinks he knows everything that's going on in this town. But he's got some big skeletons in his closet."

White teeth appeared in the beard. Was he smiling?

"He pretends he doesn't know that..." the man started to say as a loud crash came from the street.

Across the street, Ron was standing inside the tattoo shop, looking through a broken window at a skinny man lying on the sidewalk. Ron shook his fist and began climbing through the window while Ivan tried to pull him back in. I guess using the door was something that hadn't occurred to him.

Riley ran out the door with me on his heels. Ron stalked toward the man on the sidewalk, who was trying to crawl away.

Riley got in between the men. I was a few feet away. The skinny guy sat up and wrapped his arms around my legs.

"Are you alright?" I said to him as I tried to disentangle myself.

The man pointed at Ron. "He's crazy! I'm not giving a guy like that a tattoo!"

Ron was breathing hard, not from exertion as much as anger. His outer shirt was missing, and his *Justice for Pancratz* shirt was on display over a ridiculously muscled chest.

"You make bad small talk!"

Bear appeared next to us, a cell phone in his hands. "You guys know him?"

"No," Riley said quickly and easily. "I think this was just a simple disagreement."

That was the understatement of the week. Shattered glass was everywhere. The kid was lucky he wasn't cut. I glared at Ron, who didn't see it. What was he thinking? We didn't want to draw this kind of attention to ourselves!

Bear began tapping on his phone. "Police? There's been a fight."

Argh! Now the police were on their way! And those guys knew me. That's all I needed, to be seen at the scene and in the middle of a fight.

"Honey," Riley said. "Why don't you head to the car? I know you don't like the sight of blood, and you look like you might faint."

Bear shook his head. "You shouldn't get a tattoo, then."

"Right!" I agreed. "I'll head to the van and lie down. You don't need me, do you?"

"Bear and I can talk to the police," Riley said.

I practically ran to the minivan, started it up, and drove down an alley behind the tattoo shop until I came to a nearly full parking lot at The Dew Drop Inn.

Sirens wailed, getting closer as people spilled out of the bar and into the street. I texted Ivan to ask what the hell happened. He sent me a fart emoji. I think it was a mistake.

I took a deep breath as anger washed over me. How could Ron start a fight like that? I knew he was a little hotheaded. But this was my idea, so it was really my fault. And we were just about to get something out of Bear about Mordecai Brown. What kind of skeletons was the owner of the Pump & Pawn hiding? Maybe he even had something on Buddy Malone.

I punched the steering wheel. Dammit! We could've gotten something on the guy who's so perfect that you can't say anything bad about him!

"Why you punch steering wheel?" Ivan said as he opened the door to the passenger seat. "What did steering wheel do to you?"

"Get in!" I said quickly. "Why aren't you out there? What happened?"

Ivan frowned and looked toward the street. "Riley said to go find you. Ron asked about tattoo of goat wearing Chechen flag like cape. The boy said he didn't do that for made up countries. Ron threw him through window. That is not professional."

At least one of them wanted to do a good job.

"You've got that right. I don't think Riley will hire him after that. I told you guys not to hurt anyone."

Ivan shook his head. "No, I mean you do not destroy property when beating someone. That crosses the line."

"I have to stay in the van. If the cops see me, they'll find out I was involved, and it will make me look guilty of the murder."

Ivan nodded. "I will go and look."

I grabbed his arm. "Wait. You can't get close. Riley sent you away so that he could control things. We are still flying under the radar here."

"Okay." Ivan got out, shut the door, and disappeared around the building.

I was about to throw a tantrum when my cell rang. It was a FaceTime call from Ivan. He was showing me what was happening without getting too close. I stared at my phone. The two cops who had arrested me were talking to Riley and the victim. A third officer was cuffing Ron. He was a short, dumpy, middle-aged man. Kind of old for a cop. In fact, he looked ridiculous next to the tall, overly muscled goon.

Was this Bryce Vanderzee? The chief who hated me for absolutely no reason?

Riley noticed Ron in cuffs and went over to the officer. He talked to him, and the other man began to soften. Riley could charm the panties off of a warthog. It was a talent that had gotten him in trouble more than once, including with me during the extremely short time we'd dated while still working together.

I watched in amazement as the officer took off the cuffs and handed Ron over to Riley. They began to walk toward the camera, probably seeing Ivan. Within a few seconds we were all in the van, driving across town to a grocery store lot.

"What the hell, Ron?" I shouted as I parked. "That wasn't discreet! Riley and I had to end our investigation just as we were getting information."

"You heard what you wanted to hear?" he asked.

"No. We almost did. Until you threw a guy half your size through a window!"

"It's okay, Merry," Riley soothed.

"How can that be okay? He almost got arrested! And then they would've found out he's Chechen, and that he's now related to me!"

"But they didn't arrest him," Riley said. "I talked them out of it."

"I just can't believe that worked."

"Well, that and the kid didn't want to press charges."

"What did you say?" Then I shook my head. "Never mind. It's more important that we yell at Ron for messing up."

"I did not mess up," Ron said calmly.

"You did," Ivan chastised. "You threw man through window. You know we do not damage property. It was core value of our work."

"But I did right thing," Ron insisted.

"I have told you," I breathed. "That you can't do things like that here. You weren't supposed to beat him up. You were supposed to question him."

"But…"

I cut him off. "But nothing. You had a chance, and you blew it."

"But…"

"And now," I continued, "Riley will never hire you."

Riley shook his head. "Oh, I'm totally keeping them on."

"What?" My mouth dropped open. "After that display? Why?"

Riley smiled. "Because he got some good intel. Ron found out something about Tyson Pancratz that we would never in a million years have guessed."

"And then he threw the guy through a window."

"He told me to throw him out window," Ron said. "He forgot it was closed."

That brought me up short. "He told you to do that?"

"Yes," Riley said. "While we were waiting for the police, the kid confirmed it. I just told the police chief that I'd take Ron home."

Who does that? Who sees the largest man he's ever seen and says, *Hey, would you mind throwing me through that window, please?* "I don't get it."

"The only thing you have to get is that this guy is germane to the case."

Ron grinned in the rearview mirror. "He knows guy you murdered."

CHAPTER TWELVE

———

"I thought Kelly said no one knew Tyson," I said once I found my words again.

"Neil said," Riley replied, "that he didn't want to be connected to this in any way."

"Why not? Is he a suspect?" That idea was exciting. I hated being the only one accused of murder.

"That's what we're going to find out later." Riley looked at his watch. "I think the rest of the downtown investigation is a bust for the day. We'll have to come back again. Things are too hot here. And those cops know you."

"They said that?"

Riley shook his head. "No, I deduced that. Because they're the entire police force. They're the ones who arrested you."

"They didn't mind that the guy," I began. "Neil, whatever, didn't want to press charges after being thrown out a window?"

Riley shrugged. "They said they didn't want to do the paperwork. Relax. We're two steps closer. Bear said something about Mordecai hiding something. And now we know someone who knew Tyson. And Ron and Ivan don't have to pay for the window."

"That is good news," I grumbled.

"Because I'm adding it to your bill," Riley said. "Pickle Lips."

Without looking, I punched him in the face. That may seem extreme, but Ron and Ivan were a bit protective of me. I didn't want them to smack him for it. Okay, I made that up. I just wanted to punch him. I didn't hit him hard. Didn't even break his nose. And I could have.

We drove back to Who's There, digesting this new information while Ron and Ivan discussed the physics, without using the word physics, needed to hurl such a skinny guy through a window.

"Ivan." I made eye contact in the rearview mirror. "Was that all the intel you got?"

"Oh no. Ron did not mention other part. And it's good."

I almost slammed on the brakes and dragged these guys out of the van. "Why didn't you say so?"

Ivan looked at me curiously. "You never asked."

Unfortunately, that was true. "Well, I'm asking now."

"Neil said he worked the night of the murder," Ivan said.

Ron brightened. "Oh yes! He said he saw woman and boy-man park in lot and walk behind building."

I deflated. Great. That was all I needed. Another witness.

Ivan spoke up. "Neil said the woman was odd, and he did not think it was a woman."

I perked up. "Really?"

"Do not get excited. He could have meant you," Ron said. "You are very odd."

I was? "Odd, how?"

Ivan cut him off. "She walked like a man. He wondered if man was wearing wig."

"Yes! Now that's more like it!" I did a little victory dance in my seat.

"And I got this!" Ivan pulled up his shirt to show the tattoo of Lance Armstrong with bicycle tires intertwined behind his head. He touched it, and the ink smeared. "Is just drawing on skin for placement. I will get it inked next time." It was pretty good too.

Bear wasn't going to like that.

We dropped the men off at Ferguson Taxidermy to explain why Ivan wanted to get a tattoo of a criminal on his stomach.

"When are we meeting up with Neil? Was it because he saw the T-shirt? Why did he want to be thrown out of a window? Do people know that he knew Tyson?"

Riley cut me off. "I am meeting him later tonight at The Dew Drop Inn. You aren't in the picture."

"What? It's *my* problem!" Not that I had any issue with it becoming *his* problem. The too-handsome-for-anyone's-good Riley Andrews owed me for several past grievances. But I wanted to be there.

"And it's my case," he said. "People might recognize you." He pulled a copy of *The Bladdersly Beard* out of his pocket. It was so thin that it could've qualified more as a newsletter.

Who's There Native Brutally Murders Bladdersly Man was the headline by Medea Jones. And there was a photo of me eating corn on the cob. Actually, it was me stuffing my face with corn on the cob, butter everywhere. A very unflattering picture. How did she get that? I squinted to see the twins' picnic table in the background. We'd had barbecues there all summer.

Ronni must have sent it to Medea. I needed to have a talk with those two. But first, I needed to attend that meeting tonight and make sure Riley couldn't see me.

Which was why, two hours later, I walked into The Dew Drop Inn wearing a brown mullet wig, heavy black-framed glasses, a trucker cap, and overalls. I'd even given myself a bit of a five o'clock shadow. It took a while for my eyes to adjust to the gloom. It was darker inside than it was outside for some reason.

The place was packed. And it was almost all men. I congratulated myself on choosing to disguise myself as a man and shoved my way to the back. There were two tables open in an L-shape in a corner. I took the seat that put my back toward the door.

I don't usually do that. In fact, I never do that. You'll never see a spy sitting with his back to the door because how can you avoid someone coming to kill you if you have your back to them?

But I didn't want Riley to recognize me. Hopefully Riley would wander to the back of the room to choose a table out of the way, like the one next to me. It made sense since it was quieter here. But if he didn't, this was going to be a long night.

I couldn't believe he wanted to do this alone. Riley knew that I was good at disguise. I once convinced everyone at a Tupperware party in Katmandu that I was eighty years old. Two seventy-year-old women even helped me to my car. And the Prime Minister's mistress didn't suspect a thing. In fact, neither did his wife.

"Ya gonna order something or what?" A forty-something waitress with a cloud of red hair stood next to me.

"Whaddaya got on tap?" I asked in a gruff voice.

"Regular beer and light beer." She snapped her gum.

"Regular," I grunted.

And off she went.

Riley sat down behind me. How did I know this? Because I had worked with the man and knew what it sounded like when he sat down, brushed his teeth, ate oranges, and killed terrorists. Another reason I got here earlier. He'd know me too. The less movement I made the better.

"Thanks for meeting me here, Neil," Riley said.

So Neil was with him already. I risked a sideways glance. Yup. That was him.

"I don't know, Mr. Andrews." The kid sounded nervous.

"Riley. Please," my former handler soothed.

"Okay. What I mean is, I don't want anyone to know that I was friends with Tyson."

"Here. Four dollars." The waitress slapped down a mug of beer that sloshed and overflowed.

"Keep it." I handed her a five and waved her off.

Normally, I liked to over tip. But in small towns, something like that wouldn't go unnoticed. And I was undercover.

"What do you guys want?" the waitress said to Riley's table.

"Do you have a wine list?" Riley asked.

I snorted, covering it up with a cough. Did this place look like it had a wine list? They only had one kind of beer, and they didn't tell you what it was. He was doing a crappy job of blending in.

"Sure," the waitress said as she walked over to the bar and snagged a stained piece of paper.

"I'll have the 2018 Pinot Grigio," Riley said. "And you?" I assumed he meant Neil.

"Light beer. Thanks."

I nursed my beer. At least it was ice cold. If I'd ordered wine, these people would be onto me. Wearing a disguise isn't just about looking different. Your mannerisms, habits, and the things you'd order in a dive bar had to fit with your persona.

And my persona of Harvey, a lonely, hard-drinking truck driver who loved puppies and had a heart of gold, drank beer.

"How long did you know Tyson?"

Neil said, "Since school. He didn't really make a lot of friends. In fact, it was just me."

The waitress returned with drinks and then left.

"I'm sorry for your loss," Riley said.

"I'm not. Tyson was a first-class dick. Always putting on airs about things like working at Best Bye. He thought he was all that."

Oh good. If I'm going to be accused of murdering someone, at least the victim was a first-class dick.

"Tyson thought he was better than you?" Riley asked.

"He thought he was better than everyone. In fact, I stopped hanging around with him a year ago."

Riley considered this for a moment. "Is that why you don't want anyone to know you were friends?"

"No!" Neil said a bit too loudly. "I don't want that killer woman to kill me next!"

Like I would do that. I wasn't the kind of gal who murdered you and then everyone you knew. That was so tacky.

"Why do you think Tyson was murdered?" Riley's tone throughout this was soothing and friendly. It was a good tactic that worked 99% of the time. I say that because the 1% was Eunice, five seconds before she set fire to my shoes.

But Neil didn't answer.

Riley pressed on, changing the question slightly. "Who do you think had motive to kill him?"

Neil spoke up. "Oh, lots of people. He was rude, obnoxious, and arrogant."

To the point where someone would kill him?

"When you say lots of people hated him, who hated him enough to kill him?"

There was no answer. Neil was shutting down.

"The guy who threw you through the window said you saw what happened that night?"

Neil squeaked like a mouse who just noticed a huge cat in front of him. "I didn't see what happened! It was dark. I just saw two people by the shed around that time. I didn't know that it was them!"

Ask why he thought it was a man dressed as a woman!

"The other man said you thought it was a man dressed like a woman." Riley leaned back in his chair, and it creaked.

"Well, they're liars! 'Cuz I didn't say that!" Neil's voice was tight. He sounded like he was about to snap.

Riley calmly backtracked. "Can you give me any idea what happened to Tyson?"

"Some woman killed him," Neil snapped. "Why do you want to know?"

"I'm looking into this for a client."

Neil's voice went up several decibels. "Is that woman your client? She should probably go to jail!"

"She didn't do it," Riley said. I was surprised that he said that.

A chair screeched across the floor. "She was caught in the act! You're trying to make me look like a suspect!"

Oh crap. This went downhill quickly.

"Please, sit down. I'm sorry if I made you think that," Riley soothed.

"No! I gotta go. Thanks for the beer. I'll just tell the waitress you're buying!"

Riley's chair slid back, and as they walked away, I saw that he was following Neil out, most likely hoping to patch things up.

And we didn't even find out why Neil had wanted Ron to throw him through the window.

"Hey." Kurt Hobbs slid into the seat across from me and grinned cheerfully. "I'm here to take you in!"

The young man's face was lit up with a joy most likely inspired by the idea of getting to first base with Kayla.

"Do I know you?" I asked in my disguise voice.

"Mrs. Ferguson, your disguise doesn't work with me. Now hold out your hands so that I can cuff you. I've got a friend waiting outside with a camera."

"I'm not skipping bail," I hissed in my normal voice. "I'm investigating. How did you know it was me?"

Seriously! Riley didn't even know it was me!

"Trade secrets." He held up the Boy Scout sign again.

"You tailed me here, didn't you?" I asked.

"No." He shook his head vigorously. "Nope. I used my intellect and figured it out. Who are you spying on?"

"No one," I said with a sigh.

"Who's the guy who ordered wine? No one has ordered off that list in years. All the wine in back has dust on it. Gross."

"Fortunately, wine can age without issue." I got to my feet then looked at him. "How do you know that?"

"I told you—I know how everything works in town. Paper route. He*llo*!"

I sat back down. "What can you tell me about Mordecai Brown?"

He rolled his eyes. "Oh, lots. But it will cost you."

"What will it cost me?"

"You have to let me walk you out in handcuffs so that I can send the picture to Kayla." He thought about this and brightened. "Or maybe to the paper! That's a much better plan. Let's do that. I'll text Medea Jones and see if she can meet us outside."

"First of all, I'm not skipping bail. My husband posted bail, and I don't want to get him in trouble. And secondly, if you don't tell me, I'm going to tell Kayla that you said druids are idiots."

To my surprise, this worked. Kurt paled. "Okay, okay! I'll tell you."

He settled in, and when the waitress appeared, Kurt ordered a soda water with lime.

"It helps for those long nights on stakeouts," he explained. The more likely reason was he was underage.

I pushed. "Mordecai."

Kurt relented. "He's been here forever. Practically runs downtown. And he's smart too. He came up with the brilliant idea to mix the pawn shop with a gym." He tapped his forehead. "Smart."

I thought it was ridiculous but didn't say so. Who's going to go to a pawn shop to work out or a gym to pawn stuff?

"I was in the tattoo shop talking to Bear yesterday," I started.

The kid looked astonished. "Did you get a tattoo? Is it a goat? Bear's really good at drawing goats."

"No. I didn't get a tattoo. Anyway, he didn't seem to like Mordecai. He said Mordecai has skeletons in his closet."

Kurt frowned. "I don't know about that."

"Who does? Maybe his staff…or kids…"

He shook his head. "Mordecai doesn't have kids. And the only staff he has is Pastor Malone, and even he doesn't work all the time."

"Maybe he meant the shed? Maybe the closet is a metaphor for the shed?" I liked that idea, but frankly, I wished this wasn't so complicated. It had been a long day, and I was exhausted. And I wasn't looking forward to going back to Riley's, which meant I had to find somewhere else to stay in order to keep Rex in the dark.

The waitress deposited the drink on the table with a wink at the kid and a scowl at me.

"Thanks, Mom," Kurt said as he sipped from the straw.

"That's your mom?" I watched her go back to the bar. "So that's how you know about the dusty wine bottles."

Kurt leaned forward conspiratorially. "Mom is kind of my ears, if you know what I mean. You have to have connections if you're going to succeed in this line of work." He wiggled his eyebrows meaningfully before going back to his drink.

"Your mom is your informant?"

"When you say it like that it sounds stupid. But she hears everything. People get drunk and say all kinds of things you wouldn't believe."

Oh really? Did she know about Mordecai's secrets?

"But don't ask her about Mordecai." Kurt seemed to read my mind. "She won't gossip. In fact, anytime someone tries to get her to talk, she's been known to punch them. The police don't even bother with arresting her anymore."

Half an hour later I walked into my house (for lack of any sleepover ideas) still wearing my disguise. Rex was on the sofa. He looked up at me.

"Is that a new look?"

I peeled off my mullet and fake glasses. "Yeah. What do you think?"

"It really does nothing for me," he said. "I'd ask where you've been, but I don't think I want to know."

Rex got up and took me in his arms and kissed me, in spite of my five o'clock shadow. "You smell like really cheap beer and dive bars. Oh, and by the way, some young guy showed up this afternoon and gave me this to give you." He handed me Kurt's card. "He said it was a prototype, and you are supposed to give it back when you're done."

"I'll bet," I said as I headed for the dining room.

Philby was pawing furiously at Rufus's aquarium, as if he was made of tuna and she was starving. The frog just blinked at her sardonically. I checked the latch on the top and made sure it was secure before going into the kitchen to pour a glass of wine.

I made Rex promise not to ask me about the case, and he agreed a bit too readily. I was happy and offended. We went to bed after I spent an hour trying to get all the spirit gum off my face. They really should come up with something that doesn't practically need turpentine to scrub off.

In spite of my exhaustion, I couldn't sleep. I tossed and turned all night, hashing the case out in my head and jonesing to tell Riley that I'd totally fooled him. Well, mostly the first part. At midnight, when I gave up and went downstairs to get something to eat, I spotted a light on in my old ranch house across the street.

I know it's unusual owning two houses right across the street from each other, yet I just can't bear to part with my first house.

But who was there now?

CHAPTER THIRTEEN

———

Still in my pajamas, I slipped on my rain shoes by the front door, slid my key off the hook, and stuffed my cell phone in my pocket. We lived on a quiet street.

No car in the driveway or on the street, but that didn't mean anything. The intruder could've parked around the corner or on another street. Before I could even think about what I was doing or about waking up the cop in my bed, I skipped across the street, slid the key into the lock, and threw open the door.

Betty and Lauren were sitting in front of a laptop at the breakfast bar in their pajamas. They stared at me.

"You might want to close the door, Mrs. Wrath," Lauren said before both girls went back to the computer.

"Guys!" I did as they told me to and joined them. "Are we having a sleepover that I wasn't aware of?"

"Yes. You weren't invited," Betty said simply. "But since you're here…"

I looked around the kitchen and spotted a huge sign on the fridge that read:

Badass Betty's Detective Agency & Hacking Services

"What's that?" I pointed at the sign.

"It's a sign," Betty said.

She had me there. "What are you doing?"

Lauren cocked her head to one side. "Betty's hacking into the Bladdersly Police Department."

"You're what?" I asked with a bit more enthusiasm than I should have.

"Almost in." Lauren smiled at me. "Did you know they have no firewalls or security software?"

I sat down, transfixed by the screen. "Yeah, they don't lock their doors either. Everyone just leaves their keys in their mailboxes. Classic fail."

Betty paused. "That's good to know."

I decided not to ask. Instead, I studied the Bladdersly PD page that was open. There were three icons on the screen: *Solitaire*, *Angry Birds*, and one file named *Some Case Files*.

"Why are you guys here in the middle of the night?"

Betty didn't take her eyes off the screen. "Mom and Dad are out of town. Bart's babysitting."

I looked around. "Your brother is here?"

Betty looked at me as if she felt sorry for how stupid I was. "No. He thinks we're at home. I gave him the slip."

"We're starting our own detective agency, and this is our office!" Lauren said cheerfully.

There was that wiggle of fear in my gut. Kelly was always on my case for not acting responsibly or setting consequences when the girls did something cool that she didn't think was healthy. On the one hand, Betty was getting me info that Riley hadn't. I could hire her, but of course that would be wrong... As for hacking into the Bladdersly PD, it was brilliant and useful, and I was proud of them. I was also conflicted on whether or not I should report this to Rex.

Too bad he's asleep. Across the street. Guess I'll just have to wait until tomorrow.

"Here's your file." Betty pointed a stubby finger at the screen.

"Under *Some Case Files*, your file is called *Merry Wrath is a Meddling Busybody and Murderer and I Hate Her!*" Lauren frowned. "That's not very nice."

"I'll fix it." Betty stuck her tongue out of the side of her mouth and typed *Merry Wrath is Awesome & Didn't Kill Anybody*. "Better?"

I wished I could be there when Vanderzee opened the file in the morning. Then again, he might realize we hacked into his system, so maybe I should get Betty to change it after we'd gone through it.

"I'm not sure we should be doing this," I said mostly for show. "But since we are already here, it saves me a trip to break in."

The paperwork seemed to consist of photos of handwritten notes.

"Oooh!" I pointed. "Open *Witness Statement Against the Enemy of Bladdersly, Merry Wrath!*"

Betty looked at me. "We haven't discussed my retainer fee."

"Retainer? You're charging me a retainer?"

"To cover expenses in case things don't work out and you decide to shortchange me."

"I'd never do that," I said. "And I didn't know I was paying for your services. Or taxes and utilities on your *office.*"

"You called it," Lauren said, and both girls nodded.

"Called what?"

"We had a bet that you wouldn't pay up. Betty won." Lauren handed her best friend a nickel.

"Okay, guys, this is valuable intel, sure. But I don't know how ethical it is to pay you for hacking into a police department. It would look extremely bad."

"I'm not going to juvie for you," Betty warned. "Even if you are awesome."

"She has standards," Lauren added.

"Well, if I do use your services, I'll pay you. But I can't pay for this. It would make me look very guilty, and I'm sure it's illegal."

The girls looked at each other for a moment, communicating with their eyebrows. They reminded me of Ron and Ivan...except smarter...way smarter.

"Okay. This is a gimme." Betty turned her attention back to the file and opened it. Then she hit a key. A printer I hadn't noticed on the stove started spewing out pages.

"That's pretty useful," I had to admit as I collected up the pages. "Anything else?"

"Uh-oh," Betty gasped. "They're onto us." Her fingers flew over the keyboard as she backed out of the site.

"Close the curtains!" she ordered Lauren, who was already on it. "Get the weapons and go to blackout!"

Lauren turned off the lights. We sat there in the darkness as Betty unplugged her laptop.

I had to ask, "What's going on?"

"We're waiting to see if the internet police come," Lauren said in a hushed voice.

"Say," I pointed out. "Why isn't Betty talking noir?" To be honest, I kind of missed it.

Betty shook her head. "It's after midnight. You don't talk like that after midnight. Everybody knows that."

"She has standards," Lauren said.

After maybe ten or fifteen minutes in the dark, completely quiet, Betty jumped up and turned on the lights. "Okay, all clear."

"Oh good," I said. "Now it's time for bed."

The girls went into the bathroom and began brushing their teeth.

"Guys! You can't stay here!"

Foaming at the mouth, Lauren asked, "Why not?"

"Because there's no supervising adult!"

Betty rolled her eyes. "You're here."

"Yes, but I'm sleeping over there." I pointed across the street. "Come on. You guys can sleep in our guest room."

I dragged two grumpy girls across the street and took them upstairs, where I ordered Leonard to keep an eye on them. I wasn't sure what he'd do. The huge Scottish deerhound was a bit of a pushover. But hopefully it sounded tough.

I stashed the pages we'd printed off before climbing into bed.

The next morning, I found the girls in the kitchen making bacon and eggs.

"Take a load off and rest your dogs, Mac," Betty ordered. Apparently, the noir was back.

Lauren smiled. "We're going to make you and Mr. Wrath breakfast!"

Ever since I'd known them, my troop has called me Mrs. Wrath. Explaining why that wasn't accurate to a group of five-year-olds went nowhere because, even though I was in my late twenties, I was considered old. And old women were *Mrs.* It was kind of hard to argue with that.

When I did get married and became Mrs. Ferguson, instead of correcting my name, they changed Rex's. He didn't seem to mind.

"Good morning." Rex kissed me on the forehead. "Are you making breakfast?"

"These dames." Betty marched in and deposited a plate with at least two pounds of bacon on it.

"Why are the girls here?" Rex sat down and began munching. "Hey! This is perfect! Just the right amount of floppy and crispy!"

"It's Lauren," I said as the girl appeared with a heaping bowl of scrambled eggs. She must've made two dozen. "She's the bacon chef."

Each girl in my troop seemed to be good at, at least, one thing. With Lauren, it was starting fires and making bacon. Ava was a strong leader. The four Kaitlyns could balance five spoons on their faces. Inez, Hannah, and Caterina were the cheerleaders and soothers of feelings. And Betty? She could do almost anything, including appearing and disappearing in a poof. We learned the extent of her magic skills not too long ago on a trip to Behold, Iowa.

The girls sat down at the table and began digging in.

Philby, who'd been staring at the aquarium for the past twenty minutes without blinking, sniffed the air. In a split second, she'd managed to haul her immense body onto the table. I grabbed the plate of bacon and whisked it away.

The feline führer loved bacon. On multiple occasions, she'd managed to walk across the plate in an attempt to gross us out so that she could get the spoils. It wasn't going to work this time.

We didn't make bacon very often. We just kept buying it at the store and adding it to the fridge. That must be where the girls found it.

Betty tossed the cat a strip, and she devoured it.

"I didn't realize we were hosting a sleepover last night." Rex smiled good-naturedly.

"I didn't either. But here they are."

Betty glared at me. Either she didn't want me to mention the hacking or she was mad about…well, it could be anything.

"Have *you* heard anything about my case?" I asked. I wasn't going to say what I knew, but see if he knew something.

Rex shook his head. "No. And I still think it's serious. But if things go bad, I get street cred for having a convicted felon as a wife."

I grabbed another piece of bacon. "You should be so lucky."

Rex ate quickly for a few moments, then got to his feet. "I've got to go. But I'll check in with you later. Okay?"

After washing the dishes and getting dressed, Lauren asked, "What are we doing today?"

"I am interviewing a witness. You are going home."

"Don't give us the bum's rush, pally," Betty growled. "We got the goods on you."

Oh right! The police report.

"I'll go get dressed and drive you home."

The girls complained the whole way, Lauren in English and Betty in fluent noir. Although, there were some phrases I was pretty sure she made up when she told me to make like the wind and fight off Catalonians.

Back at the house, I grabbed the printouts and settled down at the kitchen table to read.

At the top, it said, *The Case Against Merry Wrath: Meddler, Murderer, Potential Serial Killer.* Well, that was unprofessional. They got my name wrong. It's Ferguson, not Wrath anymore. Yeesh. You'd think they'd get at least that right.

They weren't wrong on "meddler." I'm well aware that I've been meddling in cases ever since I'd moved back home. It might even be how I dealt with losing a career path that was loaded with adrenaline. And there had been so many murders since I'd moved home that I made Scooby Doo and the gang look like Cub Scouts.

But "murderer" and "potential serial killer" just seemed like wishful thinking on their part. I was going to prove them wrong. The word *wrong* made me cringe a bit. It was wrong to allow the girls to hack into the Bladdersly PD's mainframe. It was wrong not to use it as a teaching moment, although the only thing I can think of that it taught was valuable hacking life skills.

Okay, that sounds bad. But most of my job with the CIA had involved stealing intel. This wasn't much different than that. Oh sure, it's illegal, but that was less important than maintaining justice. And Betty was bound for the CIA. There! That was my teachable moment. I set aside my guilt and continued.

Just below the obnoxious title, there was a hand-drawn picture of the crime scene. It looked just like it had when I woke up there. I was a little taken aback by the notations, especially the one that said: *And here's where Wrath murdered Pancratz.* What happened to innocent until proven guilty?

There wasn't much here. Just one paragraph summing up Pastor Malone's statement, stating that Malone had been working his shift as security guard, making his rounds. His testimony was written by Vanderzee. Vanderzee paraphrased:

Pastor Buddy Malone reported that he had seen Merry Wrath and Tyson Pancratz enter the shed. He thought nothing of it at the time because Mordecai Brown leaves it open for public use. But later he walked by, and hearing nothing, assumed they were gone. He opened the door, saw the victim and the killer lying on the floor. He locked the door and called 9-1-1. The end.

Vanderzee had actually written, *The end.* That's what I was dealing with.

I pictured the whole thing in my mind. And something seemed off. Why hadn't Malone thought it strange that Tyson and I were sneaking into the shed in the middle of the night? There's no mention of the murder weapon. I closed my eyes to focus on what I'd seen.

If I'd killed Tyson, why didn't they find a weapon? What did I use? My charm? No, if I'd murdered the guy, the weapon would be in that room. I suppose you could say maybe I went to dispose of it and came right back. But why would the killer do that? If it had been me, I wouldn't have come back.

So where was the weapon? I pictured Tyson's body and made another realization. If I'd stabbed him in that room, where was the blood?

And why was I the only one asking these questions?

CHAPTER FOURTEEN

———

"You're absolutely right, Merry!" Soo Jin said cheerfully on the phone two seconds later.

"Before you say anything else," I said quickly. "I know that I'm not supposed to have this information. So if this could hurt your career, you don't have to tell me anything."

"I think enough time has passed. The authorities have my report. Besides, you're accused of murder! As your friend, I should tell you what happened."

"Okay." That was easier than I'd thought. "How did he die?"

"A small stiletto knife. One stab wound directly through the heart. The knife was pulled out, and he died pretty quickly."

Part of me was happy to finally get the news. The other part of me was a little freaked out because my small stiletto was still missing. Maybe I'd get lucky and Betty had taken it. Maybe I won't repeat that to Kelly.

"Soo Jin," I asked. "Was Tyson killed on-site?"

"Inconclusive. You're asking because there wasn't much blood on the floor, right?"

I nodded, even though she couldn't see me. "That's right."

Soo Jin explained, "When the heart stops, all blood stops pumping. There's no spurting or spraying. It simply drains to the lowest part of the body. So in answer to your question, I don't know. He could've been killed there. He could've been killed elsewhere and dumped in the shed. The one thing I do know is that you didn't do it."

My heart leaped. "Do you have proof of that?"

"No. I just know you wouldn't go to Bladdersly, number one, and kill someone you didn't know there, number two. That's all I need."

I pumped my fist in the air and tried to high-five Philby, who was sitting next to me on the couch. The feline führer grunted then turned and jumped off the couch, presumably to torment Rufus the frog some more.

"But Merry," Soo Jin warned. "You're going to need more than that to prove your innocence. Bryce Vanderzee was here in my office throwing a full tantrum because I wouldn't sign off on you as the killer."

What was it with this dude? "Thanks for sticking up for me," I said.

"No problem. I gave him a piece of my mind. No one yells at me about my friends."

I smiled. Soo Jin and I had had a rocky beginning when she first moved here. The medical examiner was gorgeous, nice, and all-around fabulous. Eventually, we became friends, which is good because she owns two of Philby's daughters.

"I'm sorry, Merry, but I have to go. I just pulled up to a scene."

I froze. "Is it connected to the case? Was there another murder?"

"No. Accidental electrocution on a job site. Ten witnesses saw this guy grab a live wire. But Rex is asking me to be here just in case. Bye!"

The information Soo Jin had given me helped. It answered some questions, but today was the day I was going to get a few more answers. After chasing Philby away from the aquarium once again, I grabbed my keys and headed out. It was time to go pay a visit to Pastor Buddy Malone.

I was all of six feet away from my van when a pink-haired, petite young woman came barreling toward me.

"Merry Wrath!" she shouted. "I've got you this time!"

I folded my arms over my chest. "Medea. What's with this smear campaign against me? There's no evidence that I killed Tyson because I didn't kill Tyson."

She sneered, pushed her glasses up on the bridge of her nose. "Oh right! I have an excellent source who says you *did* murder Tyson!"

I maintained my stance. I wasn't going to be bullied. "And who would that be?"

Medea scowled. "My sources are protected, and I'd die before giving them up."

That was one option available to me, but another murder was the last thing I needed. "Considering the fact that you are talking to someone who you believe murdered a man in cold blood, doesn't that seem to be a dangerous ultimatum?"

That brought her up short. I could almost see the tiny wheels turning in her brain. Then she frowned. "Don't try your mind tricks on me! I'm too smart for that!"

Right.

"Look, Medea, I really have to go. What do you want from me?"

"A confession would be nice," she asked hopefully.

I tried not to laugh. "You are never going to get one. Because I'm innocent."

"We'll see." She consulted a notebook. "Why did you have on a Best Bye shirt? Was that because you were trying to lure Pancratz to the shed by having him think you worked for corporate?"

That was an interesting theory. "No, I have no idea why I was wearing the shirt."

She squinted at the notepad as she wrote and said out loud, "Killer has memory loss. Most likely due to early onset dementia."

"Hey! Don't write that." I pointed at her notepad. "I don't have memory loss."

Medea broke out in a smug grin. "Aha! You didn't deny being the killer!"

This was getting old—fast. "Yes, I have. Several times in fact."

"Intrepid reporter gets murderer to confess!" she wrote, ignoring what I'd just said. "There's my Pulitzer Prize winning ticket to the Big City!"

"I did not confess to anything. And if you don't stop, I will…" I considered the possibilities…torture? Murder? "I'll sue the paper."

Medea looked stricken, as if she'd had no idea someone could do that. Without another word, she pocketed her notepad and walked back to her car. How had that happened, and could I pull it off again?

If the intimidation didn't work, I was not looking forward to the next paper. Who was her source anyway? It didn't matter because Medea Jones had no problem spreading lies about me. Maybe when I was done, I'd sue the paper anyway…just because.

I sat in my front seat, staring at the Pump & Pawn. I wasn't wearing a disguise because I had a special mission in mind. I was going to accidentally bump into Pastor Buddy Malone. No, I wasn't going to intimidate the main witness. I was just going to talk to him. I was pretty sure I couldn't ask about the case. But I did want to know how he knew Tyson. After all, he told the police he'd seen him specifically that night. As for knowing me, he could've seen me before in Who's There or in the paper or on the news the night I was outed.

The only problem with my plan was that bumping into him here didn't really seem that impromptu (and not because of the fact I don't go to Bladdersly if I can avoid it). I had an idea that would make it a little more believable.

Since Who's There didn't have a pawn shop, I figured I'd pawn something here. This was the nearest place. It took me a while to find something pawnable. I'd finally settled on a tiny spy camera from the Cold War. It was a souvenir I didn't really want to part with, even though I had two. But a customer in a pawn shop could change their mind, right?

I wondered if Mordecai Brown knew who I was. I had no idea what he looked like. Which made this an opportunity to meet him too. It was a win all the way around.

After a moment, I got out of the car with my purse and started to walk toward the door. It opened when I was still about twenty feet away, and an elderly man in a security guard uniform walked out and right toward me.

My heart started pounding. This was it. This was where he would freak out at running into the woman he'd accused of murder. Malone could call the cops. The last thing I wanted was Vanderzee dragging me into the station. But I needed to talk to Pastor Malone. Squaring my shoulders, I continued toward him. When I got close, the man looked me in the eye, smiled, and gave me a quick nod.

"Morning, ma'am!" he said brightly before continuing on his way.

A shock went through me. Buddy Malone, the man accusing me of murder, had no idea who I was! There was no flash of recognition!

Buddy Malone had seen me, face-to-face in broad daylight, and didn't seem to know who I was! Wow!

My mind was still racing through the possibilities. Should I go after him? Confront him? Or would that make things worse? It would probably be better if I didn't since I could bring the sheriff here and have him witness Malone ignore me. That would be much better. If only I'd thought of bringing Carnack with me.

To say I was thrilled would be an understatement. But it was time to move on to phase two, so I continued on the mission and went inside the Pump & Pawn.

The place was brightly lit, and by that, I mean blindingly. Rows of gleaming sports equipment faced me like an army. There was a free weights area on my left and two tanning beds on my right.

Nobody was working out. In fact, nobody was there. From what I'd seen of Bladdersly, people weren't very interested in getting fit.

"Over here!" A very attractive, fifty-something man with a hint of gray at the temples of his dark hair waved at me.

The pawn area was in the back. All the way back. Walking past the ellipticals and treadmills made me tense up because I never exercise. I know I should. And someday I would. It just won't be *here*.

I finally cleared the area and found myself in what seemed to be a whole new building.

It had all the hallmarks of a pawn shop, with glass display cases filled with all kinds of things.

"I'm Mordecai Brown! What can I do for you?" He smiled, and that's when I noticed a taxidermied diorama behind him, featuring a fortune-telling squirrel looking into a crystal ball while a moray eel dressed like Elvis looked on.

"A beauty, isn't it?" Mordecai must've noticed me staring. "It's a Ferguson original. Those are very rare—I never get one in here."

"The Fergusons are my sisters-in-law." I smiled. "They'll be glad to hear that."

Well, Ronni wouldn't. She'd probably burn this place down, find the address of whoever pawned it, and burned his house down too. Then she'd have me locked away, just for mentioning it.

Mordecai's smile turned into a frown as he studied my features. Then his eyebrows went up. He, at least, recognized me.

"You're that Merry Wrath Ferguson woman! The one who killed Tyson!" He didn't seem worried or appalled. In fact, he seemed to be curious.

"I am Merry," I explained. "But I didn't kill Tyson."

Mordecai grinned, smelling a customer. "If you say so. Hey, weren't you in the CIA or something?"

Now this was something I didn't mind him knowing about me. "Yes, I was. In fact, I'm going through my things and found out I had a couple of these." I took the camera out of my purse and set it on the counter. "Who needs two spy cameras?" I rolled my eyes.

Mordecai picked up the tiny camera with care. "Are you pawning or selling? No one buys cameras anymore. But this is special. And with it belonging to a murderer, I can get a very high price on it."

"Wait, you can?" I was so surprised that I didn't correct him saying I was a murderer again.

He was turning the little camera over in his hands. "Oh sure. This is small-town Iowa. You couldn't find something like this here. How much do you want for it?"

This was an opportunity.

"Tell you what. You can have it in exchange for some information."

Greed seemed to take control of the man's senses. "Perfect! What do you want to know?"

"Tell me about the shed out back. The place where I allegedly killed Tyson."

"Oh." He looked off into space. "I guess I've had it for about twenty years. The Magnolia Girls used it for their office for a while. But they moved out a month or so ago. It's been empty ever since."

"What's with the Lucky Charms and *Boats of the Midwest* books?" Okay, it probably wasn't germane to the case, but I did find a copy of that book on Tyson's nightstand.

Mordecai scratched his head. "I don't know about the Lucky Charms. Maybe some kids broke in or something. They do that a lot."

I levelled my gaze at him. "Maybe it's because you leave the key in the mailbox?"

His eyes grew wide. "So that's how you got in when you murdered Tyson! I've been wondering about that!"

It took all I had to maintain a calm demeanor. "Like I said before, I didn't murder Tyson. And how do you not know that kids aren't breaking in, they're just basically letting themselves in because you leave the key in the mailbox?"

The confusion on his face seemed sincere. "Huh. I never thought of that."

I had to ask, "Surely you don't do that for the pawn shop."

He laughed. "Of course not! I'm not an idiot. We have a combination panel. Makes it easier on Pastor Malone."

Ooooh! Was he saying that Buddy had some impairments? "Oh. Because he can't see too well, huh?"

"Nope. He has the vision of an eagle. I've never known anyone with such sharp vision. And at his age!"

I tried another thought. "Is it because of cognitive issues?"

Mordecai slapped his hand on the counter between us. "Think again! That man changes the password every week and remembers every time. He has to write it down for *me* so that I don't forget it."

Oh, for crying out loud. "Then why did you say it's easier for him?"

He feigned writing in the air with an invisible pen. "Arthritis. His right hand cramps up."

Would that be enough to discredit him as a witness? He didn't know who I was. How does someone with perfect vision see me if he doesn't know me from sight?

Ivan said the tattoo artist thought it wasn't a woman leading Tyson that night. He thought it was a man in a wig. If some young guy could see that from a distance, why couldn't Malone?

Next question. "Were you here that night?"

"No. I was checking out an estate sale in Johnston." Mordecai leaned forward conspiratorially, looking left and then right. "Did you know that there's a woman out there who has the world's largest collection of Dwayne 'The Rock' Johnson paper dolls?" He pointed to a display case featuring a paper doll of The Rock. He had five different kinds of paper wigs you could put on him. I was partial to the mohawk.

"I got the whole shebang!" He slapped the counter. "Do you know how big that guy is here in Iowa? Man! I wish she'd had some other memorabilia of him. I could retire early!"

It was interesting, and I did have some questions, but I forced myself to get back on track. "Pastor Malone was here by himself? Why, if he saw me and Tyson enter the shed, didn't he follow us in to find out what we were doing there?"

This brought the pawn broker up short. "What do you mean?"

"This is a pawn shop, and the shed is part of your property, and he's responsible for security. It's a no-brainer."

His face relaxed into an aha expression. "Oh. That's probably because so many people use that shed for meetings. He probably didn't think much about it."

He did think about it. At least enough to directly identify me.

This was new information. "You're joking. What kind of meetings do a man and woman get up to in there…"

Mordecai smiled and wiggled his eyebrows.

My mouth dropped open. "Are you using your shed as a no-tell motel?"

"Absolutely not," he said while nodding up and down.

I leaned forward in spite of the fact that the place was empty. "Is that legal?"

He shrugged. "Money isn't changing hands."

Ugh! "So *Pastor* Buddy thought that Tyson and I were…"

"I'm not saying that." He nodded again. Then his smile dimmed. He was worrying that he'd said too much.

"What else do you want to know?" His enthusiasm and patience seemed to be wearing a bit thin. I needed to end this before he figured out what I was doing—even if he was getting the spy camera for free.

I held up my index finger. "One more question. Did you know Tyson Pancratz?"

Mordecai rocked back on his heels as he thought about this. "The guy you murdered?"

Sigh. "I did not murder him."

"Yeah. I mean, I'd seen him around. Mostly at Elrond's Comics and once or twice at The Opera House. I think Harold was giving him acting lessons or something like that."

Harold knew him. I should've known.

"Would you say you knew him more than just seeing him around?" I wasn't really sure he was going to give me too much more. There's a moment when you know your informant is done with you. Beyond that, you're lucky to get anything.

Mordecai seemed to lose his casual demeanor. "Not really. He was really quiet. Worked at Best Bye. Now, if you don't mind, I'd like to put this beauty in the safe while I think of the right words to market it. I'm thinking *Ex-CIA Serial Killer's Spy Camera*! What do you think?"

I threw my arms up in the air. "Why do people keep calling me a serial killer?"

He pointed at me. "Aha! You admitted it!"

"No, I didn't." I turned to get out of this madhouse, when I remembered something. "You didn't answer my question about the boat books. Why do you only have that book and so many copies?"

"Figure that out for yourself," he said gruffly. This interview was over.

I stepped out into the sunshine with a head full of information that I needed to process. I walked over to Elrond's Comics, but the shop was closed. Glancing at The Opera House, my stomach growled, and I realized I didn't want to face Harold on an empty stomach.

Besides, I needed to write all of this down before I forgot. Back in Who's There, I picked up some fried chicken and took it to Rex's office.

"Thanks!" Rex smiled as I walked into his office. "Fried chicken! My favorite! What's the occasion?"

From his desk in the main area, Officer Kevin Dooley sniffed the air and looked at me with interest for the first time since I gave him a snack pudding in the third grade. I'd had two, or I normally wouldn't have shared.

"Should I take some to Kevin?" I mumbled to Rex as I unloaded the bag.

"Officer Dooley," Rex corrected. "How much did you get? There's enough for the whole station?"

I shrugged. "You know me. I over-order when I'm starving."

Rex pulled a paper plate from a desk drawer. He had everything in there because he often worked late. He put a chicken breast and drumstick on the plate.

"For Officer Dooley," he said as he dumped a scoop of mashed potatoes.

I snatched the drumstick off, replacing it with a thigh. "Sorry. Drumsticks are mine."

Rex laughed and took the plate to Dooley, who was now drooling. He came back into his office, closed the door, and sat down to dig in.

"How's the meddling going?" Rex asked me.

"We aren't going to talk about it," I said. "I don't want to cross some colleague confidentiality line."

He pointed a drumstick at me. How did I miss that one? "That's not a thing."

"Trust me. I'll tell you when I have enough. But not now. I don't want you compromised."

Rex sighed. "At least tell me you're talking to Jane."

I nodded. "I should probably call her."

Actually, she'd call me if she had anything. Right now, I was pretty sure I had more than anyone else in this investigation.

"So what do we talk about?" His right eyebrow went up.

"How was that electrocution victim?" I asked.

Rex leaned back in his chair. "You've been talking to Soo Jin." When he saw that I wasn't going to say anything else, he said, "Just an accident. We had ten witnesses who saw it."

I really, really wanted to tell my husband the truth about my one and only witness. But something told me I should tell Carnack first. He was the only one who'd have any influence over the case.

We ate, making small talk about the pets and Philby's obsession with Rufus. When we were done, I got to my feet and started packing up the garbage.

"Are we on for dinner?" Rex asked as he helped.

"No. I'm going to see if I can meet up with Jane for dinner," I lied.

Rex liked this idea. "Good. And by the way, the twins want to have us over for a cookout soon."

"Okay," I said as I kissed him good-bye.

In the main room, Kevin had eaten all of the food we'd given him and was now working his way through a box of Ding Dongs.

"You're welcome, Kevin," I said breezily as I walked past him and out the door. I had plans for the night. And they didn't include my lawyer.

CHAPTER FIFTEEN

"What am I doing?" I muttered to myself for the tenth time since I'd left my house.

It was getting dark out, and I was on the road to Bladdersly to visit Pastor Malone at home. Hopefully, I'd get him to explain how he didn't recognize me on the street but his eagle-eyed vision spotted me with Tyson Pancratz the night he was murdered.

I didn't want to confront the man at work because I didn't want Mordecai to influence him. Since I'd looked him up and discovered he had a house in the country, I'd thought I'd just pop on by. What could it hurt?

Everything. It could hurt everything. The man had obviously lied about me. How many retired pastors did that? If he lied to the police once, he could do it again. My end game was to get him to tell me the truth so that I could find a way to expose him as a liar without ending up in jail for harassing the witness.

Easy, right?

I found the gravel road turnoff just before Bladdersly and eased my van onto it. It was evening but not too late. Past dinner but before bed. The house was about a mile down a road that dead-ended right in front of his home.

I pulled into the drive and turned off the engine. The porch light was on. Walking up onto the wraparound porch, I thought about what I would say.

Hello. My name is Merry Ferguson. You accused me of a murder I didn't commit. How are you?

Sure. That should go over well.

I reached up to knock on the door when I noticed it was ajar. Was he waiting for me? Of course he wasn't. He had no idea who I was! But what if he was a secret criminal mastermind and he was luring me in for the kill? That made more sense.

The lights were off inside. It sure as hell seemed like a trap. What did I do now? I should call the sheriff. Carnack would have jurisdiction here. But then again, he'd wonder why I was here to see the main witness against me. And if the man was hurt inside, wouldn't that make me look just as bad?

I could go home. But what if he was injured? I'd never forgive myself if I let a man die from falling or something. I'm pretty sure that my lifetime membership in the Girl Scouts could be revoked for that. On the other hand, what if he had been attacked? And what if the attacker was still here? What if it was the real killer? What if they'd seen Malone *not* recognize me on the street and decided to take him out before I blew the whistle on him?

Insidious! But that's exactly what I would do. And I wasn't the killer.

Well, I had to do something. I texted Riley with my location and situation. At least someone should know. Rex would be mad at me, and Carnack would be forced to arrest me. But at least I'd be in County instead of the Bladdersly jail.

If the killer was in there waiting for me, I needed to be ready. Being prepared wasn't just a scout motto. It worked for the CIA too. Only, I wasn't prepared. I'd left home without my gun. Looking around for a weapon, the only thing I found was a cement garden gnome reading a Bible.

I picked it up and kicked open the door, hard. If anyone was behind it, I'd find out. No one grunted, and the door slammed against the wall. Any bad guys hiding inside would know someone was here.

"Police!" I shouted in the male voice that I'd used at The Dew Drop Inn. "The place is surrounded! Come out with your hands up, and we won't shoot! Alright, men! Be on your guard!" I was ad-libbing here, and it would be kind of fun if the situation weren't so dire. "No one shoots until I say! And that goes for you, Luther!"

I was getting a little carried away, but I thought that bit about Luther made it seem more real.

There was no sound of movement. I waited a beat before moving in, gnome at the ready, my other hand fumbling along the wall for a switch. I found it and turned on the lights.

The living room had been trashed. Couch cushions and pillows were torn apart. The couch itself had been turned upside down, and the TV was smashed on the floor.

My feelings turned to concern.

"Pastor Malone?" I used my male voice again. There was no answer. "Luther! Call for an ambulance!"

Make-believe Luther made the call. Well, in theory.

Armed with the gnome, I went from room to room but found no one. Each room was just as trashed as the one before. But I didn't find anyone in a closet, under a bed, or behind curtains. I searched for a sign of a struggle…blood, hair, torn clothing, but with everything torn to pieces, it would be hard to find.

And I was careful not to touch anything. Leaving prints was out of the question. I wasn't wearing gloves because I thought Pastor Malone might have found an accused murderer, wearing gloves and standing on his front porch, a bit off-putting.

Had someone taken Pastor Malone? Why? Because maybe he'd seen the real killer that night? Because he hadn't recognized me when I approached him up close in broad daylight? Did Malone even know that he'd "made a statement"?

What if his statement had been different? Could Vanderzee have forged it or changed the identity of the killer? The thought chilled me to the bone. If that was the case, how far would Vanderzee go to make sure I was thrown in prison?

If he was coerced into naming me, maybe Malone had changed his mind and called the killer to tell him so. These were all valid ideas. And none of them ended well for the elderly, retired pastor.

I walked into the living room to see red lights flashing outside. My heart sank. The sheriff's department. It had to be. And here I was at Malone's house, armed with a Bible-reading gnome.

"This is the police!" a voice shouted. "Come out with your hands up, and we won't shoot."

It wasn't lost on me that I'd used those same words only moments ago. What now? I could flee out the back door or hide somewhere. But my van was in the driveway. One call to the DMV, and they'd know I was here. I knew I should've registered my car under a fake name. Seems like an opportunity missed.

"No one shoots until I tell you!" the voice shouted. "And that means you, Luther!"

What were the odds?

CHAPTER SIXTEEN

———

Sheriff Carnack stood with me in the living room, surveying the damage. He hadn't arrested me…yet.

"You're lucky it's me, Merry." The big man took off his hat and rubbed his forehead.

I raised my hand. "I've got a question. When did you get a guy named Luther?"

He gave me a strange look. "He's a transfer from Oskaloosa who's been sent here for punishment. The guy's a bit trigger-happy. Arrived yesterday. Do you know him?"

"Nope." I had another question. "What are you doing here?"

"We had an anonymous tip that someone was breaking in." He sighed. "Well, according to your statement, you found the place like this. And I believe you. But you have to admit, it does look bad. Why did you come out here?"

I wasn't sure how much to admit. I wasn't ready to play my ace in the hole just yet.

"I just wanted to talk. I've never met the man, and yet he fingered me as a killer."

The sheriff sighed. "That can be considered witness tampering. Since this was an official call, I'm going to have to write it up. I'll try to keep Vanderzee from wanting your head. Please stop messing around with this one. It's my job, and you need to let me do it."

I looked at him hopefully. "You're not going to arrest me?"

"I should," he pointed out. "But there's no evidence that you did anything to Malone. And unlike Vanderzee, we don't like circumstantial evidence with nothing solid to back it up. But I mean it. You need to stop. I will arrest you next time. Got it?"

"Yes. I'm sorry."

Luther was on our right, showing off his gun-twirling skills to another deputy.

"Thank God that's a revolver and not a pistol," I said under my breath.

The gun went off—the bullet buried itself in a cornfield.

Sheriff Carnack and I looked at each other for a split second before I headed for my car.

"Nice going, Luther," I said as I passed him.

The man had the good grace to look nervous. He had nothing to fear from me. It was better that he was the target for Carnack's rage than me. I'd caused the sheriff enough headaches for one night.

Not surprisingly, Carnack called Rex out to help him with the search for Malone. By the time my husband got back, I was asleep.

Riley listened patiently. I'd stopped by his office after having a nice sleep in, packing my bag, and eating lunch—which consisted of a box of Girl Scout cookies and lemonade. By the way, those things do *not* go well together.

"They probably think," Riley said after I finished explaining all that had happened, "that you kidnapped or killed the only witness."

"But it wasn't like that. He didn't know who I was!" Why didn't anyone think that was a big deal?

My former handler put his hands on his desk. "You should've let me talk to him about that. I could've shown him photos and asked him to pick you out. If you're right, he would've failed, and we would've had credible documentation."

"I am right," I insisted. What I didn't say was that Riley was right. If I'd had him ask Pastor Malone, it would be far more credible, and maybe the pastor wouldn't have been kidnapped, if that theory held any water.

I thought about this. "Why didn't whoever paid him off show him a photo of me or something? And why didn't he speak up to the police when my picture appeared in the paper?"

My face had been connected to the case thanks to that brat Medea Jones. Surely Malone had seen it. From the look on her face, Kelly was wondering about that too. Or she was mad at me for doing something stupid. Again.

"Maybe the real killer found out somehow that Malone didn't recognize you," Riley reasoned out an idea I already had. "And that's why the real killer got rid of him."

I felt a little sick. This guy had born false witness against me, but I didn't want him hurt over it. "Do you think he's dead?"

Riley was silent for a moment. "I don't know. But if Malone grew a conscience and complained, then the killer would've felt he had no choice but to silence him."

I threw my hands up. "Great. I need another dead body that points my way."

"But Tyson doesn't point your way," Kelly said. "We still have no real motive for why you would kill him."

"Not that Vanderzee needs one," Riley scoffed. "He'd do anything to lock you away."

"About that…what did I ever do to him?"

Riley shrugged, but Kelly pulled something out of her purse and slid it to me.

"You've got to be joking," I said as I read her notes. "Mary Gold is his sister?"

Mary Gold, leader of the Magnolia Girls, hated me too but for other reasons.

Riley looked at his researcher with surprise. "Why didn't you tell me about that?"

Kelly rolled her eyes. "I tried, but you had a hot date, remember?"

Riley smiled with a faraway look. "Oh yeah. The librarian. She *was* hot."

I slammed my hand on the table. "Focus, Riley! Do you think this is enough of a motive for him to set me up? We were found in a building recently used by the Magnolia Girls."

"And," Kelly continued, "Tyson had a juvenile record, and he had committed some petty thefts about a year ago—all linked to his Best Bye job. I guess he was one of the Nerd Herd who go out and fix computers."

"What kind of thefts?" Riley asked with interest.

"The police record shows that during some 'house calls,' he stole petty cash from one of the tattoo parlors, Ella's Diner, the Pump & Pawn, and the police station itself."

"He could've stumbled onto something he wasn't supposed to see..." I wondered if it was Neil's tattoo parlor he'd stolen from. Maybe that was the reason Neil didn't like Tyson anymore.

"Which would increase the suspect pool," I said. "Why did Best Bye keep him on?"

"According to the statement," Kelly said, "he was the only one who really knew technology. He promised not to do it again. But even more interesting is that he had a juvie record before he worked there. Nothing much. Buying alcohol underage, stealing cigarettes. That kind of thing."

"That's very strange," Riley said. "I do background checks for businesses all the time. They should've known about him."

"It's *Bladdersly*," I said. "They're probably grateful to get someone who isn't a twice-convicted felon and has all of his own teeth."

"Neil would know more about this," Riley mused. "You haven't asked me about my meeting with him."

Ooops. Riley didn't know I was there and had heard the whole thing. "Oh yeah! I forgot! What did he say?"

Riley filled us in on the conversation, including the part where Neil walked out on him, which I thought was endearingly humbling. There were a few times when I was tempted to correct a word or two, but if I had pulled off the disguise, it was a tool I could save for later.

"So what do we do now?" Kelly took her notes back and dropped them on her desk.

"We need to find Pastor Malone," Riley said.

I agreed. "And I need to do a little recon at Best Bye."

"No way. You've gotten into too much trouble as it is," Kelly said. "I'll do it."

"I can come up with a disguise…" I almost said *that Riley didn't even see through* but stopped myself in time.

Riley cut me off. "No, this is a good idea. They won't know Kelly. Your photo was in the paper."

I was not going to be left out this time. Well, that he knew of. "Can we at least wire her up so that I can listen in?"

Which is how Riley and I ended up in a van in the Best Bye parking lot a few hours later, listening to Kelly as she went into the store. We had mics so that she could hear us make suggestions through an old spy earpiece I'd "liberated" from the CIA.

"Remember," Riley said into the microphone. "You need to talk to the other employees and the manager."

"Start with the employees," I suggested. "They'll be more likely to gossip. And if they balk, ask for a manager. Act like you're buying something and then pull out the ID."

"What ID?" she hissed.

"You know, your private eye identification or business card or something."

Kelly said, "Riley's too cheap to buy business cards."

I gave him a look. "You know she *needs* this for investigating."

Riley dismissed me. "I'll use the money you're paying us to buy her some when we get back."

Kelly disappeared into the store, and immediately we heard some woman very unenthusiastically welcome her to Best Bye and ask if she needed help.

"I'm looking for a laptop," Kelly said clearly. "It's a business expense."

Riley frowned. "Why does she need a laptop for work?"

"Because," Kelly whispered. "You're too cheap, remember? And if I'm going to do field work, I'll need one."

"Absolutely not." Riley shook his head, even though she couldn't see him do that.

Someone else greeted her after a beat, offering to show her the computers.

"Yes, I'd like your most expensive, top-of-the-line laptop, please," Kelly said.

Riley folded his arms over his chest. "Well, I'm not reimbursing you."

"You don't have to," she whispered curtly. "I have the agency credit card."

Riley's jaw dropped open.

"And you can close your mouth," Kelly said. "You used it for that trip to Omaha last week, and I know you weren't paying for the most expensive hotel room there for a *case*."

"I forgot about that card." Riley looked worried. "I gave it to her yesterday to pick up my dry cleaning."

"Merry," Kelly said softly. "If he makes a move to cancel it, break his fingers."

I reached into my purse and pulled out a nutcracker I carried in case I was assaulted by walnuts. "No problem."

The salesperson introduced herself as Nyla and told Kelly about the latest, most innovative laptop they had. In fact, it sounded so good that I might go back and get one.

"Thanks," Kelly gushed. "I usually ask for Tyson, but since the murder, I...well, you know."

"She's good," I said to Riley.

"Thank you," Kelly whispered.

"Don't feel too bad for that bastard," Nyla's voice spat. "No one here liked him."

"Oh?" Kelly sounded surprised and innocent all at once. She had been very good at that ever since our elementary school days when she convinced the principal that she hadn't punched Kevin Dooley in the face—he'd accidentally done it to himself. It wasn't surprising that the principal bought it. By the way, she totally had punched Kevin in the face. And he never bothered us again.

Nyla cracked her gum loudly. "He was always selling laptops to third parties—other dealers, like online sales and stuff. I work my butt off to sell one a week, and he'd sell ten to some slime bag who was going to resell them."

"Is that illegal?" Kelly asked.

"No, but it's against company policy. He was constantly being written up for it, but in the end, they didn't care because he was selling a bunch of laptops."

"Why would anyone buy them here and resell them?" Kelly wondered.

"You must not be from around here," the girl scoffed. "Nobody in this town is capable of using a computer. No one buys them, so they are always on sale. The sellers scoop them up at a discount and sell them for a profit in Des Moines or Davenport. And then there once was a missing shipment of laptops. No one knew anything, but I think Tyson was behind it."

"Ask if she has any proof!" I urged into the mic.

Kelly asked.

"No. I wish I did. I'm so sick of this place. The guys get promoted, but the women don't," the girl said.

"Well…" Kelly's voice took on a matronly tone. "I'm happy that you are getting a commission on this sale."

"Me too." The girl sounded a bit more relaxed. "I'm planning on leaving this town. I'm going to Drake University. I can use the money."

Kelly was quiet for a second before asking, "In that case, how many accessories can we load up on this thing?"

When she was finished, she had a leather case, extra power cords, a set of ridiculously expensive speakers, a wireless mouse, wireless earbuds, and a very expensive backup drive. I was so proud of her.

By the time she walked out, Riley had regained the ability to breathe. Kelly unloaded her packages and climbed into the back seat.

"What about talking to the manager?" he asked.

Kelly shrugged. "Why do I need to do that? It seems like the manager was complicit in this. He hired Tyson in spite of his record and turned a blind eye to his questionable sales."

"Good point," I said. "Besides, most management is just going to give you the dates of his employment and that's all."

Kelly flashed a grin at Riley. "Thanks for the new equipment, boss."

Riley grumbled as he started the car. "I should confiscate that."

Kelly held up a finger. "You even attempt to do that, and I'll come out here again and buy the best state-of-the-art desktop Claire has ever seen."

I changed the subject. "I told Rex this morning that I was going to stay the night somewhere else for the next two nights."

Well...I had sent him a text that said that. He had sent one back with some expletives I won't repeat here. I did promise to check in with him regularly. He wasn't happy, but it felt like I was getting close to something here. And with Carnack's patience running thin and Vanderzee on the warpath, I didn't want Rex to get in their way.

"Where are you going to stay since you're on the run?" Riley asked.

I shook my head. "I'm not on the run. Don't even breathe that, or Kurt Hobbs Jr. III Esquire will be all over me. And nobody wants that."

"Wherever you go," Kelly said. "Don't forget to keep us updated. That reminds me. I need to check in with Betty."

She did? "Why?"

"Ava texted earlier and said Betty's parents took Bart to the University of Illinois for a college visit. She told Ava that she was home alone for the next two days."

I put my hand on her cell. "I'll take care of it."

Looks like I had a place to crash after all.

CHAPTER SEVENTEEN

"Mrs. Wrath." Betty answered the door. "Do come in."

"Thanks." I pushed past her with my duffel bag. "You're not surprised to see me?"

The kid shrugged. "Not really. I figured you needed a place to hide out. That's why I engineered Bart's college visit."

"You did that?" I shouldn't have been surprised. The girl had just hacked into the Bladdersly PD.

The kid smiled. "It was easy. I just pretended to be an admissions counselor and sent Bart an email inviting him to visit. Then I emailed the admissions counselor and told them Bart and my parents wanted to visit."

I wasn't sure how I felt about the ten-year-old manipulating her family like that for a suspected murderer on the run. But it was nice that she wanted to help, and maybe Bart would get an education out of it with the added bonus of escaping his little sister.

I looked around. "Do you have a guest room?"

"Nope. But you can have the top bunk in my bedroom." She turned to walk down the hall.

"Hey. Are you over the noir slang?" I asked.

The girl shrugged. "I'm just taking a break. The other girls asked me to stop."

"And that worked?" Of course! Peer pressure. I'd have to remember that the next time Betty tried to do something like boss the girls into doing something, hack into the school records, or in one case, attempt to overthrow city council.

"Here's my room." Betty opened the door, and I followed her in.

Betty's house was about average for the Midwest—simple but comfy furniture, endless beige walls and carpet. Her room, however, was a different matter.

"Wow" was all I could think to say.

Betty was my black sheep. The girl in the troop voted most likely to master the dark arts or become a CIA black ops agent specializing in wet work. I expected the walls to be filled with photos and news articles connected with different colored yarns to one conspiracy theory after another. At the very least, I expected posters featuring the Basque regions.

I didn't expect this.

It was as if the girliest girls in the universe gathered together to decorate a room that they, themselves, would consider too girly. Everything was pink and had ruffles. Stuffed unicorns covered every surface of the white dresser, nightstand, and bunk beds. The carpet was a color I could only call "sparkly." The walls were pale pink with white lacy curtains. And the room smelled like roses.

I gave her a look. "Who are you, and what did you do with Betty?"

"What?" she asked as she stood on a ladder on tiptoe to clear the stuffed unicorns off of the top bunk.

"This!" I waved my arms around. "This just doesn't seem like you."

"What do you mean?" She came down from the ladder. "Why not?"

"Because…because…" I stammered. "You are…well, you know…"

The child put her hands on her hips and frowned at me.

"You have ninja suits and know all about weapons, and you speak in noir gangster…"

She shrugged. "I'm complicated. Now put your stuff wherever. I'm gonna go make snacks. Okay?"

I nodded, still dazzled by her room.

She paused in the doorway. "And whatever you do, don't, under any circumstances, open the closet." And then she was gone.

Oh, I was so opening that closet.

CHAPTER EIGHTEEN

———

Someone was standing over me as I lay on my back on the floor. It was hazy. Dark even. My nose was burning, and it felt like I'd been punched in the head.

"You opened the closet, didn't you?" Betty's voice floated above me.

I looked around. I was on my back on her sparkly carpet. "What happened?" I propped myself up on my elbows.

Betty went over to the open door. "Chloroform deployer. Got the idea from the movie *Mystery Men*."

"Why does my stomach hurt?" I got to a sitting position.

Betty pushed a button, and from the deep recesses of her closet came a swinging beam that was about one foot in diameter and three feet long. She stopped it with her hands after it swung back and shoved it back inside.

"You booby-trapped your closet," I said without the slightest hint of surprise.

"Yeah. I wanted the beam to hit adults in the head, but I'm not tall enough to install it."

"Makes sense," I said as I got to my feet. "What did you make for snacks?"

She didn't ask if I was mad. And why should she? She had warned me.

In the kitchen, the table was loaded with everything from cupcakes to pizza rolls. This girl knew how to eat! We sat down and dug in.

"Most people wouldn't want to spend the night alone with a murderer," Betty said as she passed me a bowl of potato chips. "But I think it's okay if it's your Girl Scout leader."

"I didn't kill anyone," I said through a mouthful of cookies. It came out like *Mfffninntkllneeone.*

"And now," Betty continued as if I hadn't said anything. "You kidnapped some pastor guy because he was a witness."

I shook my head vigorously because the chocolate-stuffed marshmallows had sealed my lips shut.

"It's okay. I know you didn't do it."

I swallowed. "Good. Because I didn't."

She tapped a spoon from the ice cream against her chin, leaving a chocolate smear. "So where is this dude they say you kidnapped?"

I washed the marshmallow down with Mountain Dew. "I have no idea."

"I have a theory. Wanna hear it?"

Why not? It couldn't be worse than anything I had…or didn't have.

Betty poured maple syrup on the pizza rolls. "I think Tyson was a spy for Spain against the Catalonians…"

And there it was. Betty was obsessed with the Catalonians.

She stirred the gooey mess with a fork. "And I think Hilly did it."

That explanation was shorter than I'd thought it would be. "Why do you think Hilly did it? She's not even here." I looked around. "Is she?"

Hilly Vinton, a tall, Amazonian assassin—who isn't an assassin because the CIA does not condone assassination—was a friend of mine. And while she sometimes turned up unexpectedly, I didn't think she was back in town.

"No, she's in Malta." Betty stuffed a Rice Krispies bar into her mouth. "We keep in touch," she said.

"If you knew that, why do you think it was her?"

Betty rolled her eyes. "Because I don't want to think it's you."

I tried to wrap my head around that. "But you just said you didn't think I did it."

"I don't. But just in case you did, I'd rather it was Hilly."

Kid logic was a puzzle I'd never crack.

The girl studied me for a moment. "Okay. I'll help you. Again."

"Thanks" was all I could think to say.

The doorbell rang, and she shot me a look. "You weren't followed, were you?"

"I don't think you should open the door." I got up from the chair, stuffing donuts into my pockets.

"Get to the bedroom, and this time don't open the closet!" She waited until I was down the hall before going to answer the door.

"What?" I protested. "That's a bad idea! You don't know who it is!"

Betty thought about this as the doorbell rang again. "It's alright. If it's a bad guy, I'll tell him you're in my closet."

That made sense...in a way. I didn't go to the bedroom but stayed just around the corner from the living room. If this was trouble, I needed to be ready in case Betty didn't have the living room booby-trapped too.

I heard some mumbling that I couldn't make out before the door closed and Betty hollered that it was safe to come out.

"Who was it?" I asked once I joined her in the living room.

"Some cop. He said he'd be back." She looked at the door. "I told him you weren't here but that you totally didn't do it."

"Thanks," I said. "I'll drop you off at Lauren's. You can't stay here if that cop is coming back."

Betty grumbled a little, but let me shuffle her out back to my van. She didn't say a word when I dropped her off at Lauren's. Lauren's mom didn't seem to think Betty dropping by in her pajamas at night was a weird thing.

I was pretty sure Betty was mad at me. It wasn't fair to involve Betty in this, no matter how much she wanted to be. Also, being there made me feel a little like I was contributing to her delinquency.

"Welcome, Bird Goddess!" Kayla held open the door of what, until recently, had been a Lutheran church. "Welcome."

She gave a deep bow with an exaggerated flourish. "To the Chapel of Despair!"

The girl pulled a flashlight from her voluminous black robe (a definite improvement over the whatever-ratty-bathrobe-you-have garb they used to wear). Kayla held the flashlight under her chin, aimed up, in an attempt to appear menacing. Instead, the weak glow made her look slightly anemic.

"Can I come in?" I looked around. I was pretty sure this would be the last spot anyone but Rex would think of, but the longer I stood out here, the more those odds would shrink.

"Enter." Kayla stepped aside, indicating a lobby with a red glow. "At your own risk!" she warned. There was a cracking sound as she threw Pop-Its on the floor.

"Very nice," I mumbled as I walked inside, closing the door behind me.

"The demigod Odious will listen to your request. He is fair and righteous." Kayla rolled her eyes and shook her head, pulling back her hood. "I can't stand these lines he has us saying. You wouldn't believe the things he comes up with! Heather and I had to reject one phrase where we were supposed to praise his abundant and evil manhood!"

"Sounds like you have grounds for a sexual harassment claim." I immediately regretted saying that. The last thing I needed to do was cause a rift between the four druids.

"Really?" Kayla's eyes opened wide at the possibilities.

I changed the subject. "Hey, do you know Kurt Hobbs?"

That caught her attention. "That guy from Bladdersly? The paper boy who thinks he's a bounty hunter?"

I nodded. "That's the one. He really likes you. He's trying to capture me to prove it."

Kayla beamed. "He is? He'd do that for me? I had no idea! I just thought he was a greaser from Bladdersly."

"Well, he is, but he's ambitious." For reasons I've never understood, Whovians refer to Bladders as greasers. We always thought this was unique until we found out that they called us the same thing.

"Should I tell him where you are?" Kayla asked a little too eagerly.

"Absolutely not. The last thing I need is him here swooning all over you while trying to handcuff me."

Kayla gasped. "Swooning? How romantic! I had no idea he was interested. He's older, right?"

"Well, yeah. I think he's like twenty or something." I hadn't thought about an age difference. "Are you still in high school?"

"An older man! And a businessman too!" She clapped her hands together before looking at me earnestly. "Do you think he'd join the cult? Stewie says we get a bonus of twenty-five dollars for every new member we bring in."

"That seems a little low considering how desperate you are," I said. "And who's paying you? Stewie? Out of his own pocket?"

Kayla shook her head. "Oh, it's not about the money. We each want to be the first one to do it. Can you believe that, even after getting all that money, a church, and a car, we still can't get anyone to join?"

I could. "Well, maybe you could have a sign-up table at school."

"The principal said no. He thinks we're Satanists." She snorted. "As if! *Those* kids are total losers!"

"Yeah." I looked around. "Is there a place I can crash for the night?"

"Oh sure." The girl seemed delighted with the idea. I'd have to make sure she didn't call Kurt and turn me in. "We have the relaxation room."

I followed her down a flight of stairs to a hallway. We passed an old nursery, a kitchen, some meeting rooms, and a large hall before she opened a door and waved me through.

"What is this place?" I asked, trying to take it all in.

The room was painted dark red, with Roman braziers blazing. It seemed dangerous until I noticed the flames were silks being blown by tiny fans. Barry White was singing through a state-of-the-art sound system, and in the middle of the room was a round waterbed.

Kayla motioned to the bed. "Stewie says he'll need it to indoctrinate new female members."

"Oh no. He's not doing that." I needed to talk to that kid. There would be no sexual harassment on my watch.

"Well, he thinks so. Heather and I decided we aren't going to stand for that when the time comes. Maybe we'll combine it with that sexual harassment suit you suggested." Kayla thought for a moment. "Do you think Kurt could swoop in and put Stewie in jail for that?"

I sighed. "Is he here?"

She nodded before continuing. "Mostly we use it for naps. Waterbeds are weird. Why did people use those in the Dark Ages?"

"Forty years ago wasn't the Dark Ages." I dumped my bag on the waterbed and watched it wobble on the bed of waves. "Let's go see Odious." I pushed her out the door.

The chapel was filled with black candles, all lit. Swathes of red fabric hung from the ceiling, and the pews had all been painted black. On the altar was a huge throne with a back about six feet in height, almost two feet taller than the diminutive Stewie needed. And there he sat. The demigod.

Stewie didn't see us come in at first. He was busy eating a corndog and watching something on his cell phone.

"*Odious!*" Kayla shouted tremulously. "The Bird Goddess has requested an interview with the great and impotent King of Evil!" She tossed a few more Pop-Its onto the ground. They sputtered pathetically.

I decided not to point out that she said impotent when she probably meant omnipotent.

Stewie jumped to his feet, which didn't change his height at all. He tossed the corndog onto the throne and held his hands high in the air, wiggling his fingers in what I referred to as druid jazz fingers.

"It's King of *All* Evil, Kayla!" he complained. "And it's important, not impotent!"

"Yeah, you're lucky that I don't call you the Butthead of All Evil," Kayla snapped.

"Come forth, Bird Goddess!" Stewie beckoned. "And speak!"

I walked up to him.

"Kneel before Zod!" He pointed to the floor.

"The guy from *Superman*?" I shook my head. "Not happening. Look, as a member of this cult, I demand, um, refuge."

I wiggled my druid jazz fingers for effect.

He frowned. "Why are you doing that?"

"What?"

He nodded at my hands. "Wiggling your fingers like that."

Was he joking? "That's what you do!"

Stewie's face turned as red as his hair. "I don't do anything stupid like that! Dread demigods don't wiggle their fingers!"

"I don't care," I said. "I need to crash in your pervert room. And by the way, you can't 'indoctrinate' female members. The braziers are a nice touch though."

Stewie sniffed. "I'm the leader of the Cult of NicoDerm. You are only a goddess. You must do what I say."

"Doesn't goddess outrank leader?" Kayla offered. "I vote for the Bird Goddess to be the Supreme Leader."

"Thanks," I said. "But I don't want that. I've got this murder investigation to deal with and my Girl Scouts are tweens, so…"

"*Mutiny!*" Stewie shrieked.

"It's not a mutiny," I said. "I'll take my stuff downstairs and move into the sexual assault room. And you and I are going to have a little talk about how women should be treated."

Stewie picked up a plastic wand and shook it at me. "I will turn you into a bat!"

"Fine," I sighed. "Whatever." I walked back up the aisle and down the stairs to the relaxation room and locked the door behind me.

No one bothered me, which was good. I had a lot to think about. With Pastor Buddy Malone missing and the Bladdersly PD hot on my tail, I needed to think. I took out my cell phone and searched the web for news of the pastor's disappearance. Oh sure, you probably thought I'd use a burner phone. But I'm not on the lam, and using my own phone seemed to back that up.

Nothing. Even *The Bladdersly Beard* had nothing.

I really should call Rex. But then he'd get upset, and I didn't like upsetting my husband. So I guess I was not calling him for his own benefit.

I needed a computer. It was too hard scrolling through my phone. Not that I was old or anything. It was just easier to stare at a monitor. There had to be an office in here somewhere, right? Someplace where Stewie wrote his humiliating scripts and ordered Pop-Its in bulk.

There wasn't anything in the basement, so I went upstairs, bypassing the nave. A short hallway on the side proved fruitful, and I found an office with a desk and laptop.

"We have Wi-Fi." Kayla appeared in the doorway. "That should be a major draw to new members."

I turned on the laptop. "What's the password?"

The first thing that came up was a video with flames accompanied by the audio of what suspiciously sounded like four teen druids screaming in agony. Stewie's head popped up with the flashlight under the chin trick, and he laughed maniacally—something made comical by his high-pitched, nasal voice.

"Kayla," I repeated. "Password."

"I am a great and powerful leader."

"What?"

She pointed at the monitor. "Write it all together. That's the password."

I typed it in. "Is Stewie losing it?"

"Nah," Kayla said. "He's just a bit full of himself now that we are all rich."

"I guess all that money can change a person," I said as I opened up the browser and typed in a social media page. I could check and see if there was anything there about the missing pastor. Our police department had a Facebook page, so maybe the Bladdersly PD did too.

I was greeted by a login request. I didn't know my login information. It was in a green Girl Scout notebook I kept on my nightstand.

"You can use mine." Kayla reached over me and logged in. "You old people never remember these things."

I couldn't argue with that because it was true. Once in, I pulled up Rex's page. He never used it. Mostly he had it because his sisters liked to use Messenger.

This is Merry, not Kayla the Terrifying, I typed. *Just wanted to let you know what's going on. I'm crashing with the druids tonight. Should be safe—it's not like people are beating down the doors to get in here.*

"Hey!" Kayla complained.

I finished up with the message and checked to see if Vanderzee had ever made a page.

Merry Wrath! Bladdersly's Most Wanted! Armed and Dangerous!

I was sorry I looked. There was my photo on a wanted poster. I thought this was a bit over-the-top, especially the skull border around it. There was an appeal to call a hotline to report a sighting of me, but they'd forgotten to add the number.

"That's you!" Kayla gasped.

"Yup." I kept scrolling. "Bird Goddess/Murderer."

There wasn't any information on Malone. Maybe they didn't update very often.

"Thanks," I told Kayla. "I appreciate that. And by the way, can you tell Stewie and the others that no one is to know I'm here?"

Kayla nodded. "I'll tell them you're on the run from killing that guy."

"I didn't kill Tyson Pancratz." I sighed wearily. Seriously? My own cult thought I was a murderer?

She looked disappointed. "Oh. That's too bad. It would've been cool to have a Killer Bird Goddess of Death. When we saw the Bladdersly paper, Stewie thought so too and started talking about ordering brochures that say that."

I got to my feet. "Make sure he doesn't send them out, and I'll see what I can do about getting Kurt here as your recruit."

She brightened. "Great! Well, Stewie and I have to go. We have a consumer ed final tomorrow. You'll lock up and blow out the candles?"

I agreed, and once the two were out the door, I went to the nave and blew out the black candles. All 167 of them.

Killer Bird Goddess. Yeesh.

CHAPTER NINETEEN

———

I awoke with a jolt and checked my phone. Ten a.m. Not good. I needed to go see some people, and I'd wanted to start early. Popping some mint gum into my mouth as a sad substitute for brushing my teeth, I grabbed my bag and headed out of the room into the hallway.

The sound of footsteps overhead stopped me in my tracks. Normally, I would've thought it was just the kids, but then I remembered that two of them had a final today. It was a school day. Kayla and the others shouldn't be here.

Part of me wanted to defend the Chapel of Despair from invaders. I mean, I was part of the cult. But the other part of me wondered why anyone would break into a place like this. Had the police found me already?

The sounds of two or more people coming down the stairs had me diving into the kitchen. After a quick glance around, I opted for hiding behind the counter that divided the kitchen from the hall.

You probably think I should've picked a closet or cabinet. Both options would be wrong because there's no way out. At least from the counter, I could scoot one way or another around the long island in the center of the room. Having your back against the wall is a bad idea.

It was a lesson I'd learned the hard way in Paraguay. A government official who was in league with the Russians was having a party at his place in the country, and I'd followed a large group into the compound, breaking away by the time they asked for invitations.

I was in the office, rummaging through his desk, looking for concrete proof that he was helping the Russians target

Americans, when I heard voices in the hallway. I ran over to the wardrobe with the intent of hiding inside.

Little did I know, the foreign pastor was in there waiting for his mistress to sneak in for a quickie. I also had no idea he would need the wardrobe until I realized it was full of sex toys. The wardrobe door flew open, and I thought fast enough to jump out and say I was his erotogram.

I began dancing, using dildos as batons, until I got to the door. Then I ran for my life. Later I found out that the foreign pastor was looking for me so that he could give me a big tip. Apparently, I did a good job. And Riley never let me live it down.

Footsteps sounded in the hallway, coming closer. I scanned the room, looking for all of my options. There was another way out to the hallway through the far corner of the room. It would take some serious sneaking to pull it off, but I should manage to get out.

"Where?" a man's voice demanded.

Were they looking for me or something else?

"I don't know," came the barked reply.

The voices sounded vaguely familiar. But it was the kind of vagueness that led me to wonder if it was someone in Bladdersly that I'd briefly met. Would I be able to hazard a glance without detection?

"We have to find it!" the first man growled. "Check the back stairs!"

There were back stairs? And "*it*"?

They ran off in two different directions. I decided to stay put in case they were going to meet up here again.

What was "it"? Was it connected with the murder? Were my druids in trouble? That was all I needed right now, for someone to be here snooping for something else. What if they found me? Would they try to overpower me to turn me in?

Footsteps ran across the ceiling and out the front door. Seconds later, a car pealed out of the parking lot. I waited a minute or two more before standing up. I had enough on my plate, but if the Cult of NicoDerm was in trouble, I had to do something. These kids were idiots.

But they were my idiots.

The Opera House was run-down looking outside and not much better inside. The lobby was badly lit, and the popcorn looked like it had been there for months. The front door was open, so I went looking for Harold.

"Breathe!" I heard him say. "Breathe from your diaphragm!"

The doors to the auditorium were open, and I slipped inside, keeping to the dark, shadowy corner until I knew who he was talking to.

Harold was standing in the middle of the stage, arms outstretched, wearing a Roman gladiator costume that looked like it would much rather be on anyone else. Flab oozed from every opening of the leather shirt he wore, and his extremely white and pasty legs gleamed through his sandals. At least the helmet covered his balding head.

"I am!" Stewie whined next to him, also dressed as a gladiator. They looked like two different sizes of the same guy, except for the bright red hair that stuck out under Stewie's helmet.

"You are not, or I would know," Harold said.

"Why are we dressed like gladiators? I'm a demon from hell!" Stewie's voice squeaked on the last word, erasing any hope of gravitas.

"We are warriors!" Harold intoned dramatically. "If you want to command millions, you need to look the part!"

"I just want to command maybe forty druids," Stewie complained.

"Just try the line again. The way I told you." Harold nudged the kid with a wooden sword.

"Fine!" he grumped. And then he held his sword aloft and announced in a wheeze, "Come at me, and find that death awaits!"

Well, at least there were no jazz fingers.

"That's better," Harold said, even though I was pretty sure it wasn't. "Now, a few more lessons and you'll be as good as I was back in my CIA days."

Stewie took off his helmet, his sweaty hair plastered to the sides of his head. "You were in the CIA? For real?" His voice had a hushed reverence that I couldn't stand.

I was in the CIA for years. Harold was in the CIA for, like, a minute. He screwed up his first assignment so badly that they fired him immediately. Only recently did I discover that he had moved to Bladdersly.

He nodded solemnly. "I was. A master of disguise too."

He had gone to a Central American dive to infiltrate a guerilla unit...dressed as an Arab. They saw through him immediately.

"Really?" Stewie gushed.

"You've heard of Merry Wrath Ferguson?"

"Bird Goddess!" Stewie whispered.

Harold placed a hand on his chest. "I taught her everything she knows."

That was it. I stood up and, in a better theater voice than he had, shouted, "Harold! Stop lying to Odious the demigod!"

Harold paled, but recovered quickly. "Merry! What a pleasure to see you here! I was just telling young Stewart here how well we worked together in the field."

"Yeah. You were a total flop. You barely survived your first and only assignment. Stewie." I walked up to the stage, past rows of battered chairs. "What are you doing here?"

"I'm um..." The kid looked from Harold to me. "Taking lessons to be more menacing when we have hundreds of new recruits."

He sounded defensive, and my problem really wasn't with him.

"Good idea," I said, much to the kid's relief. "Can you give me a moment with Harold?"

"I'll go. Time was up anyway." He turned to Harold and reached into a pocket, pulling out a couple of one-hundred-dollar bills. "Here's your fee. Next week can we dress like demons?"

Harold plucked the money from the boy's hand and nodded. "I'll see what I can do."

Stewie fled. I assumed it was to the dressing rooms to change, but I couldn't be sure.

I joined Harold on the stage and snatched the money away. "You're charging a kid two hundred dollars an hour for lessons? And is he skipping school for this?"

Harold took the money back, stuffing it down the front of his gladiator skirt. Yeah, I wasn't going to go after it there. "Half an hour. And he really has made progress."

"That's wrong on so many levels."

"No, it's not. They got the *Beetle Dork* comics rights and made a fortune. I'm in the *Beetle Dork* comics and got nothing. It's like my cut."

If anyone should make money off of *Beetle Dork*, it was *Beetle Dork*, who happened to be me. But I didn't want the money, so I brushed it aside.

I gave him a menacing glare. "Fifty is all you'll charge from here on out, or I'll waterboard you."

He looked into my eyes and knew I was serious. "Fine. Why are you here, besides to ruin my life?"

I'd almost forgotten. "We need to talk someplace private. This isn't the right place."

Harold burst into spontaneous sweating. "So you can kill me? I'm only trying to make a living!"

That brought me up short. "What? No! Just to talk! That's all!"

Without a word, he walked backstage. I followed him to a dilapidated office, where he shut the door behind me. The room was covered with theatrical posters with some suspicious photo editing. I'm pretty sure he didn't star in *Hamilton* with Lin-Manuel Miranda, and yet there he was as Aaron Burr. His head was also superimposed on a young Hamlet, which premiered at The Old Vic in London. And most surprising, as the waif-like Maria in an LA production of *West Side Story*.

Harold eased his bulk into a squeaky chair behind a splintering desk, and then he asked me what I wanted.

He was still dressed as a gladiator. I did my best to block it from my mind.

"You've probably seen in *The Bladdersly Beard* that I've been wrongly accused of a murder that happened next door."

Harold scowled. "I never read the local rag! I have standards! I read *The New York Times'* Sunday Arts and Leisure section!"

"Good for you." I eyed an enormous stack of *The National Enquirer* tabloids. "Like I said, I was accused of murdering Tyson Pancratz in that shed next door."

"Tyson?" Harold was aghast. "Tyson Pancratz is dead? And you killed him?"

I closed my eyes and counted to ten before proclaiming my innocence for the fiftieth time since the murder happened. "No, I didn't. And yes, Tyson is dead. Did you know him?"

"Of course. He took a theater class I offered at the juvie detention center. He was a terrible actor." Harold sniffed. "Refused to breathe from his diaphragm."

"Seriously," I interrupted. "Is that the only advice you have for kids?"

"Of course not!" he snapped. "Sometimes I tell them to *project* from their diaphragm."

In a minute I'd remove his diaphragm just to keep him from mentioning the organ again. Could you lose your diaphragm and live? I'd have to look that up because it might come in handy in a matter of minutes.

"Tyson. You worked with him. Please continue." Could the diaphragm be removed using a rusty trophy that I was pretty sure Harold hadn't won? How did I know he hadn't won it? Because as far as I know, there was no such award as the obviously racist *Best Depiction of Another Race or Gender* at the Tony Awards.

"He was a troubled youth." Harold shook his head sadly. "His struggle was real. An orphan. No family. Bullied and beaten by his peers. He had nowhere to turn but to a life of crime."

"Is that true or are you making that up?" I asked.

"I'm making it up." He studied my face. "Did you buy it? I'm told I can be very persuasive."

"No." I was pretty sure he couldn't persuade a starving man to eat a sandwich. "So you think he was an innocent youth?"

"Not really." Harold seemed to deflate. "He was a bad egg. Frankly, I don't know why I tried. It's just that money was a bit tight since the high school refused to work with me."

"Why did they do that?" Besides the obvious reasons. "You got the money for this place contingent on working with kids!" Now that I'd said it, it did seem like a bit of a pipe dream.

Harold gave a martyrish sigh. "I wanted to put on an authentic staging of *Oh! Calcutta!*"

My mouth dropped open. "The show where everyone on stage is nude? The one where they sing about sex? What on earth made you think that would be okay?"

"It's art," he sniffed. "You wouldn't understand. And neither did those Luddites."

It may be one of the only things I'd ever heard of done right in Bladdersly. Maybe I should send my congratulations to Bladdersly High.

"So," he continued, "I offered my services to the juvenile detention center."

"And did you attempt to do *Oh! Calcutta!* there too?"

Harold looked shocked. "Of course not! We didn't have enough people to fill out the cast."

"Never ever, ever do that again." Yeesh! What was it with him and Stewie? Or maybe that was the problem. He was rubbing off on Stewie. Either that or Stewie was watching documentaries of cult leaders like Jim Jones.

Harold promised. I made him pinky swear. If my girls have taught me anything, it's that the pinky swear is the hardest contract to ever break.

"Did you see anything that night? Anything unusual? Me?"

Harold seemed surprised. "Of course not. If I had, I would've told the police when they asked."

"The police were here? What did they say?"

"Well, that Vanderzee hates you with a passion," Harold said. "Like really, really, really hates you." He stared off into space. "Maybe he should try breathing from his diaphragm."

I took several calming, cleansing breaths before responding. "Besides hating me, which is weird since I've never met the man, what did he want from you?"

Harold continued. "He said that nice pastor, Malone, had seen you that night. Buddy really is a sweetheart. He's the one who got me the gig at the detention center."

That caught my attention. "And what did you say?"

He steepled his fingers. "I said that I knew you very well, that we had worked together, and that you probably did it, but no, I hadn't seen anything."

I blinked at him for a full two minutes before talking myself out of torturing him. And I did it all while breathing from my diaphragm.

I was leaving Harold alive and with his diaphragm intact when Rex called. I decided to take it.

"Merry," my husband said. "This is crazy. Even for you. Come home, and we can deal with this."

That was sweet. He wanted to help. But he couldn't. "I can't investigate from a jail cell. I need to be free to move around. Besides, I don't want this to affect you and your standing in the community."

"Oh?" Rex asked. "You don't think that having a wife who's a suspect in a murder investigation, who's giving the impression that she's on the run, isn't going to affect my reputation?"

"Does it?"

I could literally hear him running his hands through his short, dark hair. "I don't care about that. This is a mess. Vanderzee is furious with Carnack for not arresting you. And I've been getting some strange calls from some kid named Hobbs who disguises his voice every time he calls. And I mean a different voice every time. He doesn't seem to realize his number keeps coming up and it's the same one."

"That's Kurt. He's a bounty hunter." Why wasn't he calling my cell? Maybe I hadn't given it to him.

Rex kept his cool. "A bounty hunter? So now they think you've skipped bail. This seems dangerous."

"Only if my name is Kayla." I told him about young Kurt's aspirations.

Rex was quiet for a moment. "Riley and Jane can handle the investigation. You need to come in."

"Oh sure." I rolled my eyes. "That's what *they* want me to do!"

"That's what *I* want you to do."

Awww. That was sweet. "Well, I can't right now. I am safe. But you could give me some details. We know he was stabbed with a stiletto. Do they know anything else?"

There was a long sigh before he spoke again. "Vanderzee has asked if you have a stiletto."

"Yes, but it's missing," I reasoned. "So you can honestly say no."

"Vanderzee is convinced you killed Tyson and kidnapped Malone."

I bit my lip. "I'm sure he does, but you know I had nothing to do with that."

"Yes, I do. So does Soo Jin and Sheriff Carnack and most of the family, except for Ronni, who's turned those T-shirts into an empire. And Ron and Ivan have threatened anyone who says you did it."

"Well, that's nice," I said.

"You should come in and answer some questions. Malone's disappearance and you being at his house looks like you tried to eliminate the only witness who can place you at the scene."

I felt a stab of fear for the old man. I needed to find him. And not just because he knew I wasn't there that night, but because someone took him—because of me.

"I wonder what happened to him. Do you think the real killer kidnapped or killed him?"

Rex grew quiet. "Maybe he went on the run out of fear? Who knows? You need to go in and talk to the sheriff."

"Okay. I will," I lied.

"You will?" My husband sounded skeptical.

"Yes, tomorrow." And then I hung up. I hated lying to my husband, and I really wanted to do the right thing. Saying I was coming in tomorrow was all I could think of. And I didn't have a lot of confidence that I'd be able to solve this by then.

I was running out of clues. I needed to start from the beginning with waking up in the shed. It was time to find out what the deal was with *Boats of the Midwest*. I'd avoided it because it sounded dumb and boring. But it was showing up everywhere, including in bulk in the room where Tyson died.

I made my way back to the Chapel of Despair.

The waterbed was difficult to sit on without creating mini tsunamis every time I shifted. Pulling out my cell, I ordered a massaging recliner from Amazon. It would arrive the next day, and the kids would have something far more comfortable.

The author of the book wasn't listed on the cover. I opened it up and found the cover page, which listed the author as Anonymous.

The copyright indicated that it had come out this year. So it was a new, boring book. I opened up a can of pop and a bag of chips and turned to the first page.

Three hours later, I was finished and felt like I needed to wash my eyes out with soap. Far from being dull, *Boats of the Midwest* was either a badly written novel or a complete diary charting all of the scandals in a town called Intestinally, Iowa.

Was that a very badly disguised Bladdersly? Were these the town secrets? It would explain the pen name. This little, two-hundred-and-fifty page book charted the history of Bladdersly to present day. And the history was very different than the one we'd heard before back in Who's There.

Apparently, Bladdersly started off originally as Wanderwee. Hmmm…the name of the police chief. Was he a descendant?

Anyway…Wanderwee was founded by a gold prospector of the same name, who, on his way out West, got tired and decided he didn't want to go any farther. Obadiah tried panning for gold in Idiot Creek, a trickle just west of here, but didn't get more than a few leeches and some typhus from drinking out of it.

He built a one-room cabin and set up a trading post. And even though it wasn't on any routes for any travellers, he kept things afloat and managed to lure a few others to settle there. Most of these people were down on their luck too and decided a second or third chance in the middle of nowhere couldn't be any worse.

When Who's There was founded, along with a lumber mill and tavern, Wanderwee had nothing but losers and a mysterious and endless cycle of cholera. Wanderwee attempted a sort of resurrection. His idea, mainly because they couldn't compete with the lumber mill or tavern, was to set up a brothel.

The idea backfired when they couldn't get any of the town's forty-seven women to even consider the world's oldest profession. In fact, the town drummed Wanderwee out of city limits and decided to rename the town Intestinally after the mayor's wife, Intesta.

Obadiah lived outside of town in a shack. He married some unfortunate woman who gave him twelve children before dying. And eventually those descendants returned to Bladdersly, or Intestinally, and have lived there ever since.

The badly edited book then jumped forward two hundred years to the year 2000. And that's when things got interesting. Whoever wrote this had insight into the secret lives of most of the town.

I knew it!

There were tales of inbreeding (which made a lot of sense to me), bizarre fetishes (did you know some men are actually turned on at the sight of a pretzel?), countless love affairs, and murder. It read like those tabloid rags in Howard's office.

None of this information was backed up with hard evidence. It all seemed to be hearsay. And yet, it was pretty damning. I could see someone killing to keep this book quiet. Which made me think of the books in the shed. Was that the entire print run?

Had someone killed to silence the author? And was that author Tyson Pancratz?

I jumped to my feet to do a little victory dance at the idea of having solved this, but the waterbed had other ideas and launched a wave worthy of a professional surfer that sent me tumbling to the floor.

I got to my feet and continued the dance because this was big. This was huge. This could break everything wide open!

Unfortunately, I spilled my pop and crushed my chips. So I headed to the church kitchen to get the bottle of wine I'd brought in. Fortunately, none of the kids had tapped into it yet, so I broke the seal, unscrewed the cap, and poured it into a glass.

Where were those kids anyway? School must've been out by now. And I was pretty sure these guys didn't have anywhere to go. I needed to talk to them about the break-in earlier and see if they knew what it was about.

I'd probably ban them from the building until I could guarantee their safety. A little pang hit my stomach. Sure, they could be annoying, but I had a soft spot for this little troop of druid wannabees. In fact, I should put in place some security measures that would keep it safe...at least while I was here.

I could run to my ranch house and get the various tools of my trade, which I'd stolen from my former employer and hidden in the basement. But if the police were surveilling the house, that was a no-go. I'd just have to use what I had here.

The kitchen cupboards didn't have much, but there were a couple of things I could work with. The tin of popcorn kernels would be especially useful. Although I had to wonder, who made popcorn the old-fashioned way anymore? Was that a thing? Or was I lazy in using those microwaveable bags that only popped half of the corn?

I found twine, scissors, thumbtacks, a staple gun, and plastic bags. This was going to be fun! Just like the time Riley and I holed up in an old office supply store in Budapest!

"What are you doing?" Heather startled me from the doorway. Her face was scrunched up as if something smelled bad. Mike walked in behind her and stared at the bottle of wine on the counter.

"You can't have any." I snatched it away and put it back in the fridge. Great. Now I was going to have to open the fridge to get it back out.

"I don't want to drink alcohol." Mike waved his hands in front of him. "My dad said it leads straight to juvie and, before you know it, adult diapers."

Maybe the kids weren't the weird ones. To be honest, I'd only ever met Stewie's dad, who labored under the delusion that Stewie was super smart and popular.

Heather shook her head. "My mom said that wine is medicinal, especially if you drink it out of a box."

"That's right," I said as I took a swig. "I'm taking my medicine."

Mike looked confused, so I added, "Of course, Mike's dad is right too."

"He is?" Mike's eyes grew wide. "I'll have to tell him Bird Goddess says so. He'll love that."

"You guys can call me Merry," I said. "Seriously. You call each other by your real names. I've even heard you call Stewie Stewbutt. Merry is fine."

"It's one less syllable." Heather seemed to agree.

"See? I'm making things easier on you already. Oh, and by the way, I ordered a massaging recliner for the relaxation room. You're welcome."

Mike and Heather high-fived each other. Kayla and Stewie pushed past them into the kitchen. I hadn't even known they were there.

"I need to talk to you guys." I clapped my hands to get their attention, something that sometimes worked with my troop. "Something strange happened today."

"Did you commune with demons?" Stewie burst into the center of the room eagerly. "Raise the dead? Contact aliens?"

Kayla put her hands on her hips. "That's our problem right there. We have no consistent message!"

"Kayla's right," Heather said. "I mean, are we into demons or zombies or aliens? You change it all the time, Stewie."

Mike shook his head. "I think we should keep all options open. I mean, what if we're having a meeting with demons and an alien walks in? Do we just kick him out?"

Stewie nodded his head and pointed at Mike. "He's right! We have to be open to all things strange and unusual."

"What if the demons are jerks?" Kayla folded her arms over her chest. "What if they're sexist?"

"Like you!" Heather pointed at Stewie.

"What are you talking about?" The diminutive redhead seemed genuinely confused.

The girls brought up the language about manhoods and indoctrinating females. Stewie's face grew redder, and for a moment, I was worried he'd explode.

"Manhood means I'm a man," Stewie insisted. "And indoctrinating means giving a person a place to take a nap. Women need naps. My mom told me that."

I needed to meet Stewie's mom. "Besides the fact that I'll be buying you a dictionary soon, why do you think women need naps?"

"To rest their cosmic auras," Stewie said. "Duh!" He made a circular motion on the side of his head as if to imply that I was crazy.

I was starting to wonder if I was.

After I explained to the kids what those things actually meant, Stewie began to sputter.

"I didn't know that!" His face was flushed and his eyes wide. "How would I know that?"

"You should read more romance novels." Heather nodded. "Then you'd know what a manhood was."

"Okay." I held up my hands. "We need to talk about something else."

In truth, I was greatly relieved that Stewie was only *inadvertently* sexually harassing girls. I herded the kids to a table in the hall, and we all sat down. Then I told them about the men invading the Chapel of Despair.

"Recruits?" Stewie leaned forward eagerly.

"I don't think so. They seemed to be older guys."

The kids looked at me questioningly.

I sighed. "Like me."

"Ahhhhhh…" the girls said in unison.

I toyed with accusing them of ageism, but decided we didn't have time for that. "If I had to guess, I'd say they were professionals."

"Men in Black!" Mike slammed his hand on the table. "We've attracted the attention of the dudes from, like, Area 51!"

Stewie drooled a little. "We've done it! We've hit the big-time! Now a secret government organization is after us!"

"Cool!" Kayla said.

Should I ruin their excitement and tell them these were not Feds?

"These guys said they were looking for something they called 'it.' Any ideas what they want?"

"Do you think we have the Holy Grail or an alien egg here?" Stewie asked hopefully.

It was so tempting to say yes, but that would only encourage them. "No. I don't."

Kayla looked at Stewie. "Why would aliens have eggs?"

Mike nodded. "I think they have babies, like people."

"They could have eggs!" Stewie stormed. "They could be marsupials! Who knows?"

I raised my arms. "Guys. We are getting off track. Let's say for the sake of argument that you're all right…"

"We can't all be right." Kayla frowned.

"Yeah!" Mike added. "Which is it? Babies, eggs, or marsupials?"

"I don't care." My voice had an edge. "The real question is where could whatever 'it' is be?"

Heather spoke up. "I don't know. There was a lot of junk when we moved in. We tossed a lot of it. But I think we stashed some stuff in the old nursery."

Huh. So we were getting to babies. Albeit not alien babies. "Let's go," I said. "First, we need to lock the doors. And we need to keep locking the doors every time we leave here. I'm going to need a key."

The kids looked at each other and burst out laughing.

"What's so funny?"

"You! You actually think we have keys! That's so 2010!" Mike wiped away some tears.

I closed my eyes and pictured myself removing his diaphragm. It helped.

"What do you use instead?"

Stewie pulled out the latest version of the iPhone and tapped until an app came up. He showed it to me. The logo had a goat's skull on it with the words *Security for Your Peace of Mind* written in red, dripping letters.

"This guy at MIT invented it," Stewie explained. "We use the app to lock and unlock the doors."

"And you didn't understand what *manhood* meant?" I asked.

"Give me your phone." Heather held her hand out.

I handed it over.

"Uh, what is this?"

"It's my phone." I paused.

She handed it back to me. "Well, I can't put an app on that. You have an old phone. Last year's model can't handle this app."

"That's really primitive," Kayla said.

"My grandma has that phone," Stewie added. "And she's got dementia."

"Well." I took it back. "This is what I have to work with. I guess you'll have to give me a key."

"Don't worry," Mike said. "We have a failsafe. There's a keypad under the skull to the right of the door. Just enter the secret code."

"Which is?"

"666."

I blinked at them for a moment. "Guys, don't you think that's a little obvious?"

"Oh" was all Stewie could say. "I hadn't thought of that."

"How about 999?" Kayla offered.

"Yeah!" Mike said. "Good idea!"

Heather hesitated. "Maybe that's too obvious too. I mean, it's just 666 upside-down, right?"

I smiled at her to reward her for saying something intelligent.

"Well, I don't know if I can remember something harder than that," Stewie whined.

"How about…" I held up my arms. "Something like 1212?"

The kids started laughing again. I was really regretting staying here.

"Too obvious!"

"I know!" Stewie held up a finger. "0804!" He turned to me and explained, very slowly, "That means August fourth. That's the date the *Beetle Dork* comic came out!"

This was greeted by a roar of agreement and my sigh of let's-never-do-this-again. Mike changed it with his phone, which apparently sent the message to the keypad. These guys were smart enough to have an app that locked and unlocked doors but not smart enough to not use 666 for a demonic church.

I decided not to say anything about Stewie's tone, implying that I was too ignorant to know how a date was written. We didn't have any time to waste. If these guys were coming back, I wanted to find whatever "it" was before they could. So instead, I led the way to the nursery.

"Well, this shouldn't take too long," I said as I walked in. There was a pile of junk along the back wall.

"What are we looking for?" Mike asked as he picked up a doll with two fingers as if it were on fire.

"Should we wear our robes?" Stewie asked hopefully.

"I don't know." I shrugged. "Anything that strikes you as very strange or very valuable. And no to the robes. They'll just get in the way."

Stewie removed his robe to reveal he was still in the gladiator costume.

The kids laughed for ten minutes while I started digging through the wreckage.

Searching any place can be tedious. You don't just open drawers and look through them. You pull them open and search for hidden panels and see if there's something taped to the bottom.

The life of a spy seems exciting, but a lot of time is spent looking for things. I've had to search everything from a very messy and cluttered office to an igloo. And the amazing thing was, I found more in the igloo than anywhere else. The Finnish general who'd hid out there had secret plans, two sticks of dynamite, and a disturbing stash of reindeer porn (images of mating reindeer—what did you think I meant?) stashed inside blocks of snow.

What he hadn't anticipated was an unseasonably warm front that came through and melted everything. Mother Nature had been my wingman.

After an hour, we had nothing. We'd waded through old toys, newsletters, hymnals, and boxes of golf pencils. There was nothing there that seemed valuable or even interesting.

"Is there another stash somewhere?" I set down the last case of golf pencils.

"We know what's in all the other places." Kayla scratched her chin.

"Just our stuff." Mike shrugged. "Nothing else."

Had I gotten this wrong? Maybe the men had. Maybe they were looking for something in the wrong place. If this was about the murder in Bladdersly, why would anyone look for something in an old church owned by four teen druids in Who's There? The only connection to them was Kurt. And that was only because he liked Kayla. But as far as I knew, they'd never really had any kind of relationship, and he'd never been here.

On the other hand, this could mean that Kurt was involved. I needed to give this some thought. My stomach rumbled.

"Oh well," Stewie said. "We need to clear out the altar. I have big plans for this place. Are you in, Bird Goddess?"

I fled to Bladdersly. I wanted some time to sit and think, and I was hungry, and I still hadn't been to the diners there. Three birds with one stone! Which was one better than the old saying.

Ella's Diner was half full in spite of the hour. Peering out the window at Ela's Diner across the street, I could see that place was half full too.

"What can I get ya?" A red-faced, heavyset woman with light brown hair pinned up in a bun smiled at me. She had to be in her fifties. Her nametag said *Ella*. This was the owner?

"What do you recommend?" I asked.

"The meatloaf. I make the best meatloaf in the state." Her pen hung in midair over her pad.

My stomach rumbled in agreement. "Ok, that sounds good. Is the food here better than Ela's?"

Ella scowled. "You're damn right it is! That idiot couldn't pour ketchup out of a bottle without burning it."

"It's kind of strange," I continued with no regard for my own safety. "That you have two competing restaurants with the same name."

The woman wrote on her notepad. "Yeah, well, that's what you get in this business. Just when you think things are going well—*Bam!*" She slammed her hand on my table, making me jump. "Some kid comes along and thinks they can do it better!"

I put on my most sympathetic face. "That sucks. So you've been here a long time?"

Ella stuffed the pen and pad in her apron. "Thirty-two years. And that fraud across the street has only been here five."

"You have my sympathies," I said.

The woman responded by sitting down across from me.

"That's nice of you since you aren't from around here. But I do know who you are. You're that woman they think killed Tyson."

I decided not to deny it. "That's right. But I didn't kill him. No matter what Pastor Malone says."

She cocked her head to the right. "Do you think, if you go to prison for the crime, you could give me an endorsement? That cow across the street would faint if she thought I had the endorsement of a murderer."

"I'm sorry to disappoint you," I said firmly. "But I didn't kill him."

Besides. I'd like to try the food first.

"Who do you think killed him?" I asked.

Ella's expression grew stormy. "Hell, I'd have done it if I could've gotten away with it. You did a service to this town by taking him out."

I fought the urge to insist on my innocence. "Why's that?"

"He was a bad seed. He robbed businesses, including his own store. He was rude and obnoxious. And I'm sure he would only have gotten worse if you hadn't killed him."

I sighed. "I didn't kill him."

Ella struggled to get to her feet. "Whatever. Your meatloaf will be up soon."

As she walked away, I looked across the street again. A much younger, thinner woman was waiting tables there. So that was Ela. Maybe I'd go there for dessert after interviewing Elrond.

In the meantime, I needed to think about the break-in at the church. I really should've confronted the men. Then I'd know who they were. However, if they'd had guns and I wasn't able to disarm them, well, I'd have died for nothing.

The big question was if Kurt was involved. The kid seemed to know everything about this town. And he was under my feet half the time. Could he be smarter than I'd given him credit for? Was he just following me around to stay one step ahead of the investigation?

The theory had some merit. The problem with it was that if it was correct, what did Kurt hide in the Chapel of Despair? It had to be something valuable. That didn't necessarily mean something physical. It could be information.

Argh! All of this was a stretch. Connecting him to the Chapel was tenuous. Was I going off the rails into crazy town just to dodge the rap? Yeesh. I was starting to think like Betty now. I filed this information away mentally and waited for my food.

Sure enough, I didn't have long before a plate with meatloaf and mashed potatoes appeared next to me. Ella lingered, so I took a bite.

"Oh wow! This is fantastic!" I said between mouthfuls.

It really was. Meatloaf is one of those Midwest staples. You'll find hundreds of different recipes in Iowa alone. And this one was possibly the best I'd ever had.

Ella softened. "Thanks."

I was so busy devouring my lunch that I didn't even notice she'd wandered away. I moaned with each mouthful, rolling my eyes. It was that good.

"Are you okay?" Kurt sat in the seat Ella had occupied earlier.

"What are you doing here?" I asked. And how strange that I'm thinking of the guy and he shows up right here, right now.

He looked at me curiously. "You're not very bright, are you? I told you…I'm sticking to you like glue so that I can bring you in when you run."

I thought about stabbing him with my fork. "Considering that I've told you repeatedly that I have zero interest in running, it seems like you're the not very bright one."

Kurt shrugged. "So what's next?"

Maybe he could be useful. "Tell me about Elrond."

"Oh, that's easy. He's this guy who's into comics and opened his own shop."

"I know that," I said through clenched teeth. "What else can you tell me about him?"

"Well." Kurt tapped his chin. "He's lived here all his life…like everybody else here. After he graduated from high school, someone died and left him money, and he opened up the shop."

"Is his name really Elrond?"

Kurt nodded. "He changed it a few years back. He doesn't use a last name, but it's Anderson if you need to know."

"Did he know Tyson?"

"*I* didn't know Tyson. But maybe? A lot of guys hang out in that shop. And Tyson was in the Nerd Herd at Best Bye."

I speared the last bite of meatloaf. "I'm going to Elrond's next—since you need to know where I am at every moment."

"I can go with you." Kurt brightened.

I thought about this as I polished off the potatoes. "Why not?" There wasn't really a reason not to. Besides, maybe if there were other people in there, Kurt could draw them off so that I could talk to Elrond alone.

"Alright, kid. Give me a few minutes to pay my bill, and then we're out of here."

Elrond's smelled like paper and dust. The shop was dimly lit and the shelves stocked with a dizzying array of comics and graphic novels.

A tall, skinny man, maybe in his midtwenties, stood behind the counter. He had long, thin, stringy hair hanging limply over his shoulders. The pale skin told me he didn't get out into the sun much. This kid might be a good recruit for the druids. Would Stewie give me $25 for recruiting him, or was the Bird Goddess exempt?

"Hi," I called out brightly. "You must be Elrond. Do you have any *Wonder Woman* comics?"

The kid froze, staring at me. He didn't respond.

"They don't get many women in here," Kurt whispered.

I could see that.

"Are you alright?" I approached the counter, and he backed up nervously.

Kurt stepped forward. "Dude! You're making a bad impression on my bail jumper."

It shows how magnanimous I was that I didn't immediately fashion a comic book into a shiv and impale him. I could've done that. You can make a lethal weapon out of just about anything. But I didn't. And I'm kind of proud of that.

Elrond snapped out of it. "Fine. You want *Wonder Woman*? I don't usually stock it."

Was this sexism? How could you be a comics shop and not have *Wonder Woman*? "Why not?"

He shrugged. "I don't get a lot of call for it here."

That's when I noticed his skinny bicep with a tattoo of Lance Armstrong as a Native American chief.

"Nice ink." I pointed at his arm.

Elrond frowned. "I didn't want that one. Bear insisted. Even gave it to me for free." He rolled up the sleeve of his other arm. "This is my favorite. It's Beetle Dork. You're probably too old to know who that is."

"You might be surprised," I mumbled as I looked closer. Sure enough, it was the entire cover of the first edition.

"It's pretty cool since it's all about Harold and all." Elrond gave a weak smile.

"Yeah." I narrowed my eyes. "I'm familiar."

"That's because *she's* Beetle Dork." Stewie and Mike emerged, hidden by the stacks, and pointed at me.

Elrond did not seem convinced. "That's not funny, guys. You're just saying that because you own the rights."

"It's the truth," Mike said. "That's Merry Wrath Ferguson. She's Beetle Dork."

For some reason, I felt I had to explain. "Not because I wanted to be, that's for sure."

"That's so cool!" Elrond's face opened up into an almost pleasant expression. "Wait." His face fell. "Did he say Wrath? You're the chick who murdered Tyson!"

"No." My hands curled into fists. "I didn't kill Tyson."

But Elrond continued as if I hadn't said anything. "He was one of my best customers!" He waved limply at Mike and Stewie. "Except for these guys."

"I didn't kill Tyson," I reiterated.

"Bird Goddess," Stewie sniffed authoritatively, "wouldn't kill anyone."

"Wait." Elrond did a cartoon doubletake. "You are Beetle Dork, you killed Tyson, and you are these guys' cult's Bird Goddess?"

"It's not a cult!" Stewie's voice went up about fifty decibels.

"Two of those three are correct," I said. "I did not kill Tyson Pancratz."

The four of us stared at each other. Stewie wiggled his eyebrows at me, intimating that we were somehow communicating with our minds—although what we were saying was a secret to me. Mike shrugged and went back to the stacks.

"Okay," Elrond said at last. "We don't have *Wonder Woman* though."

"Why not?" Betty shouted from the doorway, with Inez hot on her heels.

"Because no one buys it." Elrond rolled his eyes.

"What are you doing here?" I asked the girls as they walked over to me.

"Buying comics," Inez said. "Same as you."

"You know," Kurt said. "You've never had this many women in here at once."

Elrond's eyes shot daggers at him, but then he seemed to reconsider and finally nodded as a way of giving in.

"Why don't you have comic books written about girl superheroes?" Betty stepped forward.

"Yeah!" Inez crossed her arms over her chest.

"I guess I could order some…" he offered, hoping no one would ask.

"No! It's too late," Betty snapped. "What we really want to know is, why did you kill Tyson Pancratz?"

I stared at her. "This guy did it?"

A responsible adult would've dismissed the child's ranting. But I wanted someone else to take the heat, so I was interested.

"I didn't do it!" Elrond's hooded eyes opened wide. "What makes you think I did it?"

Betty leaned back. "I have my reasons."

"And they are?" Kurt asked curiously.

Betty stuck her tongue out. "I don't have to tell you."

"I didn't do it!" Elrond blustered. "Sure, I was here that night, and sure, it happened not far from here, but it wasn't me!"

That caught my attention. "Did you see anything?"

He shook his head so hard that he became dizzy and stumbled a bit. "No! I told Vanderzee that!"

"Do you have video footage of that area?" Inez asked.

We all gasped and looked at her. It hadn't occurred to anyone else to ask.

"Um." He looked up and to the left. "Only of the alley. But The Opera House blocks my view of the Pump & Pawn."

"You do?" I turned to him. "You have footage?"

Elrond didn't seem to know how to answer. "Yeah. Probably. Maybe?"

"Did you hand it over to the cops?" Stewie asked.

"No. They didn't ask when they interviewed me. But remember, I can only see the alley out back. I can't see the shed."

We were already coming behind the counter. Elrond had no choice but to allow us into his back room, where we stopped cold.

"No *Wonder Woman*! You're a dirty, rotten fink!" Betty stomped. "I should plug you, but I gassed my heater. Your lucky day, bub!"

The noir speak was back.

It was true. The office was papered, floor to ceiling, with images of Wonder Woman.

"Don't touch that!" Elrond ran over to Betty, who had picked up a coffee mug that said, *Wonder Woman's BFF*. There were figurines of the superheroine scattered across every surface.

"I think this is my favorite." Kurt winked and gestured to a picture.

On the desk was an 8"x10" framed photo of Elrond in Wonder Woman drag. The costume hung limply on his skinny frame, but he made up for it with enthusiasm as he smiled broadly with both thumbs up.

"Forget about that." I brushed it all off. "Show us the footage from the night of the murder."

"What time did it occur?" Inez asked.

"The coppers squealed," Betty said. "Pops Malone said this dame dusted the lug in the shed around two in the morning."

With a heavy sigh, Elrond sat in his Wonder Woman upholstered desk chair and turned on his Wonder Woman laptop. He clicked on an icon labelled *The Secret Diaries of Diana Prince* and pulled up the footage for the night of the murder at two in the morning.

"Back it up to 1:30," I insisted. "And run it through three a.m."

Betty pushed the man out of the chair. "Scram, ya rube. I'll be the gumshoe."

She found the right time stamp and fast-forwarded. There was no traffic.

"If you came in through the front parking lot or exited out the other end of the alley," Elrond said, "we wouldn't see you. It's a one in three chance that I caught you on camera."

"I. Didn't. Do. It," I said through clenched teeth.

At 2:05 a.m., a car raced down the alley in the direction we were looking for.

"Back it up!" Inez insisted.

But Betty was already on it. She found the vehicle, froze the frame, and blew it up.

"What's he doing there?" Kurt wondered.

Bryce Vanderzee was in a black sedan driving down the alley. In the front seat next to him was a shadowy figure we couldn't make out.

Stewie squeaked, "That puts the police chief at the scene of the crime at the right time."

"Yes, but we don't know if that's just a coincidence. Maybe he was driving around town. Malone said he saw me at two. This is a few minutes later."

Kurt leaned closer to the monitor. "If Vanderzee did it, he could've scared Malone into falsely accusing you."

I pointed at the screen. "Who's in the front seat? Is that Tyson?"

The image was too dark and murky. It was impossible to tell. "That's why the chief didn't ask you for your footage. He knew he was in it."

Inez nodded. "And hoped you were too stupid to even think of it."

"Vanderzee is scary," Elrond said with a shudder.

"He's just loud and obnoxious," I dismissed.

"No, he's, like, really scary," Elrond insisted. "There's rumors about him and stuff."

That was interesting. "Like what?"

Kurt spoke up. "There have been rumors for years that he's tried to shake down people."

"Blackmail?" I asked. Oooh! That was a great motive!

"I don't know." Kurt seemed doubtful. "That's just it. I've heard of this vaguely, but never any specifics."

It was possible that these were just normal rumors in a small town. Last year, there was a rumor that Officer Kevin Dooley ate the evidence from the theft of a Cheetos truck. But I didn't believe it. Mostly.

My mind reeled back to *Boats of the Midwest*. I needed to do a deeper reading of that later.

"I've emailed you a copy of the footage, complete with time stamp," Betty said as she slipped a DVD into the computer. "And I'm making a copy of the whole evening, just in case Wonder Woman here screws up and erases it." The noir was gone, but it made sense. They didn't have any of this technology in the early twentieth century.

"You know," Inez said. "I'll never look at Wonder Woman the same way again."

Glancing at Elrond as Wonder Woman in the picture, I had to agree.

CHAPTER TWENTY

———

I headed over to Ela's Diner for dessert and information. Unfortunately, a small crowd followed me.

"I need a table for one," I told a bored, gum-cracking waitress.

"Three," Betty said.

"Four," added Kurt.

"What do you mean?" Stewie asked. "There's six of us!"

Which is how I ended up sharing my table with two Girl Scouts, a bounty hunter, and two druids. It sounds like the foundation of a joke, even though I couldn't come up with a punchline at the moment.

"What'll ya have?" A pretty, young waitress came over and smiled. Her nametag read *Ela*.

"Desserts," I said, pointing to Stewie. "He's buying, so bring him the check."

Stewie started to protest.

"It's because you outed me as Beetle Dork," I said.

"Oh. That." He nodded at the waitress. "I'll take the check."

Mike stared at him, mouth open.

"What?" Stewie snapped.

"You've never paid the check for anything! At cons, you always 'forget your wallet.' Last week, you had *me* gas up the hearse! In fact, you always have someone else fill up the hearse!"

Kurt's eyes grew wide as, for the first time since running into the guys at Elrond's, he realized that he was sitting with Kayla's cult members. "You guys know Kayla?" he asked, in case there was more than one cult in Who's There.

"Duh," Mike said. "And then there was that time at Area 51, when you tricked Heather into paying for your lunch."

Stewie wasn't listening. His ears perked up at the prospect of a possible recruit. "That's right. Kayla is a member of our sect. Are you interested in joining?"

Kurt thought about it. "How often do you guys meet?"

"We practically live at the Chapel of Despair," Mike groused.

I studied Kurt's reaction to the location, but he didn't seem to recognize the name of the place.

"Because it's awesome!" Stewie squealed.

Kurt and Stewie fell into a conversation about the merits of membership.

Ela brought over menus, and we divvied them up.

"What do you recommend?" I repeated the question I'd asked earlier. A familiar aroma wafted from the kitchen. "Hey, is that meatloaf?"

Ela beamed. "Best meatloaf in the state!"

"It smells like the meatloaf I had for lunch at Ella's." I pointed across the street to make my point.

Ela sighed. "That would be just like her to steal our recipe!"

"She stole your meatloaf recipe?" Betty asked. "I can help you with security. Do you have any heavy logs that could swing out of your kitchen?"

"I don't know how she did it." Ela ignored the girl, which was for the best. "Well, she doesn't have the recipe for my triple-chocolate cheesecake!"

"I'll have that," I spoke up.

Around the table, everyone asked for the same thing. Ela collected the menus we hadn't even looked at and left.

"It's so weird," I mumbled.

Kurt looked at me curiously.

"You have two tattoo shops with the same name and theme of Lance Armstrong art. You have two cafes, across the street from each other, named Ella's Diner…"

"Ela and Ella," he corrected. "They're totally spelled differently."

"What is it about Bladdersly?"

He shrugged. "I guess I never really thought about it before."

I pressed him. "Why not? It's such a strange thing. It kind of stands out."

Kurt seemed a bit defensive. "I don't know. I guess it doesn't stand out to us."

"And you hardly have enough business to support these places and The Opera House." As soon as I said it, I wondered how could I overlook something so bizarre?

Bladdersly was a ridiculous town. That was a given. But the businesses on this street went beyond simply quirky.

"Remember the police report?" Betty said. "Tyson went to juvie for burglarizing these places."

I hoped Kurt didn't pick up on Betty saying she'd seen the police report. "Which gives them motive to want to punish him," I said. "But enough to kill him?"

"I think Vanderzee did it," Stewie said.

Mike nodded in agreement but said nothing.

"And then there's *Boats of the Midwest*," I mused.

"That book really made people mad," Kurt said. "Lots of people were on the warpath wondering who'd written it."

Ela came over with a platter and dropped off six slices of triple-chocolate cheesecake. There was a reverent six minutes of silence as we ate.

"Maybe Tyson wrote it?" Inez asked. "What's it about?"

I was proud of Inez for coming up with a very valid idea. Maybe I was rubbing off on these girls. I was like a role model— a little more like Wonder Woman and a little less like Bird Goddess of the Cult of NicoDerm.

"Scandals." Kurt shoved his plate away. "Whoever wrote it seemed to know an awful lot about the people around here."

I wondered. "If Tyson wrote it and people were mad, anyone might have killed him."

Kurt suggested, "Or they might have killed him for robbing them."

I sighed heavily. "That just opens up the suspect pool to more suspects."

"But Vanderzee was driving through the alley at the right time with someone in the car with him," Stewie said. "He could've killed Tyson."

"Yes, but why?" I pressed.

"Because he was in the book?" Stewie suggested.

I really needed to do an in-depth reading of *Boats*.

"Because he robbed the police station?" Betty added her thoughts.

Kurt nodded. "There's a crooked cop in the book. And a scandal about someone named Bella, who seems an awful lot like Ella. But then again, there's dirt on half the town in that book, so it could be anyone."

I pushed my empty plate toward the center of the table. "Who would be most likely to kill over that? I mean, the cat's out of the bag, so they wouldn't be shutting him up."

Inez said, "Revenge."

"That's good too," Betty agreed.

To his credit, Stewie paid the bill. I discovered that Inez and Betty had been dropped off by Inez's mother, so I gave the girls a ride back, followed, as ever, by Kurt. Mike and Stewie went back to Elrond's for reasons they didn't explain. Maybe Stewie was going to give Elrond a pitch to become a druid.

I walked in the door of my house stuffed from a heavy lunch of meatloaf and potatoes, topped off with cheesecake. In the dining room, Philby was again sitting, staring at Rufus, but she seemed hairier for some reason.

"Philby?" I asked.

The cat slowly turned to face me. She was wearing the beard from my disguise at The Dew Drop Inn. There must've been some spirit gum still stuck on it. And it fit her perfectly. I didn't wear it that well.

"It's so you," I said as I scratched her head. "Does the beard intimidate the frog?"

Rufus stared at me and swallowed. I guess not. Philby gave me an irritated look.

"I don't get it. Why don't you try to be friends? I'm not going to let you eat him, and you're never going to get into that terrarium. So what's the point?"

At that moment, Leonard bounded into the room, racing over to me to pepper my hands with kisses. That was odd. The deerhound was never in the same room as Philby. She tormented the poor guy.

"Ah," I said to Leonard. "Because she's working so hard to annoy the frog, she doesn't have time to torture you."

Leonard barked happily. Philby ignored him. Martini, Philby's daughter, jumped up onto the table. After I gave her a quick scratch, she flopped onto her back, legs akimbo, and passed out. A total narcoleptic, Martini slept more than the usual amount. The vet said there was nothing wrong with her, besides the ability to pass out anywhere.

Philby turned back to the frog, staring more intently than ever. Maybe this was a good thing. After all, the cat…

The cat. It hit me with a cartoon *boing*. Effie. I needed to solve the Effie puzzle. There was so much to this case, what with the scandalous book, thefts, murder, and kidnapping. I hadn't had time to think about Effie the cat.

A pang of guilt hit me. I also hadn't spent much time thinking of Pastor Malone. He was my witness—the one who'd nailed me and had the potential to free me. I called Riley. He answered on the first ring.

"Wrath," he said. "Any news?"

"I was hoping you had something. Especially on Malone."

Riley sighed. "I've listened on the police bands. They have no idea where he is or if he's still alive. There's been no ransom request."

I needed hope. I needed to believe that Malone was alright and would set things straight. "Do you think he did a runner? When he realized that he didn't know the person he'd declared to be the killer — maybe he figured out who the real killer was. It's possible he's afraid of the real killer."

"At this point?" he asked. "I don't have any leads but lots of questions. I'm leaning toward the idea that the killer kidnapped him to keep him from talking. This is one convoluted case."

I filled him in on what happened at Elrond's and Kurt's mentioning the book.

"Do you have *Boats of the Midwest*?" Riley asked.

"Yeah. I'm going to go through it again. I really like the idea that Vanderzee is behind this."

Riley laughed. "Just because he hates you."

"A girl can dream, right?"

"Do you want me to read through *Boats*?" he offered. "To save some time?"

"No, but I do have some footage from a security camera I'd like you to go over." A text popped up on my cell. "I've got to go. My attorney wants to touch base. I'll have Betty email you the footage."

We hung up, and I called Jane.

"Hey, Merry," she said. "I just wanted to check in. I don't have anything new, but from what I understand, neither do the police."

I let out a breath. "Well, that seems like good news."

"Not really," she admitted. "Vanderzee has asked a judge to move your trial up early."

"How early?" I asked warily.

"Way too early for my comfort," the attorney said. "They think that they have enough to push it through."

"That can't be right," I protested. "They don't have their star witness. If the witness is missing and can't testify against me, what case can they have?"

Jane's voice was soothing and calm. She really was an amazing attorney. I made a silent vow to use her for all future issues, hoping that I wouldn't need her.

"They're going to push through using his sworn statement," Jane said. "It's highly unusual, and I have a strong case for fighting it. They also have the phone call, but I think I can get around it too."

I thought for a moment. "That all sounds good. Why do I get the feeling you are still apprehensive?"

"Because the judge agreed that you'd be tried locally. Merry, the trial will take place in Bladdersly."

Considering that everyone from Bladdersly kept repeating the lie that I'd killed Tyson, that did not look good.

I had to move fast.

CHAPTER TWENTY-ONE

———

"That's bad." Riley shook his head when I dropped off the DVD. "We need to move things up."

Kelly patted my arm. "We'll get this solved, Merry."

Claire walked over and handed me a platter of artistically arranged Hostess snacks and walked away. It was scary awesome how she knew when I was coming by and what I needed.

"I hacked into some security cameras at the gas stations at the roads in and out of Bladdersly," Riley explained. "I've been going through them to see if I can spot Malone. No luck yet."

"He's got to be somewhere," I said hopefully.

"What are you going to do now?" Kelly asked.

I put my arms protectively around the platter. "I've got to see a man about a cat. Or…a woman. Or two people. Well, at least a person…"

Riley held up his hand. "Just get going. I'll see what we can do with this." He held up the DVD. "And, Merry, be careful this time."

"Who are you?" A thirty-something guy in a bathrobe peered at me through a crack in the doorway.

I stood on the stoop of the other half of Tyson's duplex. It was still daylight, so breaking into Tyson's place seemed like a bad idea, considering I was his alleged killer. And since the duplex shared an open basement, I figured that I could bluff the neighbor into letting me in.

"I'm a friend of Tyson's. His brother, Mike, sent me to see if there's anything left of his to pick up."

Of course, Tyson didn't have a brother. And for a moment, I wondered if using Mike as the name was a stupid move, considering Mike and Tyson together made it sound super fake. But maybe the neighbor wouldn't know much about Tyson and think it all made sense.

The door opened all the way. The man was scruffy, unshaven, and possibly unwashed. And he didn't appear to have anything on other than the bathrobe. Maybe this wasn't the best idea.

"Why don't you have a key?" he asked.

"Mike had to turn in the key to the landlord. But he realized he hadn't searched the basement. Tyson told him you shared the basement."

"Okay." He opened the door a little wider and walked inside.

Huh. I was surprised that worked.

I followed, closing the door behind me. "Thanks, um…"

"Frank. And you are?"

"Molly"—I thought quickly—"Molly Nixon. Were you friends with Tyson?" Part of me wanted to get downstairs so that I could leave. This guy was seriously creepy.

"Not really. He was kind of an ass." Frank paused, looking me in the eye. "Sorry. I shouldn't speak ill of the dead since he was your friend and all." He belched. "Come on."

I followed him to his door that led down to the basement, and then I followed him downstairs.

I stared at the back wall. "That's all his?"

Frank nodded. "Yeah. I was surprised this stuff was still here."

There were—all sealed with tape and labelled *Private*. How very mysterious. Would any of these have a clue that would solve this case?

"Oh," I said, remembering. "About the cat. Effie?"

Frank's eyes glazed over. "What cat?"

That's what I'd thought. When I'd been here before, I hadn't seen any evidence that a cat lived here. And yet, somebody retrieved a cat named Effie.

"Oh wait. I remember." Frank scratched his head. "He was cat-sitting or something. Some guy knocked on my door with the cat and asked me to give it to Tyson."

"And did you?"

"Nah. I just put it down here. Since we shared a basement, I figured Tyson would grab him sooner or later."

"You didn't say anything to Tyson about it?"

"I hate cats." He shrugged.

And from that moment on, I refused to feel bad if this went south and came back to haunt Frank. Who hates cats? Somebody like this loser.

"Well, thanks," I said. "I can take it from here."

"Whatever. You can take them through Tyson's place so that you don't bug me." Frank belched again and made his way upstairs, slamming the door behind him.

I tiptoed up Tyson's stairs, emerging into his living room, just to make sure no one was there. It was a good thing I did. Because Neil, the guy who hadn't been friends with Tyson anymore, was sitting in Tyson's living room watching TV.

Now that was interesting. Why was Neil here? Frank must not have realized anyone was in Tyson's apartment. Or he didn't care.

I slipped back down to the basement. Damn. Both exits were cut off. I really wanted to take these boxes home and go through them. But Neil had lied to me to put me off. And that made him a person of interest. And Frank had already insisted I go through Tyson's place. Ignoring his request could make him check me out more closely.

There was no evidence of Effie here. And Frank's story about cat-sitting did sound plausible. Effie wasn't as important right now as me getting out of here undiscovered. The last thing I needed was yet another confrontation with the Bladdersly PD for being somewhere I wasn't supposed to be.

Until I came up with a plan, I might as well search these boxes. Stepping up to the first one, I used my keys to cut through the tape. Prying back the box flaps revealed a stack of boxes of laptops. Still in their original packaging.

The other eleven boxes revealed the same thing. There were sixty laptops in all. Not one of them had been opened.

What was it Nyla said? That Tyson sold the laptops to people who would just resell them? And that it was unethical but not illegal, and since he'd moved laptops, it was okay?

Why did he have sixty brand-new computers in his basement? Was this the missing shipment? Was I being too hopeful in thinking he might've been killed for that? If these were top-of-the-line laptops, they could add up to $60,000. But then someone at Best Bye would have noticed if all those premium computers were missing.

I took one of the laptops out and restacked the boxes. Maybe Riley could look this over and tell me if there was anything unusual about it. It could be better than what I was originally looking for.

Maybe Effie's presence here was just that—Tyson was watching the cat. It seemed kind of crazy. But then, nothing in this case was normal. And the only way to find out about Effie would be, what, to put something out on social media asking for information on Effie the cat?

At the moment, I was far more interested in the computers. I just had to get past Neil. Sitting in this basement for hours while he hung out was a waste of time.

My cell rang, and I answered it immediately.

"Merry!" Ivan's voice was jovial. "Ron and I want to go to that tattoo shop where I got my ink. Would you like to join us?"

"What?" I whispered. "No. I do not want to join you."

Ivan acted as if I hadn't just said I didn't want to go. "You should get tattoo of something meaningful. Like your cat, Philby."

Ron shouted in the background, "Or your little paramilitary group."

"Paramilitary group?" I couldn't help but ask.

"Yes," Ivan answered. "With the scary little girls. That Betty could be Chechen strongman now."

I was intrigued as to what a tattoo of Betty would look like. She could be riding Cookie the horse while waving a Catalonian flag. Of course, then you run into the dilemma of where to put something that would have to be pretty large.

Maybe on the back? Betty would love that. I'd better not give her any ideas. I could wake up with it after the next sleepover.

"No thanks. I'm good." An idea hit me. "You guys are coming to Bladdersly now?"

"Yes. Be there in five minutes," Ivan said.

"Maybe you can help me out. Is your heart set on the tattoo shop you went to?"

Five minutes later, I heard the TV go off upstairs and the front door slammed. Neil must've gotten the call that Ron and Ivan wanted tattoos at his place. Huh. The guys got this one right. I'd have to thank them later.

Quietly, I made my way upstairs and peered through a crack in the door. No movement. I wasn't taking any chances. After letting myself out the back door, I walked down to the end of the alley before turning to go to my van, parked in front of the duplex.

"You got this from Tyson's?" Riley stared at the box.

I'd gone directly to Riley's office and handed it over. A box of my favorite donuts was sitting on a nearby table.

"Claire said you'd be coming back." Kelly smirked as she joined us.

I picked up a donut. "How does she know that every time? And can she move in with me?"

Claire, as usual, completely ignored us.

"Anyway, Tyson has sixty laptops. All like this," I explained once I'd chewed and swallowed said donut. "Can you tell me anything about them?"

Riley typed something on his keyboard. After a few moments, he spoke. "Not really. They're kind of generic. It's a basic model that is mostly used by students."

I rocked back on my heels. "That doesn't seem helpful. Do you think Tyson stole these?"

Riley thought for a moment. "I can scope out a few databases to check the serial numbers to see if they were stolen."

"Okay." I pulled my car keys out. "Oh hey, is there any way to find out who owns a particular cat?"

Kelly's eyebrows went up. "A cat?"

"Yeah. Tyson was watching a cat named Effie for some guy. I don't know if it is relevant."

"Probably not," Riley said. "Sounds like a waste of time. What do you want us to do? Take out an ad in the paper?"

"I'll take care of it," Kelly said quickly.

Riley shrugged. "I think it's a dead end."

"Well." Kelly sniffed. "Good thing I've got all this new, state-of-the-art equipment."

Riley had the good grace not to say anything.

I clapped my hands together. "Great! I've got to get back to the Chapel of Despair to read a book."

Claire, for the first time ever, turned to look at me. Like, really look at me. "That druid place? Used to be a Lutheran church?"

Claire had just spoken to me? "Yes. You know it?"

What would ultra-cool, super-refined Claire want with that place? Was she related to one of the druids? I really knew very little about her, and she knew so much about me.

"I find it very interesting," she said before turning back to her computer.

An image of the stunning redhead walking into the place, asking for information on membership, and Stewie promptly exploding, popped into my head.

"Maybe I'll see you there," I said awkwardly. "I'm their Bird Goddess."

Claire didn't acknowledge me speaking. Hopefully, she hadn't heard me.

"That went well," Kelly whispered.

"Hey," I asked her, "how are you going to find this cat, Effie, out of all the cats in Bladdersly?"

"I have an idea." Kelly winked before returning to her desk. As she sat down, she looked me over. "Are those the shoes you were wearing the night of the murder?"

"Huh?" I looked down to see the white canvas shoes on my feet. They had some fancy name with a patent leather swoosh on the side. "I guess I was wearing these."

"It's the only pair you've worn all summer," my best friend said.

I gave her a dry look. "I've worn other shoes."

"Maybe once or twice," Kelly corrected. "But you've worn these 99% of the time. You always get fixated on one pair until you wear it out."

"I do not!" I totally did. I just didn't want her to know that she was right.

Kelly got up and took off her sport sandals, handing them to me. "Let me check those out. You can wear my shoes."

I couldn't think of any reason not to swap, so I handed them over and flounced out the door. As the most responsible of the two of us, she probably knew what she was doing. And we wore the same size shoes, so why not?

Back at the Chapel of Despair, I punched in the code and let myself in. There was no one around. I found my copy of the book and made my way home.

"You're home?" Rex was feeding the cats. "Hey, I thought you threw the werewolf mask away. Philby's got it on."

Sure enough, the feline führer was sitting next to the frog's aquarium wearing the werewolf mask she'd commandeered from us after a Halloween parade a while back. I had no idea where she'd kept it. She hid it somewhere in the house where I suppose she thought we'd never look. Which was silly since we had no intention of taking it from her, and I'd certainly never throw it out.

"She's trying to intimidate Rufus." Rex kissed me.

"Is it working?"

"No. Leonard, however…" Rex pointed to the corner of the dining room, where our Scottish deerhound was sitting in a corner, face to the wall. "Is appropriately terrified."

I sighed and walked over to the dog, who nuzzled my hand. And he'd been so happy earlier. "Poor Leonard. Philby is so mean to you. Come on. Let's get a treat!"

After a wary glance at the kitty werewolf, Leonard followed me to the kitchen, where I gave him three dog treats. He wagged his tail and trotted out to the living room.

"Would you mind filling me in?" Rex asked. "I promise not to tell Carnack or Vanderzee."

I was tired. This case was like the Hydra—chop one head off and two more grew back. There were too many suspects. Too many threads to follow.

"Why not?" I told him about what I'd found in Tyson's basement.

My husband frowned. "I don't remember hearing anything about stolen computers. And a haul that large would've come in to me."

That was a surprise. "Even if it's outside of your jurisdiction?"

Rex nodded. "It's kind of a specialty of mine. The other small-town PDs often help each other out. I reach out to neighboring towns all the time for info."

That was interesting. "But Vanderzee never asked?"

"No. Maybe it hasn't been reported. Or maybe this theft was from somewhere else. Like Des Moines or Omaha or the Quad Cities."

"Well, Riley is looking into it. Maybe it's relevant. Maybe it's not." Back in the living room, I stretched out on the sofa. "You didn't say anything about me sneaking into Tyson's basement or using your brothers-in-law to get me out of there."

"That's because it isn't my jurisdiction." Rex joined me on the couch and took my hand. "I've decided that if I want to have you home and want to keep track of your antics, I need to leave the job at the office."

"Good idea. I know I'm a pain in the butt."

"Yes, you are." Rex kissed me again. If I didn't have to reread this book, I might go for an all-out make out session on the couch.

Wait a minute… "Why are you being so nice to me?"

Rex gave me a long look. "Because we're going to a cookout tonight."

I sat straight up. "Yay! Steaks? Are we taking wine? Is it Kelly and Robert's house?"

Rex shook his head. "With Randi, Ronni, and their husbands. At their place."

I slumped against the couch. "Oh."

My husband put his arm around me. "Out of the four of them, three love you. Remember that."

"Why are we going?" I grumbled.

"Randi has been chewing Ronni out for her dislike of you. She wants to make it up to you."

"Dislike is far too weak a word to describe it." I held up the book. "And I've got some serious reading to do."

"You have half an hour. I'll get everything ready." Rex started to walk into the kitchen. "Hold on." He held up the beard that Philby must've discarded earlier. "What is this? I almost shot it when I walked into the kitchen when I got home."

I took it from him. "My disguise from the other night. The one you didn't think was sexy."

"Oh. Right," he said. "And why are you wearing someone else's shoes?"

CHAPTER TWENTY-TWO

———

Rex and I walked around to the backyard, where Ron was standing at the grill with an apron that said *Kiss the Chef Or I'll Break Your Legs*.

"Rex! Merry!" Randi flew over to us, pulling us to her in an embrace. "We are so happy you're here!"

"No, we're not!" Ronni shouted from inside the house.

Ivan and Ron came over and crushed me in a group bear hug. Once I got free, I noticed that they only shook Rex's hand. There was no doubt that they loved him too. They just treated him a little more respectfully than they did me.

Rex took food inside with Randi while I pulled the guys aside.

"Thanks for bailing me out today," I said.

Ivan frowned. "We did not bail you out. Were we supposed to do that?"

Ron added, "We thought you wanted distraction."

"I did. And you crushed it."

The men looked at each other doubtfully.

"It means you did a good job," I added.

"Really?" Ivan asked. "Because crushing is bad."

They were still struggling with American slang. Once, in the taxidermy shop, a customer told Randi that she'd recently dumped her husband. The men got excited, asking where people dumped bodies around here. And on multiple occasions, I'd had to explain that being shredded had nothing to do with an industrial chipper or that having a blast didn't mean blowing up the local utilities in an effort to strike back at Russia.

I wasn't worried. They'd figure it out. Eventually.

"Did you get tattoos?" I asked.

They grinned wildly and showed me their biceps. Each of them sported a small Chechen flag.

"Those are normal!" I smiled. "I like them!"

"Good," Ron said as he flipped the steaks, "because Ronni said she would divorce me if I got any more weird tattoos."

"She said any tattoos," Ivan corrected.

Ron paled. "Really?"

Ivan patted his friend and brother-in-law on the back. "She does not seem to care, dude."

Ivan's adding of the word dude was jarring. But I kept that to myself. "Did Neil say anything to you about Tyson?"

"He said he is leaving town soon. Says he does not like Lance Armstrong."

Ron said, "We threatened to break his legs…"

"Because we still needed to get tattoos," Ivan added helpfully.

"But Neil said no. He is selling business to other guy."

Now that was interesting. Was Neil fleeing the coop before the case was solved? Was he leaving because he was Tyson's killer? Or was he leaving to fence the laptops?

"Hey, guys!" Kurt strolled around the corner, carrying a sheet cake.

"What are you doing here?" I asked.

Ivan took the cake from the kid. "We invited. We are thinking of going into bounty hunter business with this guy."

Kurt nodded eagerly. "I'm going corporate."

"You haven't had one single case!" I protested.

He set the cake down on the table. "That's just splitting hairs. Besides, if Kayla is impressed with me being a bounty hunter, imagine how she'll feel toward me when I'm CEO of the most powerful bail recovery agency in the county!"

"We can catch bad guys!" Ron said. "And bust their heads!"

Kurt laughed. "Aren't they great? And so big! No one is going to go on the run with these two on their tail."

I wasn't sure this was a good idea. "I thought you were thinking of working for Riley?"

Ivan shook his head. "We changed minds when Kurt sent us the first season of *Dog the Bounty Hunter*."

"I might get mullet!" Ron said.

"And spandex pants!" Ivan added.

Ron frowned. "No spandex. Too weird."

This from a guy who was putting ketchup on his steak…while it was still on the grill.

I looked at the house. "And what do Randi and Ronni think of this?"

The two men looked at each other before Ivan replied. "We weren't going to tell them."

Great. I didn't want to be in on secrets kept from my sisters-in-law. "Why not?"

Ron held up his index finger. "We are men. We bring home money. That's how it is."

"That's sexist thinking," I protested.

Ron frowned. "It is not sexy."

"It would be if we wore spandex!" Ivan brightened.

"Not sexy. Sexist. Saying that you are the man…" I gave up. "Forget it. Go with the spandex."

"I don't think spandex is a good idea," Kurt mused. "Unless you think Kayla would like it."

"Who's Kayla, and what would she like?"

Randi, Rex, and Ronni appeared with plates, food, and a tablecloth.

"One of my druids," I answered Randi as I took the other end of the cloth and helped her spread it over the table.

Randi looked thoughtful. "Druids? We just got a big order from some local druids. I wonder if they're the same ones?"

I wondered what the twins would do for the druids. They were very creative. Recently the twins had finished a huge project—the recreation of the Nuremburg Trials, featuring meerkats as the Nazis and flamingoes as the prosecutors. It's almost tasteful.

Why did people believe that there could be more than one? "There's only one druid group in town that I'm aware of. What did they want?"

"A Stonehenge diorama with Sasquatch and aliens!" Randi clapped her hands together with glee. "I'm so excited! We've never done anything weird before!"

I thought about the one in their kitchen where snakes, dressed as little girls with curly blonde wigs, are playing with Barbies. I still have no idea how they did that without hands. And yet the twins thought what they did was perfectly normal, until this order.

I was curious. "What are you thinking about using?"

"We just got six goats in from a farmer who accidentally mixed poison with his feed. And goats are very otherworldly. They'll be the pagans. And there's a cougar that the Department of Natural Resources had to euthanize because it ate someone. And he'll be Sasquatch." She looked concerned. "I'm not sure about the aliens yet. But we'll come up with something."

"That sounds cool!" Kurt enthused. Apparently, he had never seen their work before.

"You must be Kurt!" She noticed the young man and hugged him. "Nice to meet you! The boys have said you own your own company and you're thinking of giving them jobs doing landscaping!"

Kurt, the guys, and I all exchanged about ten full seconds of meaningful glances.

"I want them to get dental!" Ronni shrieked.

Kurt, to his credit, decided to run with it. "Oh sure. In fact, Merry here is hiring me to redo her old house."

I was? And how did he know about my old house?

Ron jumped in. "Oh yes! We will do topiary trees shaped like giant iguanas!"

Ivan even got caught up in the web of lies. "And very large cactuses! We will turn front yard into a desert!"

Rex turned away, and from the shaking of his shoulders, I could see he was laughing.

"Well," I said, going against my instincts. "We're not fixed on the details yet. I'm not sure desert plants will survive a Midwest winter."

"But we can still do iguana topiaries, right?" Ron asked hopefully, seemingly forgetting this was all a lie.

"We will see," I said.

Ronni took off her sweatshirt, and I noticed that she had on one of her *Justice for Pancratz* shirts. I wondered if she was making any money.

"Ronni!" Randi chastised. "I asked you not to wear that today!"

Ronni threw her arms up in the air and screamed, "*I have to be true to my beliefs!!!*"

"Dinner!" Rex shouted as he scooped the steaks off the grill.

I silently thanked him. And we ate, mostly in peace. Randi took to kicking Ronni every time she brought up the murder, and for some reason, it worked. Kurt was bombarded with questions about his new "landscaping" business and managed to handle it so well that even I was convinced.

As everyone else cleared the table and cleaned up, Kurt drew me aside.

"Do you think they bought it?" he asked me, his eyes nervously following Ronni.

I nodded. "I do. How do you know so much about landscaping anyway?"

He shrugged. "I have two cousins in the business."

I studied him for a moment before saying, "You know, you could be a suspect in Tyson's murder."

Kurt frowned. "Why would you think that? I didn't know him!"

"Which is exactly what the murderer would say."

"But I really didn't know him."

I changed tactics. "Okay, then you wrote *Boats of the Midwest*."

Getting someone worked up into protesting their innocence on one thing when you really wanted to know about another had worked well for me in the past. It catches them off guard. You have to start with an accusation that shocks them. Then you hit them with what you really think they did, and they're usually so relieved to be off the hook for the worse accusation that they will cop to the lesser plea. I was hoping this would work with Kurt.

His mouth opened and then closed. "Again, why do you think that?"

"You know everyone in town." I ticked off my fingers. "Your mom is a bartender at The Dew Drop Inn where, you have told me, she hears a lot of gossip. And I'll bet that, with only a paper route, you had enough time on your hands to write it."

I let this sink in.

After a few moments, he said, "Those are all good arguments."

"Are you admitting that you did it?" I asked hopefully.

He shook his head. "No. But I can see how you might think that. I do know a lot about most people in Bladdersly. And Mom is my informant."

"But you didn't write the book," I sighed.

"No. But I could have. In fact, I could corroborate most of the stuff that's in there. Not with proof, but from what I've seen."

That might turn out to be helpful. "I think you could be useful to Riley if he ever has any cases in Bladdersly."

Kurt jumped up and down with glee. "Yes! I could run the Bladdersly office as a branch of the office here!"

I held my hands up and looked around. "Keep it quiet. You don't want to bring on the wrath of Ronni. She thinks you're giving her husband respectable work."

Kurt stopped. "Being a bounty hunter is respectable work. Look at *Dog the Bounty Hunter.*"

"That's exactly what I'm talking about. Ron and Ivan are impressionable. They think that show is real."

"It is real." Kurt's eyes widened.

I lowered my voice even more as Ivan and Ron came near. "No, it's scripted reality TV."

"Oh," was all Kurt said.

"Merry." Ivan threw a thumb over his shoulder. "Rex says he is ready to go." He looked at Kurt. "What is business casual? Can I beat up a guy in such clothes?"

I left Kurt to answer him. Personally, I wasn't sure. In Estonia, I once fought off three women while dressed as a banana, but I wasn't going to tell them that.

CHAPTER TWENTY-THREE

———

I finally sat down to really read *Boats of the Midwest*. Now that I knew kind of what I was looking for, it was surprising what stood out (and what I'd missed the first time).

There was a town police chief named Wamsee, who had a barely legal, ethically questionable racket on the side. Wamsee had invested in all of the businesses on Main, including the tattoo shops. And as an investor, he insisted, for insurance purposes, that each place have security cameras with sound. Once a week, he collected all the footage and screened it.

According to the author, Wamsee used this intel to apply pressure on everything from donating to the Benevolent Police Fund to writing an insane amount of tickets with dubious claims that people paid so as not to have sensitive info leaked. Of course, this was all speculation with no actual proof behind it, but it did give me ideas.

"I think you need to read this when I'm done." I nudged my husband, who was reading in bed next to me. "You might have to share it with Carnack."

Rex looked up from his book. "That good?"

"I'm not sure." I turned the page. "The author might have made it all up. But there has to be some real truth in there somewhere."

I continued on. Next, there was Stella, who was hooking up with half the men in town in the very shed I allegedly murdered Tyson in. While not explicitly stated, the author implied that she might be taking money for her favors, which would basically mean she was the town prostitute. Huh. I'd always assumed there was way more than that in Bladdersly.

Mordecai Brown seemed a lot like the character Menachem Black, who did not hold pawned items like he was supposed to but sold them online for a high price, only paying the owner a pittance when challenged. He also trafficked in stolen merchandise.

Had Tyson stolen the laptops from Best Bye for Mordecai? That would make sense. And then Mordecai could fence them online, and no one would necessarily be the wiser. I sent a text to Riley, accompanied by a screenshot of that page.

Pastor Malone even made an appearance as Father Murphy, a gullible priest who was taken advantage of by half the town. The book claimed that he was manipulated by his congregation to get what they wanted. In retirement, however, it said Menachem was paying him next to nothing, and Murphy just couldn't get the courage up to ask for a decent wage.

Was Vanderzee one of those manipulating him, either by blackmail or something else, to lie about seeing me that night? Another idea popped into my head. Was Mordecai the one who convinced him to do it? Either Vanderzee or Mordecai could have killed Tyson—especially if they thought he'd been the author. Sure, half the town had probably read it, but Tyson was ambitious. He could try to bust out with it and hit a larger market. Then everyone would know the truth about Bladdersly.

If the book was the motive, since Kurt knew everyone in town, it was possible that the police chief or pawn shop owner thought Kurt had written the book. A nugget of an idea formed in my brain. I filed it away in hopes it would germinate.

Vanderzee and Mordecai had a lot to lose if the book took off. The names were so thinly veiled that even those morons in Bladdersly could figure it out.

I kept reading. And then there was Kurt Hobbs. Nero Fobbs, as I suspect he was named, wasn't just some kid with pie-in-the-sky hopes of finding the perfect job and landing Kayla as a girlfriend. It turned out he had a past.

And that past included Tyson Pancratz—or Byron Dantz. That was interesting. According to the book, Nero and Byron knew each other. They'd met in juvie.

I slammed the book closed. Rex arched an eyebrow at me, but when he realized the wheels were turning, he went back to what he was doing.

All this time, I'd bought it. I'd believed that Kurt had no idea who Tyson was. And knowing that he'd been in a juvenile detention center, I'd thought nothing of Kurt's denial. But here, in this book, the two were in corrections at the same time. I opened the book and continued on.

Nero and Byron were believed to have worked together on a scam that targeted the two tattoo shops in town. Now that was interesting. Everything in the book was confidently put forward as a without a doubt fact. But this was not. Did that mean it was just a rumor?

According to *Boats*, Nero and Byron convinced Antelope (which I assumed was Bear) and Bob from the other tattoo shop (was that Neil?) that for $10,000, Lance Armstrong would visit their shop and sign autographs. The trick was, besides the fact that Lance Armstrong wasn't coming because he had no idea, that each man thought they would be the only one to have the disgraced cyclist. But maybe the worst trick would be that Nero and Byron would make $20K and run off into the night.

But the scam fell through when Antelope privately reached out to Lance Armstrong to offer him a lifetime of free tattoos, only to find out that Lance had no idea what Antelope was talking about. The tattoo artist told Bob, and they confronted Byron to cancel the deal. And in something I wished I'd seen, both punched Byron in the face at the same time.

Had Tyson written *Boats*? Had he thrown this story in to throw folks off the scent? And was that why he was murdered?

The next chapter was just about Stella—and not her many liaisons. In fact, it was very interesting. My mind turned back to that amazing meatloaf. I needed to have lunch at Ella's tomorrow, I thought, as I turned out the light and went to sleep.

I was in Ella's Diner the minute it opened at 11 the next morning. I ordered the meatloaf again and moaned with delight the entire time I ate. My goal was to confront the owner after eating so as not to spoil the culinary experience. In my opinion, Ella needed to write a cookbook.

"How was it?" The large woman came over and topped off my water.

"Excellent!" I gushed. "And surprising. Almost as surprising as something I just learned about you."

Ella sat down across from me. "And what might that be?"

I placed my napkin on my lap. "You own both Ella's and Ela's."

She didn't protest or throw a fit. Ella merely looked tired as she asked, "How did you find that out?"

I pointed at the plate. "Same meatloaf recipe."

Ella's right eyebrow went up. "That's it?"

"No, that's not it." I took a sip of water before continuing. "I have another source of speculation, but the meatloaf was the kicker."

"Huh. No one in this town has noticed that in five years. And some of them act like they only patronize one diner or the other, but really, they hit both places."

I had to ask. "Why did you open another restaurant with the same name and menu across the street from your current place?"

She shrugged. "Competition."

Either Ella didn't really understand how competition worked or she had an odd business sense.

I leaned forward. "You went into competition…with yourself?"

Ella smiled wearily. "Of course! Starbucks does it all the time. There are places in the world where there's a Starbucks across the street from another one."

"Oh. Right," I said.

She tapped her forehead. "And that's what gave me the idea. See, business was kind of slowing down. People were getting bored with the same old thing, and since there was only one restaurant in town, they started going to Oleo's in Who's There. Why they'd want to eat in that train wreck of a town, I'll never know."

I was about to protest that it was actually Bladdersly that was a stinking cesspool but realized that might stop her from continuing her confession.

"So I thought, what if I just invented a brand-new restaurant and made it look like major competition for my place, and it worked."

I still couldn't wrap my head around it. "It did?"

Ella nodded. "Sure! People who wanted something new went across the street. They stayed in town. And to my surprise, some folks were mad and decided to demonstrate loyalty by coming here more often."

That prompted another question. "So if you own both places, who is Ela?"

"A cousin's kid." Ella waved me off. "Grew up in Muscatine. No one would know her here."

I tried to wrap my head around her logic, but this wasn't why I was here.

"I have to admit that I got some of the idea from that book, *Boats of the Midwest*," I said.

Ella's face darkened with fury. "What a load of crap! And it isn't true either, about me being a hooker! The nerve of that guy!"

So she wasn't upset that it gave me the idea for splitting her business, but she was convinced that Stella, the town prostitute, was supposed to be her.

I pressed. "Do you have any idea who wrote it?"

With complete certainty, she said, "Mordecai Brown. But I can't prove it."

"Mordecai?" So she didn't think it was Kurt or Tyson. "Why do you think he wrote it?"

She slammed her hand onto the table. "Because Pastor Malone was in here one day laughing about how people had been pawning their copies, while Mordecai has boxes of the stuff in the shed! I told Vanderzee that, but he said that's not proof of anything!"

This wasn't going down how I'd expected. I thought Ella would think Tyson wrote it. But Mordecai? Okay, it made sense. Even though I hadn't seen boxes of the book, I'd only seen a dozen on a bookshelf.

Had Mordecai written the tell-all? He had seemed smug about the things he knew about the townsfolk. But as a pawnbroker, he'd know all kinds of things—who pawned their wedding ring, their grandmother's silver, etc. And he allowed hookups in the shed.

Why hadn't this occurred to me before?

Ella was still ranting. "...and if I did have proof, he wouldn't be alive anymore, I can tell you that!"

I let this settle in the air a bit. "What did you think about Tyson Pancratz?"

Her stormy look turned darker. "That no-good bastard! He's stolen from every single store in town. He knows things—" Ella's face was filled with confusion for a moment. "I guess he could've written the book."

She came to that conclusion easily but seemed surprised by it. Which meant maybe she hadn't killed him.

"Huh," she went on to say. "I guess I should stop putting laxatives in Mordecai's triple-chocolate cheesecake."

I was rethinking ordering dessert. "You've been doing that?"

She nodded. "For a year now. I heard he's been seeing a doctor in Des Moines about digestive issues." Ella smiled. "But I guess, until we know more, there's no point in poisoning him."

"Considering that it's probably assault and battery, that's a good idea," I said.

Ella studied me. "Do you think I should come clean? About the diners?"

I waved her off. "Nah. What they don't know won't hurt them, and you've got a booming business because of it. I won't say anything."

The woman got to her feet and picked up my empty plate. "Do you want dessert?"

For the very first time in my life, I said no. It seemed like the safest option.

After lunch, I parked in the lot across the street from the Pump & Pawn. Mordecai may have been the author of the book. Ella certainly thought so, and she'd know more than I did.

Mordecai had been on my suspect list for Tyson's murder. But did the two things tie together?

I guess they could. Perhaps Tyson had been blackmailing Mordecai because he found out he had written the book. How would he have found that out, I wondered. Notes. There had to be notes. And maybe among the notes Mordecai had used to write the book, there were pieces of evidence that backed things up.

That would be a threat. I could see Vanderzee locking Mordecai up and throwing away the key if he thought the pawn shop owner had the goods on his crooked scams. I wouldn't put it past the corrupt police chief.

After all, he had iffy evidence against me. I never made a phone call threatening Tyson because I hadn't known who Tyson was until I woke up in the same room with his corpse. I wouldn't put it past him to set Mordecai up.

I still was unsure of my idea that Vanderzee kidnapped the pastor in order to keep him from admitting he lied about seeing me that night.

Time was running out. Malone was in danger, and Jane said the Bladdersly PD was rushing my case through the system at breakneck speed. If I was going to solve this, it had to be soon. Now I just had to psychically convince Mordecai to leave work and lead me to the truth.

Easy, right?

CHAPTER TWENTY-FOUR

————

I pulled a mint tin out of my glove box. Inside was a tracking device I'd been playing with that looked like a wad of chewed-up gum. It was an old piece of technology from my CIA days. Back then, we didn't disguise them because they resembled a bit of wire that, when attached, looked like it belonged on the underside of the car.

Since I had some time on my hands, I'd played around with some of my own spy toys. After finding a wad of chewing gum under my breakfast bar, it gave me an idea.

By the way, I never did find out who did that. The girls strenuously objected when I accused them. Betty even volunteered to do a DNA swab. But in the end, Kelly suggested that, with my lack of diligence in cleaning, it could've been left there by the previous owner, and I dropped it.

I wasn't sure what Mordecai's car looked like, but there was only one vehicle in his parking lot—a very expensive, shiny, tricked-out black pickup. For a moment, I thought that maybe a wad of chewing gum would be noticed by someone who was so fastidious about his vehicle. Then again, it was only for one day. Maybe he wouldn't notice.

The trick was to cross the street and place it without being noticed. In broad daylight. I exited the van and backtracked down the alley behind the bars, diner, and tattoo shop. Turning left, I crossed the street and walked a block down.

I figured I could follow the alley to the lot and the truck. But I remembered that Elrond had a security camera. Did I waste time, and possibly miss Mordecai leaving, by disabling the camera?

Screw it. It was go time. I walked confidently down the alley as if I belonged there. The truck was actually closer to The Opera House, facing the Pump & Pawn, so I had a little cover as I crouched down and crept to the back of the truck.

The gum-like substance was sticky enough, so it wasn't hard to reach under the flatbed and place the tracker. I slipped back to The Opera House and turned the corner, only to run smack into Harold.

"What are you doing?" Harold asked.

"Nothing," I said as I went past him.

"Merry, you're up to something," Harold warned.

I backtracked. "Yes, Harold. I'm up to something."

We stared at each other for a long minute.

Harold broke into a grin and clapped his hands together. "Is it a surprise for me?"

I wasn't sure whether it was better to smack him in the face or agree. I opted for the safest bet.

"Why yes, Harold. It's a surprise for you. You've really helped Stewie become a better…um…gladiator. And I thought I'd thank you for that."

"I knew it!" Harold squealed. "What is it? Is it money? An award? A case of petrified duck heads?"

That gave me pause, but I recovered quickly. "I can't say right now. Just wait. You'll see." And without another word, I fled.

A case of petrified duck heads? I climbed into my van and closed the door. At least I hadn't told Harold when he could expect…whatever I was going to give him. The important thing was that I got away quickly so I could be ready whenever Mordecai left the shop.

I was afraid it was going to be a long wait…which it ended up being. That's the problem with surveillance. You never knew what the person you were following was going to do. And never, ever, in my history with the CIA, did a stakeout last less than three hours.

I passed the time checking the news on my phone, listening to a couple of true crime podcasts, and staring at the building in hopes of sprouting Jedi powers to tell the man to leave. It didn't work.

It was just after dark when Mordecai locked up. I ducked down behind the steering wheel, waiting to follow him.

I wasn't really sure what this was going to prove. Maybe nothing. It just felt like I needed to do something. Confronting the man would be my next plan. I just didn't want to jump straight to that.

There's a lot to be said for taking things one step at a time. I once built a rock-solid case against a Latvian wrestler named Pavlis the Marauder, who was passing state secrets to his contact at wrestling meets. He would do it by signals and codes. So if he broke a chair over his opponent's head, it meant he had technology intel. A chokeslam meant military secrets. And a Boston Crab, I later found out, meant absolutely nothing.

I had to attend twenty-three matches just to pin down who he was signaling and about what. And then it took ten more matches for me to get the goods on him. That was a very long November in Latvia.

Acting like you aren't following someone when you are the only two cars on the road in a small town is tricky on the best day. So I pulled over as he was leaving the city limits and turned on my tablet to track him.

I was holding my breath and crossing my fingers in hopes this little device would work. Once he was about a mile ahead of me, I started the car and headed his way.

I know every gravel road around Who's There. And the roads surrounding Bladdersly weren't too much different. Walls of corn hid you and those you were seeking. When I noticed he'd stopped, I turned off my headlights and proceeded with care.

He was at a house in the middle of nowhere. I drove past quietly and backed into a cornfield. Then I hiked back, keeping just inside the perimeter of the cornfield. It was a good thing I was wearing dark green today. That was a stroke of luck that I didn't always have. It's the reason I never wear neon colors if I can help it. You really stand out in a wheatfield in Russia when you are wearing an electric yellow hazmat suit, believe me.

The house was simple, a one-story frame house. It wasn't fancy like the big black truck. Maybe Mordecai wasn't flashy about his house. It made sense in a way. Iowans aren't big on having a house that's more than they need.

The curtains were closed, but I knew he was there. Were the curtains drawn because he was hiding something? Was it stolen merchandise? Was he playing host to Pastor Malone? I remained frozen in place and strained to listen.

It was quiet. Too quiet. In my experience, that implied that there was a trap. In fact, I had no idea if this was Mordecai's primary address or not. If it was, was there any point in spying on him? If it wasn't, what had I stumbled on?

Headlights flickered through the corn, and I melted farther back into it, out of sight. It was a police cruiser, and it pulled into the driveway. The sedan parked, and Vanderzee got out. He looked around very carefully. And for just a fleeting moment, I thought we had locked eyes.

I held my breath and didn't move, hoping I'd imagined it. The police chief finding me here was the last thing I needed. After a few moments, Vanderzee locked the cruiser with a beep and went inside.

Now that was interesting. What were these two doing here together? It was possible that they were just hanging out in the middle of nowhere. However, since both of these guys were suspects in my book, it wouldn't hurt to take another look.

But first, I needed to test something. Vanderzee hadn't tripped any motion-sensitive security measures, but maybe he'd turned them on once he was inside. There were two fixtures on the outside of the house that looked like possible security.

I picked up a rock and tossed it into range.

Bright light flooded the yard, and Vanderzee and Mordecai dashed out onto the front porch.

"Who is it?" Mordecai shouted.

A squirrel chattered at the men before running up a tree.

"It's a damn squirrel!" Vanderzee said. "You're too paranoid. Running out here like an idiot looks suspicious."

"To who? The squirrel?" Mordecai groused.

Then the two men went inside.

My cell buzzed, and I retreated farther into the field. Rex wanted to know where I was and when I'd be back. Kurt had called for the millionth time to ask if I was on the run, and if so, could I please tell him where I was so that he could hunt me down and bring me in?

I wasn't going to learn any more here today. I texted back that I'd be home soon and headed to the van. I just needed to make one stop first.

"I need to know who owns this property." I handed Riley an address.

"Why?" He took the address from me.

Was he joking? "Why? Because I've paid you a retainer to work for me."

He waved me off. "Sorry, I meant why as in, what's the story here?"

I filled him in on my visit to Ella's and following Mordecai home. I mentioned the security measures he had in place on the house.

"That tracker worked?" Riley pulled out his cell and scowled. "I've never had any luck with that. It craps out on me at the worst times."

I put my feet up on his desk. "You need the upgrade." I looked around. "Why are you here so late?"

Riley relaxed back into his chair. "I'm working."

"Where's Claire?" I asked.

"Look for yourself." He pointed at her desk.

I walked over and noticed that the usually minimalist desk had a skull on it. The business card clenched between its teeth was from the Chapel of Despair.

"She's gone druid?" I ran my fingers over the skull. "I thought she was smarter than that."

Riley shrugged. "She went over yesterday and came back with that. She's back there again today."

I needed to ask Stewie what was going on. Claire was a catch that group didn't really deserve.

Riley began typing away. I took a granola bar from his desk and began munching. Ugh. How did he eat this cardboard stuff? I was starting to regret not taking the risk of having the cheesecake at Ella's.

"I don't know why you eat this boring, flavorless food."

"Because it's healthy," Riley answered without taking his eyes off the screen.

"I know it's healthy." I smoothed out the wrapper. I could actually pronounce the ingredients, which was depressing. "I just asked why it tastes so bad. You'd think they'd throw in some sugar or something…"

"That would defeat the whole purpose of it being healthy," Riley said. "Sugar is way more addictive than nicotine or alcohol. Did you know that?"

I tossed the wrapper into the garbage can. "Because sugar is awesome!" Sugar was my favorite food group.

"Okay, it looks like it is owned by Mordecai Brown." He squinted at the monitor. "I can't tell if it's his primary address or not though."

"That's all I needed to know. Maybe it was a dead end."

"It's something. As you well know, all these little bits of information can come together in the end to form a big picture."

I glared at him. "Yes. I know that. You and I were both trained by the same agency."

Riley ignored my jibe. "I did find out that the laptops are stolen. Kind of."

"Kind of? How do you kind of steal a laptop?" I asked.

He pulled out the box from under his desk and pointed at the label. "That serial number is listed as being currently in the inventory at Best Bye. They don't know it's missing, so they haven't reported it stolen."

"But it is. I mean, it's not in their inventory, unless by their inventory you mean a dead employee's basement."

Riley steepled his fingers. "It could mean that Neil is in on it. Maybe he killed Tyson so that he wouldn't have to share the profits?"

Argh! "We have a lot of suspects and motives, but we still don't know for sure what happened."

Riley cocked his head to one side. "Well, officially, you murdered Tyson for unknown reasons. And then you kidnapped Malone so that he couldn't testify." He smiled. "But that's just conjecture from the Bladdersly PD."

I got up and started to pace. "So here's what we have. Tyson could have been murdered by Mordecai because Mordecai wrote *Boats of the Midwest*, Tyson knew that and blackmailed him. It's also possible that Vanderzee helped Mordecai kill

Tyson. Vanderzee and someone were spotted in the alley at the time of the murder."

"Or." Riley held a finger up. "Neil killed Tyson over the laptop heist."

"Or"—I paused—"Tyson wrote *Boats* and was killed for that by anyone in the town who recognized themselves in it."

"Maybe this wasn't connected to the book?" Riley wondered.

"It's possible." I shrugged. "I do think that the pastor's kidnapping was connected to Tyson's murder, which makes Vanderzee the most likely suspect. He either coerced Malone to make a false statement…"

"Or," Riley interjected, "Vanderzee invented the false statement and Malone found out."

"But Mordecai could still be in on the whole thing." I sat back down. "But if Neil killed Tyson, why would Mordecai and Vanderzee pin this on me—someone they don't even know?"

Riley shook his head. "Not a clue. There are too many variables involved." He stood up and stretched. "I think I'll need to sleep on it."

"Riley, we don't have much time. Vanderzee could bring me in at any moment."

"Then I suggest." Riley put his hands on my shoulders. "That you keep thinking." He shut off the computer and ushered me toward the door. "I've got a hot date tonight."

"I thought you said you needed to sleep on it," I complained as he pushed me out the door.

"Yes." He grinned as he locked up. "But I didn't say I'd be doing that alone."

CHAPTER TWENTY-FIVE

————

Rex had homemade macaroni and cheese waiting for me when I got home. He heated up a plate for me, and even though he'd already eaten, he sat at the table. We chatted a little about the case, but I think Rex noticed that my mind was elsewhere. He didn't press the matter the whole time we cleaned up or even when we went to bed. My husband understood how I thought. Which was either awesome or scary.

Lying in bed, I just couldn't sleep. The pressure of solving this case and hoping Pastor Malone was still alive bore down on me like a rabid hippopotamus with anger issues. I tossed and turned but couldn't put two and two together.

When thinking doesn't work, I've always considered action a solid substitute. I needed to do something. Lying here wasn't helping me in any way. Without turning on the lights or making a sound, I got dressed and slipped out of the house to my property across the street.

I'd recently acquired a fanny pack that had a secret compartment for my gun. It had a hidden rip cord that would expose the gun for a quick draw. And I'd need it tonight. Because tonight, I was going to check out Mordecai's house. There was something very wrong with that place. I just didn't know what it was. And because I am me, I was going to go alone…like an idiot.

The house was pitch dark outside and in. The truck wasn't in the driveway, but it could be in the garage. I crept along the edge of the cornfield, hugging the covering foliage, going slowly so that I wouldn't make any noise. A light went on in the basement, drawing me up short. I waited and listened.

There was a partially opened window that was covered by what I guessed to be an opaque film.

The sounds of a man softly sobbing floated to me on the breeze. Was it Pastor Malone? If so, it meant he was still alive, which was a relief. But was he alone?

It is never a good idea to underestimate your opponent. Just when you think you've got them on the ropes, they can charge you with a curling iron. And then where would you be? With burn marks on your arms and an unnatural fear of hair-styling implements.

And yes, I'd had some experience with that. Never trust a hairdresser in Turkmenistan. Especially when they are the dictator's mistress. Well, one of them anyway. Yuliana had pouted and made me believe she was resigned to getting busted. And I'd almost bought it too. Right up until I saw her hand move toward her styling station.

I still had one scar from it. Which is why, to this day, I just wash and drip-dry my naturally curly short hair.

There were no other voices that I could hear. Just the man crying. I needed to get up to that window and see what I was up against. It was a run in the open to get from the cornfield to the house, and there was the risk that the motion sensitive security measures were on. But I needed to chance it. It would be pretty stupid if they weren't, considering that Mordecai seemed to have a kidnap victim in there. But I wasn't going to criticize his idiocy since it would work in my favor.

Pastor Malone was the one person who could drop the case against me. As the main witness, who obviously had no clue who I was, he could explain that I wasn't the one who he'd seen that night. I was pretty sure I was dumped in the shed after the fact. After the killer murdered Tyson.

There was no other way in, other than landing on the roof and deactivating the security from above, but I was fresh out of helicopters. So I ran for it. Hopefully, I could dart to the house unseen. No lights came on outside, which was a huge relief. Within seconds, I was plastered against the siding. After catching my breath, I got down on all fours and crawled over to the window.

Very slowly, I eased forward to see what I could and assess the situation. I could just see through the slightly open window.

"No!" Malone wailed at something out of my line of vision. "Please! I won't tell anyone!"

He was seated in a chair across the room, facing me. His hands were behind his back, and his eyes were red from sobbing. And he was very clearly staring at someone. The elderly man looked exhausted and terrified.

I drew back. He wasn't alone. Was it Mordecai? Vanderzee? Both? It was possible that I could not only rescue Malone, but I could also nab the real killer. My heart pounded with excitement. I could save the pastor and myself in one shot.

My fingers brushed my fanny pack. The rip cord was ready to go, and my pistol was fully loaded. I was armed and ready. And I had the element of surprise on my side. The killer wouldn't see me coming. Yay!

"Please!" Pastor Malone's voice had an edge of desperation to it. "I won't say anything! You have to believe me!"

Whoever he was with mumbled back an unintelligible reply. I had no idea who it was. It didn't matter because soon I'd find out. I don't like people who kidnap and torment innocents. And whoever this was would feel the great rage that was welling up inside of me.

Malone shrieked, and I took the risk of looking again. He was sweating, eyes wide as he stared at whoever threatened him.

It was go time. If I waited any longer, the killer could silence the old man forever, leaving me without a witness and the town of Bladdersly without a beloved, retired pastor—which, of course, was the most important thing. I pulled out my cell, but just my luck, it was dead. There was a charger in the van, but I couldn't drive the van into the house. I'd just have to juice it when I got back into the van. At least I had a gun. I gave myself points for that.

I slipped around the house to the front door and gingerly climbed the two concrete steps. The door was slightly ajar, as if the killer wanted to make an easy getaway. It was totally possible that he was here to kill Malone. Tonight. I needed to act fast.

I tiptoed into the house, leaving the door ajar. It was very dark. The only light was a glimmer beneath a door at the other end of the room. That had to be the door to the basement, which meant that I would be walking over the ceiling to get there. If I wasn't careful, the bad guy would hear me. And I didn't want that.

Crossing over a floor above someone you want to take by surprise isn't easy. In fact, during our training at the Farm, the CIA had told us that if you had to, shoot through the floor on your way over it. This was never a good idea if you didn't know who was in the room below. And it wouldn't work tonight because an innocent was down there.

I had a good idea of where Malone was tied up, but I wasn't sure. There was another option. I could go back outside and run around to the back of the house to see if there was another way in. But that would take time.

I needed a distraction. Something that would startle but not alarm my target. But what would that be, here in rural Iowa? I didn't have a lot of hope that a cow would bust in and walk around.

Mrrrrowwww.

A cat began purring and winding around my legs. I looked down and, in the dim light, spotted the same eyes that had been under Tyson's bed. Effie! The cat was Mordecai's?

Effie and I stared at each other just as we had under Tyson's bed at the duplex. She was interested in me. And that gave me an idea.

"Squeeeeeeeak!"

My impression of a terrified mouse was pretty good. Then I scooped up Effie and tossed her halfway across the room. She landed on her feet, thankfully, gave me a dirty look, and galloped away.

And as she did so, I ran after her as silently as possible. The basement door was now next to me. And if it all had gone as I'd hoped, Mordecai downstairs believed his cat was after a mouse.

Grasping the doorknob, I turned it. Locked. And even worse, it squeaked. Loudly. Damn.

The pastor screamed below, and I heard what sounded like furniture being tossed aside.

Oh well. No time like the present. If I died here, at least I did so clearing my name, provided I managed to help the pastor escape.

Yanking on the rip cord to my fanny pack, my fingers closed on the gun grip as I reared back and kicked the door in. Did you know that doors have a weak spot? Would you believe that it's where the lock is? Don't ask me why. I'm no physics major.

The door crashed against the wall, and I flew down the stairs, gun drawn. No one was there but Pastor Malone, who appeared to be unconscious. At the other end of the room was a small flight of stairs. And at the top was a cellar door, flung open to the night.

I could go after the killer, and maybe I'd even catch up with him. But the way the pastor sagged had me worried.

"Pastor Malone!" I shook his shoulders gently.

He groaned. That was a good sign. I spotted a knife on the floor near me and grabbed it. Without looking, I cut through the rope around his hands, with my eyes and most of my attention on the open cellar doors. Just because Mordecai had run off didn't mean he wouldn't come back to surprise me.

In fact, if he was smart, he'd come back and shoot us both. Then the elderly man in the chair couldn't rat him out.

The man's hands reached up for his head, and he groaned. After a moment, he looked at me, confused.

"Who are you?" His eyes were unfocused, as if he'd been drugged.

"I'm Merry Wrath Ferguson," I explained as I ran across the room and slammed the cellar doors shut. It probably wouldn't stop Mordecai, but it would give me a few seconds' advantage.

He squinted at me. "Who?"

I knelt down so that he could see my face clearly. "Merry Wrath. The woman you allegedly saw take Tyson into the shed." I helped him to his feet. His knees creaked.

"No, you're not." Malone's eyes were focusing on my face.

I spoke gently so as not to alarm him. "Yes, I am. And I'm here to help you."

Taking my gun back out of the fanny pack, I asked, "Can you walk? My van isn't far."

But Pastor Malone was staring at the pistol as his skin went pale.

"It's okay," I insisted. "I'm here to help you! Can you walk?"

After another glance at my face, he nodded. "I'll try."

I had no idea how long the man had been stuck in that chair, but his legs were a little wobbly. Malone hung on to my arm as we made our way across to the stairs. Gradually, he got his legs back.

This was the man with the eyesight of an eagle and the brain of a twenty-year-old? It made me wonder. Either Malone was in shock, weakened from drugs or torture, or he really was feeble. Had Mordecai told the pastor it was me he'd seen that night? And had he lied to me about his ableness?

I wanted to confirm that his captor was his employer, but he was concentrating so hard on putting one foot in front of the other that an interrogation seemed a bit unimportant.

Besides, we had to get up the stairs and out of the house. And then we had to worry about being ambushed by the killer out in the darkness. No. I'd better keep my head in the game. For both of us.

After a brief struggle, we managed to get the man up the stairs. As he caught his breath, I had him wait near the door as I ran through the house, or at least the ground floor, to make sure it was empty. There was no time to really reflect on my surroundings. There was just one room on either side of the hall and a kitchen in the back.

After clearing the house, I went back and helped Malone to the front door. A table stood next to the doorway with a stuffed animal on it. I flung open the door and threw the toy into the yard and waited.

Nothing happened. No flood lights came on, and there wasn't any gunfire. Hopefully, that meant the killer had fled. And that was fine because I was driving Pastor Malone to the hospital in Who's There, where he could tell Sheriff Carnack everything.

It seemed to take forever to cross the yard and head into the corn and back to my car. I kept my gun ready, which got a little easier as the pastor's mobility improved. Neither one of us spoke. Me, because I didn't want to tip off an ambush. Him, because he was concentrating on moving.

Once I got him into the passenger seat and buckled him up, I looked in the back seat to make sure I didn't have any unwanted killers in the car, and then I got in and started driving. Pastor Malone passed out, slumped forward, restrained by his seat belt. I felt for a pulse in his neck. He was alive, but weak.

On the way to town, I charged my cell, called Sheriff Carnack, and told him what had happened. He said he'd be there right away.

He beat me to the hospital.

"I understand you've been hiding out?" Carnack looked at me dubiously as he watched the nurses and doctor take Malone away on a gurney. My fingertips brushed my fanny pack to make sure the gun was hidden once again.

I slumped against a wall. "I haven't jumped bail, if that's what you mean."

"You have left town though." Sheriff Carnack looked me over.

The adrenaline was gone, and I was spent. "Technically, I haven't. I mean, I live in Who's There, but the crime was committed in Bladdersly, so both towns count, and the place where I found the pastor was between the two."

Ed Carnack sighed heavily. "Well, hopefully Pastor Malone can clear you of his kidnapping."

I held up one finger. "And of Tyson's murder." I told him about casually running into him on my way to pawn some things and how Malone hadn't recognized me. "And he didn't have any idea who I was when I rescued him either. Which means his witness statement falls apart."

The sheriff took off his hat and rubbed his head. "If that's true, then I guess it does. But the statement was made to Vanderzee in the Bladdersly PD."

"Which means," I sniffed. "That Vanderzee is lying."

He looked at me for a moment. "Between that statement and you saying Brown kidnapped Malone, those are some serious charges, Merry."

I shrugged. "I suppose that Malone could've said he'd seen me."

"And you were there," the sheriff said. "At the scene of the crime with the body."

"But what if Malone didn't make a statement? What if Vanderzee made up the whole thing?"

Sheriff Carnack looked away, staring into space for a long moment before replying. "I guess we have to wait to see what Pastor Malone says."

"In the meantime…" I noticed a vending machine down the hall. I was hungry. I was always hungry. "You need to go check out Mordecai's house. That's where I found Malone."

Carnack nodded. "I plan to do just that. And you'll need to give a statement."

I fiddled in my fanny pack for money, trying to make sure I didn't inadvertently give the lawman sitting next to me a glimpse of my gun.

"Are you saying you don't believe me? When have you ever known me to lie about something so serious?"

Carnack held up his hands. "I do believe you, and I'll head out there soon. But we have to do things the right way. You need to put your statement on record."

Nope. No money. I did have my driver's license, but no cash.

"Fine. I'll come in in the morning. By the way, you don't happen to have any money on you I could borrow, do you? I want to hit the vending machines."

The sheriff shook his head and reached for his wallet. He pulled out four one-dollar bills.

"I'll pay you back," I swore as I got to my feet.

The large man smiled. "Consider it a gift. You did good work tonight. Well, you did it the wrong way. You should've called us to take care of it."

My eyes grew round. "I'm pretty sure he was about to be murdered. I didn't have time and, in fact, my cell was dead."

"Okay," Sheriff Carnack said. "Thank you for saving Pastor Malone."

A nurse appeared. "Sheriff, he's asleep. The poor man is suffering from shock and exhaustion. I'm afraid you'll have to wait awhile."

I didn't like the sound of that.

"Alright," he said. "Sounds like it might be a few hours. You know how to get hold of me. I'll have someone stand guard. Call me the moment he wakes up."

"I'm staying," I said. I wasn't letting Pastor Buddy Malone out of my sight until he cleared me.

The sheriff shrugged. "At least, for once, we will know exactly where you are." And with that, he walked away.

After retrieving four Ding Dongs from the vending machine, I was just settling in on a bench outside the man's room, when Vanderzee blustered into the hallway.

"What"—he pointed a stubby finger in my direction—"is she doing here?"

I looked around. I was the only one there.

"You must be talking to me," I said calmly, setting down my snacks. I picked up a magazine and began leafing through a four-year-old copy of *Better Homes & Gardens* magazine. "And I'm here because I rescued Pastor Malone from the *real* killer."

His face turned bright red. "You rescued him from your own kidnapping! And now here you are, ready to pounce when he comes to so that he can't testify!"

"I'm afraid I don't care for your tone," I said casually. "And you're wrong. I *rescued* him. And guess what? He had no idea who I was."

The man turned an alarming shade of purple.

"I want you out of here! I want you locked up! I—" he screamed.

The nurse who'd spoken to us earlier reappeared. And she did not seem happy. "You need to stop shouting, or I'll have security escort you off the premises!"

"You can't do that!" Vanderzee sputtered. "I'm the law!"

"Not here you aren't." Rex appeared, and my heart skipped a beat. "This isn't your jurisdiction. It's mine. And I'd appreciate it if you didn't throw around baseless accusations. My wife has a pretty good lawyer..."

"The best lawyer," I interrupted.

"*I'm not leaving until I throw your wife in prison!*" Vanderzee howled.

"That's it!" The nurse picked up a phone and made a call. "Security is on its way. I don't care if you are the President or the Pope. I'm the law in this hallway."

Vanderzee stormed off, and my husband took a seat next to me.

Rex looked at my Ding Dong pile. "Had quite a night, didn't you?"

How did Rex know I was here? A little light bulb went off in my mind. "Carnack called you, didn't he?"

He nodded. "Carnack called. I'm taking this shift. I thought you'd like to have someone to bounce your thoughts off of."

It felt like a huge weight had been lifted. "Thanks. I was going to call you, but all of this happened so fast."

Rex put his hand over mine. "You called the sheriff, which was the right thing to do. It's his jurisdiction. But I wish you'd told me where you were going. I could've come along."

My eyebrows went up. "You would've come along to surveil someone's house outside of your own jurisdiction?"

My husband sighed. "I'm not the bad guy, Merry. I want to help you. You're my wife first and foremost."

"But you could've gotten in trouble." I shook my head. "Besides, I had no idea I was going to find Pastor Malone there."

Then I filled him in on what I knew. Rex listened carefully, with his eyebrows rising when I mentioned the dangerous bits.

"He didn't recognize you a second time?" Rex rubbed his chin. "That's good. And once he wakes up, we can get an official statement from him."

"Mordecai kidnapped him, and Vanderzee might be in on it," I said, repeating what I'd told Carnack.

Rex put his arm around me. He didn't usually go in for public displays of affection when he was on the job. And since he said he was taking first shift for the sheriff, I was pretty sure he was on the job.

"I don't like the man, Merry, but that doesn't make him a killer."

"Well," I grumbled, "he's *something*."

Rex hugged me before pulling back. "Merry?"

"Yes?" I was finally tearing into my snacks.

"Why are you wearing a fanny pack?"

I'd totally forgotten to leave my gun in the car. "Oh. It had, um, these snacks in it. You know how I get hungry." I jumped to my feet. "I'll take it to the car."

"Okay," he said amiably. "Make sure the safety is on on your *snack*."

CHAPTER TWENTY-SIX

———

Pastor Malone was in bad shape. Looking through the window into his room, I could see that the nurse had hooked him up to an IV and was monitoring his vitals. As badly as I felt for the guy, I really wanted to talk to him. If he named his kidnapper and explained why he didn't recognize me even though he'd said he'd seen me, all of this could be over.

"You're pacing again," Rex said.

I stopped and looked at him. "Not my fault that all of my snacks are loaded with sugar."

Rex asked, "Why is it you don't remember anything from the night of the murder?"

I sat down next to him. "I don't know. Isn't that weird? I mean, I should at least remember what I was doing before whatever happened to me. And I still have no idea why I was wearing that shirt."

I'd been so wrapped up in trying to find the real killer, and saving pastors from kidnappers, that I hadn't stopped to think about how I'd gotten into the shed in the first place.

"Do *you* remember what happened that night?"

Rex thought for a moment. "Only that you'd left your favorite water bottle at the old house after a troop meeting. Just before I fell asleep, you said you were going to go get it. I passed out and only woke up when Carnack called me."

Huh. My insulated, stainless steel Girl Scout cup had been a gift from the troop. "Have you seen it at home? I haven't."

Rex ran his hands through his hair. "No. And since I've been doing dishes with you out galivanting around, I should have."

I got up. "Stay here. Let me know what happens. I'm going to go look for it. And something else."

"That's probably a good idea. What's the other thing?"

I winked at him. "Whatever shirt I was wearing. I'm sure I didn't go to bed in a Best Bye shirt."

"No." Rex shook his head. "You were wearing your Dora the Explorer pajamas. You changed from the bottoms into jeans so that if someone spotted you, they'd think you were dressed. I haven't seen the top either."

I might have broken a few speed limits on my way home, and I didn't bother with our house, focusing on my old house across the street. After unlocking the door, I stepped inside. Nothing looked any different.

Had the killer rendered me unconscious in my own house? That took some nerve. I searched the place in a few minutes but didn't spot the shirt or tumbler. Maybe I hadn't made it inside? Maybe the killer caught me before I entered. I'd have grabbed it if I had been inside my old house, and it would be lying in the yard. Then again, maybe I *had* retrieved the cup before he grabbed me. That would mean the killer had my cup!

I wandered back outside and sat down on the front stoop. The killer must've taken both things and tossed them. Closing my eyes, I tried hard to remember what had happened, but my memory refused to cooperate. For some reason, the idea that the killer had taken my cup seemed more and more plausible.

How had he gotten me from here to the shed? And why bother taking my shirt? Why change what I was wearing? What was the significance of the Best Bye shirt? And why had he taken the cup?

His fingerprints must have been on it, and instead of taking the time to wipe them off, he just took it with him and pitched it somewhere. Dammit. I loved that cup.

I got to my feet and stared at our house across the street. I had left to come over here. The cup was missing, which definitely meant that I went inside, got the cup, and then the cup and I vanished.

Argh!!! I was exhausted. I could take a quick nap, but I wanted this over and done with.

What if I retraced my steps? It couldn't hurt. I got into the van as if I'd been kidnapped and lay there for a moment on the passenger seat.

But you can't drive when unconscious, so this reenactment wouldn't be perfect. So I turned the key and took the most direct route to Bladdersly, keeping an eye on the sides of the road for the cup or shirt.

I drove slowly, shining a flashlight on each side of the road as I went. I was halfway to Bladdersly when I spotted something shiny in a ditch. After pulling over, I ran to the spot where my insulated cup lay. My cup! Yay! I ran back to my van for a pen and, upon returning, used it to pick up the cup and stick it in my console.

The muddy water had probably washed away any fingerprints, but I'd leave that to the professionals. Getting back into the car, I continued on to Bladdersly. If I'd found this piece of evidence, perhaps I'd find something at the shed that might jog my memory.

My Dora shirt was still missing. When I pulled into the parking lot where the shed was, the sun had started to come up. After getting the key from the mailbox, I let myself inside and closed the door behind me.

The table was still there, and everything looked the same except for the missing box of cereal. A little door in my mind opened just a smidge. There had been a box of Lucky Charms at my old house. I remember that I'd worried it would go stale just sitting there and had wanted to bring it to the other house!

I remembered something! This was good news! But why just that fragment? Why not the whole thing? Closing my eyes, I willed the rest of my brain to wake up. I gave up after a few minutes. If that came back to me, maybe other stuff would too.

The bookshelf still sported copies of *Boats of the Midwest*. Maybe Mordecai bought out the print run in hopes of hiding the book because he hated how he was portrayed. That would make sense since his alter ego, Menachem, had committed some pretty serious infractions. This was his shed. I was becoming more certain that Tyson was Anonymous.

Had Mordecai lured Tyson to the shed and killed him? Vanderzee and an unknown person had driven past here at the time. Mordecai and Vanderzee had been together at Mordecai's house. Perhaps Vanderzee brought Tyson here. Or was it me? If Vanderzee was the one who'd kidnapped me, I could be the hazy figure in his car.

It made sense. But besides my finding Malone tied up at Mordecai's, there was no real proof that he was the killer with Vanderzee assisting.

How did the killer lock us in the room from the outside? I curled my fingers into a fist, and it hit me as the key bit into my palm. Oh, duh! The killer locked me in from the outside and stuck the key in the mailbox. Well, that answered that. Seemed pretty obvious, and for a moment, I was embarrassed that I hadn't thought of it before. Maybe that's because the police had said I'd locked the door from the inside. And I'd fallen for that.

While it was great to have that part of the mystery solved, there were many other questions. Why frame me, besides Vanderzee's obvious dislike of me? Why change my shirt?

I took a few deep breaths. *Think*, Merry!

After ten more minutes of searching the shed, I had nothing. Maybe I'd think of something on the way home. Or maybe I'd drive past Mordecai's house. It was possible that the sheriff had found something since I'd last talked to him.

About five minutes later, I pulled into Mordecai's driveway. The house had crime scene tape wrapped around it. The lights were out. That was a quick investigation.

I brightened. The sheriff must've gotten Mordecai to confess, and they took him in! I could be in the clear! Turning to the house, I got the feeling that I should take a look on my own. The sheriff would never know I'd been here.

Grabbing a pair of rubber gloves from my van, I went around back to the cellar doors. For some reason, even though this led down to the actual crime scene, there was no tape on them. That was weird. You'd think that this area in particular would at least be dusted for fingerprints. It was…

Oh, for crying out loud, Merry! You don't care! Just go in!

I pulled open the door on the right, turned on my flashlight, and made my way into the basement for the second time in one day. There was the chair, right where we'd left it, with the ropes I'd cut off of Malone's hands pooled on the floor behind it.

Crime scene tape blocked off the stairs that led to the main floor. I'd only been in here a short time, and that had been taken up with watching for Mordecai's return and getting Malone to move.

A table across from the chair was littered with various knives. A shudder ran through me. Torture. I hated torture. At least I got the pastor out before Mordecai started in on him. I walked around the basement. Were there copies of *Boats* here? If so, I couldn't find them. Just the usual crap people have in their basement. Including a litter box. Effie really did live here.

Poor cat. Her owner was going to prison. Maybe Rex would let me adopt her? With that thought comforting me, I walked over to the chair. It was a sturdy oak chair, the kind Grandma Wrath kept in her house for when we needed to add to the dinner table or to sit on when tornadoes came around.

I bent down and picked up the rope, fiddling with it like a fidgety kid. There was nothing here. Nothing, at least, that could tell me more about Malone being held here for the last couple of days.

Effie meowed upstairs. I guess it couldn't hurt to make sure the cat had food and water. It would only take a minute to check. Ducking under the tape, I made my way upstairs and into the kitchen.

Sure enough, the cat dishes were empty. Effie jumped onto the kitchen table and eyed me suspiciously. I didn't blame her. The cat had only seen me two times. Once in the dark when I was hiding under the bed, and again, in the dark, as I threw her through the air.

"Hey, Effie." I scratched her chin, and her eyes rolled back into her head.

I still had the rope in my other hand. I stuffed it into my pocket so I could put it back after feeding the cat. I found a bag of dried cat food and poured some into one bowl, filling the other one with water. Effie attacked it, gulping it down as if she'd never been fed a moment in her life. This was a lie. I knew that because Philby did the same thing, twice a day—as if I'd forget that I'd already fed her once.

After turning the kitchen light back off and sneaking down the stairs, I pulled the rope out of my pocket. I was about to drop it onto the floor when it hit me like the log in Betty's closet. I sank down onto the chair as the various puzzle pieces that had been floating around finally fit themselves together in my head.

Oh. Wow. I knew who'd killed Tyson, and I had a pretty good idea why. I still couldn't remember how I had gotten to the shed or why I was wearing the blue shirt. But I knew the important stuff.

I ran to the van and roared out onto the gravel road, skidding a little as I did.

As I came close to Who's There, a text popped up on my cell. I didn't have time to look at it, and I was driving too fast on a gravel road, which meant that needed my attention for the moment.

Another ding indicated that there was another text. It was probably Rex wondering where I'd gotten to. Or maybe Pastor Malone had come to at the hospital! I was just pulling into the parking lot when my cell dinged again.

It was Kelly. She had news and wondered why I wasn't responding. I read the texts. And then I smiled.

I knew who'd killed Tyson. And now I had proof.

CHAPTER TWENTY-SEVEN

———

Did you know that setting the stage for a big reveal isn't as easy as you'd think? Oh, I know that in the movies it's easy for the detective to gather everyone together in the parlor so that he could explain everything.

But people in real life have real schedules. Which meant I needed to beg, whine, and finally threaten to get everyone in the same spot. Sheriff Carnack got the folks from Bladdersly to join us at the hospital. Rex helped me get the others.

The hospital had been very helpful in providing a conference room, and they wheeled Pastor Malone into it. Maybe they were just worried that there'd be another screaming match and thought this was the best way to keep us away from the other patients.

The ex-pastor was conscious, but mentally unavailable. The doctor explained it as shock. He said it could wear off at any moment and made me promise to keep things calm. I had no trouble with that.

Everyone was here. And then some. I hadn't realized that Ron and Ivan were coming. Or that Ella had been invited. But the rest needed to hear what I had to say. Bryce Vanderzee, Kurt, Kelly, Betty, and Lauren—who I also hadn't realized were coming—Riley, and Mordecai were present.

"Hey." Kurt raised his hand. "Why didn't you invite Ela? I mean, Ella's here. It seems only fair."

I ignored the comment. It was up to Ella to explain that she was Ela too.

"Thanks for coming," I started. "And thanks to the hospital for giving us a space. They told me Pastor Malone here couldn't be moved just yet. So I appreciate the folks who made the trip from Bladdersly."

"So." Kurt raised his hand again. "Who killed Tyson Pancratz?"

The others nodded. Damn. I had planned to do this whole, long story with crazy twists that would make me look amazing. But as several people consulted their watches or looked at the clock, I decided to cut things short and keep them simple. Next time, I'd do a dramatic thingy. Next time.

"The killer is…Pastor Buddy Malone," I said a bit dramatically.

The room gasped as everyone turned to look at the man. He was sitting in the corner hunched over, eyes out of focus, and drooling. *Oh, he's good.*

"Merry," Sheriff Carnack warned. "You had better be absolutely certain of this."

Vanderzee began to shriek, "You're just saying that because he saw you! He knows you did it!"

Rex gave me an encouraging nod.

Ronni began chanting, "Justice for Pancratz! Justice for Pancratz!" How did she get in here? She wasn't invited. Then I noticed that Ron and Ivan had brought the twins with them. Rex walked over and whispered into his angry sister's ear. She scowled, which wasn't much different from the look she always had on her face, but kept quiet.

Malone drooled a little but just sat there with his eyes unfocused.

Betty leaned over to Lauren and stage-whispered, "Yup. He looks like a creeper."

"I am absolutely certain of this," I said. "I'll admit that he's very good. He had me thinking Vanderzee and Mordecai were in on it."

"You take that back!" Vanderzee sputtered, pointing an accusing finger at me.

Mordecai looked puzzled.

"Take it back! Take it back!" Ronni started chanting. Ron, thinking this wasn't a slam against me, started to chant with his wife, until Ivan shot him a look that shut him up.

I continued my monologue. "When I first walked up to Malone on the street, he acted like he didn't recognize me. When I *rescued* him and told him who I was, he said I wasn't Merry Wrath. And because the Bladdersly police chief insisted that Malone had identified me, it made me wonder if Vanderzee hadn't made up the whole thing."

The police officer lunged toward me, only to be grabbed and held back by Ron and Ivan. Ronni was furious but said nothing. I guess there's a line she wouldn't cross with her husband. I'd have to remember that.

"Let go of me!" The man writhed and screamed.

"No!" Ivan said. "You have to listen to Merry. Then we beat you. Then we let go."

"Sheriff!" Vanderzee shouted. "I'm being assaulted."

"Oh, shut up, Bryce," Ed Carnack snapped. "I can't believe I'm saying this, but while Mrs. Ferguson often interferes with investigations, she's never wrong."

That's it. The sheriff is now getting a lifetime supply of his favorite Girl Scout cookie.

Vanderzee clammed up, but his eyes bulged as he thought this over.

"I said," I clarified, "that I'd *thought* it was you. Obviously, since I'm accusing Malone, I'm saying you are innocent. You were lied to, and you aren't very bright, but you're not the killer or the kidnapper."

Kurt raised his hand. "Why do you think it's the pastor? What could possibly be his motive?"

I silently thanked him for moving things on.

I held up my copy of *Boats of the Midwest*. "Because he wrote this."

It was as if the air had been sucked out of the room.

"Buddy Malone is the author of this sordid tell-all that reveals the dirty secrets of half the town."

Betty started making notes about the title of the book.

I confiscated the notebook. "Don't order that. You're not old enough to read it."

"But it's excellent blackmail material," the girl complained.

I'd have to deal with that later.

"As I was saying, Buddy wrote the book and published it as Anonymous. Kelly Albers called the company that printed the book and discovered that the author's real name—Buddy Malone." I left out the part where Kelly promised the guy she talked to two cases of Girl Scout cookies. That didn't seem like something everyone needed to know.

"Huh," Kurt mumbled. "I always thought my mom wrote it."

I asked, "You did?"

"Well, sure. People who serve drunks often hear a lot more than they should."

I nodded. "So, it turns out, do pastors. Isn't that right, Malone?"

Buddy refused to budge from his comatose act. In a weird way, I couldn't blame him. The slandered citizens of Bladdersly would probably show up at the county jail with pitchforks, calling for a good old-fashioned lynching.

I went on. "I don't have the exact information, but I'd be willing to bet that this man has heard a lot of crazy stories from his parishioners over the years. And since he needed a job to get through his retirement, he probably thought he could write this to make some extra money and no one would be the wiser."

"How does that connect him to the murder?" Randi asked. She smiled and gave me a thumbs-up. "By the way, dear, you're doing a great job!"

I thanked her and explained. "Because Tyson Pancratz found out and started blackmailing him. Harold had told me that Malone got him a gig teaching acting at the juvenile detention center. The same place that Tyson did time. And Tyson was behind a number of petty thefts throughout town. Somewhere along the line, whether it was from a Nerd Herd visit or something else, Tyson had stolen his laptop. And as a member of the Nerd Herd, my guess is he stumbled upon the manuscript.

"However," I said. "He wasn't the only one interested in the book. Vanderzee was desperate to find the author's notes. Which was why he sent deputies to the Chapel of Despair."

Kurt was confused. "Kayla said something about old people in the church. Why would Vanderzee look for the notes in a druid chapel in Who's There?"

I looked at the kid. "Because he thought *you* were Anonymous." I had to tread carefully here because this was more theory on my part. But there was the chance that the police chief might confess, so I kept it in.

"Vanderzee knew you were courting Kayla, the teen druid. I think he thought you had hidden it there. Those notes would've been valuable because they might have offered proof of his illicit activities."

I turned to Bryce Vanderzee, who was still struggling against Ivan's iron grip. To his credit, my brother-in-law didn't seem to exert any energy in holding him there. He'd make a fine bounty hunter.

"And you created the fictitious phone call where I allegedly threatened Tyson. You knew you had only Malone's statement. You needed more proof to lock me up."

"But somebody kidnapped him," Mordecai pointed out.

"He did that himself," I answered. "There was no kidnapper. He laid out the trail of breadcrumbs…"

"Breadcrumbs?" Lauren asked. "That's *so* Mother Goose!"

Betty shook her head. "Birds eat breadcrumbs. I'd use BB gun BBs."

"And I followed it. He put on one hell of a show too. Begging, sobbing, faking another voice. But it was the ropes that gave him away…granted, much, much later. I was pretty distracted when I went up to him, worried that the kidnapper would be back. So I just cut the ropes. When I examined them later, I noticed that they hadn't been tied in a knot. If they had, they'd have fallen to the floor that way. But no, all I found was a long piece of rope with cut marks."

"He faked the injuries!" Ella snarled. "Well, he won't fake the ones I give him!"

"You can't attack him," Sheriff Carnack said quietly. "He's in my custody as of now."

"My jurisdiction!" Vanderzee snapped.

"You are going to be facing an ethics panel," the sheriff said as he held up a copy of the book. "Detective Ferguson lent this to me, and I've read it. I'm not leaving him with you."

My eyes narrowed. "And to throw Medea Jones off the scent, you leaked false information about me to the press!"

"You were our number one suspect!" Vanderzee said. "I can do that."

"That's not why you're going to be investigated." Ed Carnack pointed to the book. "I've read that book. And there's a corrupt police chief in it."

Vanderzee opened his mouth and then closed it.

"So Malone pinned it on you and made a statement to back it up," Rex said. "To make sure no one found him out."

"How did he get you to the shed?" Betty asked.

I swung around to face the comatose, drooling pastor. "We will have to ask him that. I'm still not sure. But that's what he did."

"Yeah," Kurt asked, "but how do you know?"

"Because Buddy's fingerprints were on Merry's shoes," Riley said. "They'd never met before. How had his fingerprints gotten onto Merry's shoes?"

"Exactly!" I said, explaining that Kelly had asked for my shoes and had them dusted for prints. She also found out Effie belonged to Mordecai by calling all the vets in Bladdersly, but while that was inspired work, it was too late. I'd buy her dinner later.

It didn't matter because Buddy got to his feet. "Well, I guess I can't poke a hole in that story." The drool and vacant look were gone. "Looks like it's time to face the music."

My jaw dropped. Seriously? Fingerprints on my shoe was all it took to get a confession?

"Why did you have to kill Tyson?" Kurt stood up. "Why couldn't you just pay him off?"

Buddy shook his head. "I did at first. But the fee kept going up. I'm a retired pastor who has to work a part-time job at the pawn shop to make ends meet. I couldn't afford it."

"But the book…" Kurt pressed.

The pastor frowned. "Self-published. Oh, half the town bought it when it came out. But I didn't make much money off of it. I thought it would be more successful than that. Maybe it was the title. At any rate, Tyson came to the pawn shop the night of his death. He confronted me, demanding an outrageous sum of money. There was no way I could pay it. I got so angry, and something in me snapped. It didn't seem fair that this was happening to me. It's funny. I've counseled folks for decades about keeping a lid on their anger. And then I spotted the knife. In a fury, I plunged it into his chest."

There was a moment of silence as everyone processed the idea of the beloved town pastor straight up murdering someone.

"When I realized what had happened"— Buddy drooped a bit—"I knew my whole life, everything I'd worked for, all the good I'd done, had been thrown away." He looked at me. "That's when I remembered what Medea had told me about you. And I had the idea to put the blame on you. Tyson really wasn't worth all the efforts people had put into him over the years. And you were a former spy. You'd probably killed people. You weren't as good as *me*. It seemed like the way to escape prison was to pin the blame on you. You were CIA, which meant you were a bad person who'd done terrible things. It made sense."

"Yeah!" Ronni yelled.

Every head in the room turned to face me, studying me with new eyes. To be honest, it felt like I'd been sucker-punched. This man had killed in cold blood and thought that it made total sense to pin it on me. He thought I was the bad guy. He thought I deserved to go to prison in his place.

That seemed judgmental and more than a bit petty.

Here was a man who'd been beloved by his community for maybe forty years. He'd baptized babies, married young couples, counseled them when things were tough, and conducted their funerals. He'd worked with juvenile offenders in an attempt to do good.

And at the end of his well-lived, well-loved life, he was rewarded with a tiny pension and the need to work a part-time shift at a pawn shop. People knew who he was but had moved on with their lives.

So he wrote a tell-all book, proclaiming to the world all the sins he'd heard. People read it and were angry with the author. And he hadn't made much money on it.

Here comes bad-apple, Tyson Pancratz. A rotten kid who didn't care about anyone but himself—so much so that he was more than happy to bleed dry a man who'd tried to help him.

I was just a no-good patsy to pin this on. And it stung.

"Mrs. Wrath is a good person!" Betty stepped forward, chin in the air. "She's the best Girl Scout leader ever! And you're a bad guy because you killed some guy over money!"

Lauren nodded. "The evils of money and all that…"

Pastor Malone studied the girls, and after a second, his face fell. It was as if his justification for what he'd done had just fallen apart. Maybe he'd realized there are all kinds of gray in this black and white world. Perhaps he just now figured out that a life well lived was no excuse for the crime he'd committed—and that a life like mine could find redemption in a group of precocious little girls in a small town in Iowa.

Sheriff Carnack asked, "Did you fake the kidnapping? Did Mordecai know?"

Buddy nodded. "I did. Mordecai had nothing to do with it. He wasn't even home."

"How did you get in?" I asked.

"I've had a key for years. Sometimes Mordecai makes me pick up his dry cleaning and drop it off. I never liked doing those personal errands. So I thought using his basement was a way to get back at him."

Riley asked, "Why did you call the book *Boats of the Midwest*?"

The former pastor shrugged. "I thought it was a catchy title and would draw readers. Everyone loves boats."

Riley's right eyebrow went up, but he didn't question the man's unusual logic.

"I have one question. How did you get me there, and why was I wearing a Best Bye shirt?" Okay, so that was really two questions.

Malone smiled as if he was honored to answer. "When I grabbed you, you were wearing a Dora the Explorer shirt. Who'd believe that someone dressed like that would murder a guy in cold blood? And it had the added benefit of throwing the spotlight on his coworkers."

Memories flooded back to me. Where had they been all this time?

I clapped my hand to my forehead. "That's right. I was at my old house that night. I'd forgotten my cup there. And I saw you outside on my way back home!"

He nodded encouragingly. "I spotted you in the front yard and asked for your help in finding my lost dog."

It all came back to me, except for how he had knocked me out. "What did you use on me?"

Betty whipped out another notebook, pen poised in the air. I didn't confiscate it this time.

"I roofied you. You had a water bottle, and you handed it to me so that you could lock up the house first. I think I put too much in, but it was lucky that you didn't remember until now. And before you ask, I had those drugs because I'd found them in the shed. I'm guessing one of the people who used it as a motel put them there." He looked at Ella, who shouted something unintelligible about not being the town prostitute.

Well, at least I was right about not being chloroformed. "Where did you get the shirt?"

"Tyson had a couple in his car. I am sorry about all this." He turned to everyone else. "And I'm sorry about the things I wrote in the book. I didn't want to spend my retirement working as a part-time security guard."

"Come along, Pastor," Sheriff Carnack said as he guided the man by the shoulder. "It's time to go."

"You alright?" Rex whispered in my ear as he put his arm around me.

"I never finished my monologue," I grumbled.

"You don't have to. Malone confessed."

"I guess so."

"You do know that he's wrong, right?" My husband tipped my face up to his. "It doesn't matter how good someone has been for his entire life. He made a terrible decision. And now he's a murderer. Nothing in his past can cancel that out."

"That's true." I still didn't feel any better.

"Merry," Rex insisted. "You are a good person. The work you did was part of your job. And now you're making a difference with these girls."

"Well, maybe not Betty." I nodded at the girl, who was acting out the stabbing with Lauren.

"And you've solved a lot of murders around here," my husband said. "You've helped put killers away."

I hadn't thought of that.

I ran over to Buddy Malone and shoved a card into his breast pocket. "Here."

He seemed surprised that I'd give him anything. "What's this for?"

I patted his arm. "A lawyer. And a good one. You're going to need it."

They took him away with Jane Monaghan's card in his pocket. If anyone could help him, she could.

EPILOGUE

———

A lot happened within the next few days.

Sheriff Carnack found *Boats of the Midwest* to be very useful. He found proof that Mordecai was scamming his customers. I'd thought this was because who would work out in a place where people pawned stuff?

Carnack did instigate an investigation into Bryce Vanderzee's activities, with manufacturing evidence to put me behind bars. But Vanderzee refused to go down without a fight. I made sure Jane wouldn't even take his calls.

The sheriff even investigated Ella but couldn't find any men in town who were willing to talk to him about her. I don't think he tried real hard after trying her meatloaf. I don't blame him.

I found out that Nero Fobbs wasn't Kurt Hobbs but Neil…whatever his last name was. I can't believe I never found out. Anyway, Neil and Tyson had stolen the laptops and were getting ready to sell them to a Best Buy in Davenport, Iowa. As for the question of why he asked Ron to throw him out the window? Neither man would say. I'm chalking it up to a weird, being thrown through a window fetish, but that's just my personal theory.

They never did find the murder weapon. Malone simply couldn't remember what he'd done with it. I, however, did find my missing stiletto. It was hidden in the air fryer. Unfortunately, I didn't remember that until after I'd tried to make pizza rolls.

Kurt launched Lone Wolf Bail Bondsmen the next week, complete with real business cards that could be given away. He hired Ivan and Ron, and the three of them have been working on marketing plans. I tried to point out that *Lone Wolf* and

Bondsmen were conflicting words, but the guys really, really liked it, so I let it go.

Randi and Ronni were disappointed that the guys weren't going to be doing landscaping. They'd come up with an idea of turning people's shrubs into animals doing human activities — which just seemed like what they were already doing with taxidermy, except with plants.

When I pointed out that a bail bondsman needed money to post bail for people, the twins decided to back them. Which was good because I'd already shelled out enough money on this investigation.

Kayla was so impressed by Kurt's entrepreneurial skills that she agreed to a date. Stewie even let them use the hearse to go to the drive-in. Of course, it was vandalized while they were there—someone painted *Druids Drool* on the side of it. Stewie placed a curse on the culprits at the next meeting. When two bullies from school came down with scabies, he considered it a sign from Sasquatch that he now had wizardly powers and tried to give them back acne via a spell that he made up.

Claire turned out to be a perfect fit for the Chapel of Despair. Mike and Stewie were so gaga over her that they named her High Priestess. Heather and Kayla didn't mind at all because the first thing Claire did was have a little "chat" with Stewie on the evils of sexism. Which of course, he continued to insist he hadn't realized he'd been doing.

The unveiling of the Ferguson sisters' latest artwork was held at the Chapel of Despair a few weeks later. Rex, Ron, and Ivan helped deliver and install the piece, which was then draped with black silk until the ceremony.

We stood in a semicircle around the altar with my husband's family and Kelly, Riley, the druids, Harold (for moral support for Stewie), and Kurt. Claire looked magnificent in her dark robes and hood. I wasn't sure, but it looked like there was some sort of French designer's logo all over it like a watermark.

"She's got a friend at Chanel," Riley explained, reading my mind again.

Stewie raised his arms in the air and did his demon fingers, which Harold thought was a vast improvement on the druid jazz fingers. It looked the same to me.

"I am the dread demigod Odious!" he intoned in a deep, slightly threatening bass voice.

Harold applauded enthusiastically. I guess the lessons were paying off.

"Tonight! We consummate…" Stewie started.

Claire gracefully floated over to him and whispered in his ear.

Stewie turned bright red but continued in his thundering voice. "Tonight! We consecrate our new altar!"

Mike and Heather threw down some very mild pyrotechnics that were a bit better than the Pop-Its they usually used. I wasn't sure if this was Harold's or Claire's influence, but it was an improvement.

"Why are you dressed like a chicken?" Kelly whispered in my ear.

"I'm the Bird Goddess," I replied with as much dignity as I could muster. The wonderous outfit Kurt had tipped me off to turned out a little less phoenix and a lot more chicken than I'd hoped.

Kayla tugged on the silk, and it slid to the floor.

We all gasped.

"It's a masterpiece!" Kurt's eyes grew wide.

I had to admit, it was pretty good. An almost full-scale semicircle of stones surrounded the goats that were all dancing on hind legs while covered in black cloaks and hoods. I have no idea how the twins managed it, because some of the goats were on one leg as they held hooves and danced in a circle.

In the background, lurking behind two stones, was the cougar in a Bigfoot suit, posed in the traditional Sasquatch stride.

But it was the aliens that were the pièce de résistance. A UFO loomed over the dancers with lights flashing in some sort of pattern. A beam of light appeared at the bottom, and there was the whirr of mechanics.

"This one has motion? The twins really outdid themselves," I said to Rex.

"Well, it helped that the druids paid a *lot* of money for it," my husband whispered back.

A platform came down, and a green llama with three eyes and a silver spangled suit was lowered into the middle of the circle.

We gave it a standing ovation, which in hindsight, wasn't saying much since we were already standing.

For the reception in the basement, I changed out of the chicken suit, using what I liked to think of as my old room, and joined the others for ominous snacks of black Rice Krispies bars and dark purple Jell-O. Claire had redecorated the sleazy waterbed room into a tasteful library with overstuffed chairs (they moved my massage chair to the office for Kayla) and a fireplace—which worked and was weird because there hadn't been one before.

"What in the hell is that?" Riley pointed to my arm.

"It's not as bad as the one you can't see," I admitted as I looked at my newly inked Girl Scout trefoil surrounded by flames, with a banner that said *Born To Sell Cookies*. "In fact, I really rather like it."

"What happened?"

"Bear wasn't happy that we weren't there to really get tattoos, and he didn't like that we were faking it to get information. I apologized, but they felt the only way to show I was sincere was to get two tattoos."

Riley's eyebrows went up. "And what's the other one?"

"That is none of your business," I said blithely as I walked away.

There was no way I was ever going to show him the ink on my left hip, of Dora the Explorer rearing up on the back of a goat that had bicycle wheels for legs. Bear had wanted Dora to be riding on Lance Armstrong's back, but I said no.

That would have just been tacky.

ABOUT THE AUTHOR

Leslie Langtry is the *USA Today* bestselling author of the *Greatest Hits Mysteries* series, the *Merry Wrath Mysteries,* the *Aloha Lagoon Mysteries,* and several books she hasn't finished yet, because she's very lazy.

Leslie loves puppies and cake (but she will not share her cake with puppies) and thinks praying mantids make everything better. She lives with her family and assorted animals in the Midwest, where she is currently working on her next book and trying to learn to play the ukulele.

To learn more about Leslie, visit her online at:
http://www.leslielangtry.com

Enjoyed this book? Check out these other reads available now from Leslie Langtry:

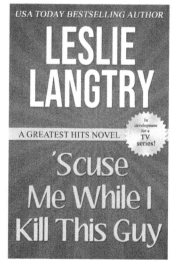

www.GemmaHallidayPublishing.com

Made in the USA
Coppell, TX
15 October 2021